Raining [

MW00940053

*Naomi*
*2019*

# Raining Delusions

### A Catskills Novel by

2/6/19

# MICHAEL GOLD

*Here's a Big Bowl of Borscht (BELT) for you!*
*Warm Wishes,*

Copyright © 2019 MICHAEL GOLD

ISBN: 9781791726317
Imprint: Independently published

# In Praise

"*Raining Delusions* is brilliant. You write unsparingly and are fearless with your bawdy, ribald, shameless, often hilariously poignant dialogue and character descriptions. (Eat your heart out Woody Allen.) The whole book is spot-on accurate. I know these people, and although I didn't live their life, my cousins did. From first page to last, the story is incredibly rich in emotion and your *Full Power and Authority* chapter is a standout worthy of an Isaac Bashevis Singer tale. Resoundingly wonderful!"

—**Hester Mundis**, former head writer for *The Joan Rivers Show*, author and co-author of twenty-five books, four-time Emmy-nominated daytime TV writer and stand-up comic.

"As Noogie reports, the villagers of his Catskill childhood speak a sassy and even ribald mix of English and Yiddish. His grandparents, Pesach, the village blacksmith and Lena, his wife, are central to these funny stories of pointy bras, farty neighbors, brassy insults, endless arguments, heartfelt grief, and food, food, food. And Michael Gold has combined them all with love, love, love."

—**Virginia V. Hvlasa**, Ph.D., author of *Faulkner and the Thoroughly Modern Novel.*

"A keenly depicted, evocative, affectionate slice of life in pre and post WWll Yiddish Catskills culture rarely portrayed in fiction. Humorous and filled with raw vernacular, this poignant novel recalls a time and place that shaped the Jewish American experience and influenced American Cuture as a whole."

—**Phyllis R. Freeman**, Ph.D.

"I have completed reading *Raining Delusions* and it is an amazing book! I found it to be enlightening in telling a great story of a rural cross-section of life in a tiny Jewish community. The description; details and nuances of the town, cars, movie theater, food, women and men and their period attire, fighting, hugging, kissing, love making, spontaneous, earthy humor and highly charged groping are wonderful.

I could not help myself from crying and then laughing and crying again. You put me on an emotional roller coaster without restraint, of family, happy and sad, life and death, of exquisite humor laced with creative profanity in both Yiddish and 'Catskill-ish' that I held onto tightly, hoping it would never stop. I think this book will be an instant classic. I'm placing it next to my copy of *Catcher in the Rye*."

–**Maurice W. Dorsey, Ph.D.,** author of *From Whence We Come* and *Businessman First*.

"Full of heart, humor, profanity and love. A visit with vivid characters in a bygone era."

—**Robert M. Osgood, Esq.**

"Michael Gold is a formidable writer. He captures the Catskill culture of his youth inhabited by so many colorful characters. Everyone should read this book."

—**Claude Samton**, architect, photographer, writer and illustrator of eight books.

# DEDICATION

My poor wife, Linda. What I put her through. She's such a lady and I have all these schmutzy, obscene words and titillating scenarios and she tries to remind me that I have daughters and I have to tone it down and she shakes her head and wonders who the hell did she marry, especially after having read this book.

But I've always been on the buckin' bronco and I ain't got thrown yet. She tells me through her laughter and tears that it's terrific, and I'm sure I couldn't have written such a raw saga without her encouragement and love and eye-rolling incredulousness. She's my best pal, the love of my raucous life and the best companion, chef, partner and greatest mother/granny to my gorgeous daughters and granddaughters. Besides that, she gets more beautiful with every passing year.

To Gabrielle, Arianne, Juniper, Magnolia, Dane and Andrew: you are the dearest family any two people could ever wish for, and I love you all a million billion dollar... stores.

# CONTENTS

# ACKNOWLEDGMENTS

My immense gratitude to the following contributors who selflessly gave their time and expertise in helping this book become a reality:

—First: My best bro, author Burt Gold, who contributed numerous facts I had forgotten or was unaware of, and sister/cousin Jeanette Fein, the first to read the raw, unexpurgated (still is) manuscript, mouth agape.

—Second: Hanna Kisiel, professional copy editor and Vivi Hvlasa, Professor of Writing and author, Queens College, who both edited me with love and kindness, time after time, as they held their ears and whipped me into shape. They are two extraordinary women who gave selflessly and patiently until they were satisfied with the final results. I could never have written this book without their encouragement and understanding.

—Third: Senior Editor of St. Martins Press, Hope Dellon, who encouraged me to write a novel while I was a member of her writing group at Yale's First Writers' Conference.

—Cathy Hull, cover Illustrator and incredibly brilliant artist

—Laurence Carr, award winning author, editor and mentor of Creative Writing at SUNY New Paltz. Mr. Carr gave me the encouragement and impetus to finish the "Max" story about Max's surprise World War II homecoming.

—Rabbi Irving M. Goodman, who assisted me with the Yiddish translations and whose advice was invaluable.

—Dr. Scott Morrison, optometrist, for his invaluable knowledge regarding eye diseases for the "Raining Delusions" chapter.

—All my fellow writers of the historical fiction group at Yale who reviewed the "Yutth" chapter and provided me with their invaluable and astute advice.

Also to a number of most special advisors and friends:

—Rick Meyerowitz, illustrator and author, my great pal with whom I shared numerous eye-popping experiences.

—Isaac "Yits" Kantrowitz and his beautiful wife, Gloria, stars of the *Yutth* chapter.

—Maurice M. Dorsey, author, for his enthusiastic encouragement.

—Andrea Barrist Stern, fellow photographer, writer, activist and incredible supporter.

—Susan and James Fertig, Esq., cousins, who provided invaluable World War II information about Susan's father, Nainie Shabus (Julius) and brother, Max.

—Phyllis Freeman and David Krikun, insightful supporters.

—Hester Mundis, author of twenty-seven books

—Marcy Goulart, writer, with whom I shared stories and astute insights.

—Robert M. Osgood, Esq., advisor and supporter.

—Sherry Ames, my supportive sister-in-law.

—Stan "Yogi" Rubin, a super star in the novel.

—Phyllis Rubin, whose contributions on Jewish culture were invaluable.

—Sharon Rudolph Gardell, who added important facts to the chapter that mentioned her late father.

—John Conway, Sullivan County, NY, Historian, who

provided me with critical information about Murder, Inc. and late various members who frequented Sullivan County.

— Neil Janovic, for his never-ending encouragement

— Fred Mayo, Ph.D., New York University Professor of Hotel and Tourism Management, and my co-author for our *Modern American Manners* book.

— Charles Heenan, Esq., for his insightful advice.

— Martin Walker, Media research expert.

— Lindsay and Alan Kraus, gourmet friends and enthusiastic supporters.

— And last, to my late cousin Shirley Ullman, who died just a couple of years ago at 95, who was my greatest inspiration, and inadvertently provided me with the title of the book with an innocent comment. She was a brilliant storywriter, had her own TV cooking show and was a loving second mother. We cooked *kreplach*, stuffed cabbage, lentil chopped "liver" and "Grandma's Cookies together. Besides herself, her own mother, Ray, played a most critical role in *Raining Delusions*.

# INTRODUCTION

My name is Noogie Ernstein and I grew up in the big, at least I thought it was big, brick house my grandfather built on Maple Avenue in Woodridge, NY, a village of perhaps seven hundred people. We didn't know Woodridge was referred to as a "small town." That is simply pure bullshit.

Small town? Waddaya crazy, small town? A few grocery stores, deli, fish and produce markets, candy store, couple of luncheonettes, movie theater, two drug stores, two barber shops, hairdresser, bakery, shoe store, three butcher shops, printers, bank, O&W train station, dairy, three fuel companies, steam laundry, liquor store, four bars, gas stations, two dentists, two doctors, lawyers, accountants, insurance agency, clothing store to dress them all, and in the outlying area, farms, hotels and bungalow colonies.

It was our world, however small and insignificant it may have seemed to any outsiders, mostly city people from Manhattan, the Bronx and Brooklyn who came up for the summer to stay in bungalow colonies and small hotels to escape the swelter and lack of air conditioning in their city tenements, and blessedly left on Labor Day weekend. They had no idea what our Borscht Belt village was like. We had the feeling that to them we were thought of as just a bunch of mostly Jewish hicks. Fuck them.

During the spring and summer months, night after

night, people gathered and sat in the cool darkness. The streets were without lights, there were just the lit cigarette and cigars' red tips and smoke hovering and slowly swirling in the air with tobacco pungency to accompany the laughter and sarcasm and political banter from all those shadowed voices at the Shabus home on Maple Avenue in Woodridge.

The darkness gave the voices permission to speak.

Life in Woodridge, a microcosm of America, of immigrants and first generation Americans, whose lifeblood, besides the family stories all had to share, was politics, politics, politics, gossip, gossip, gossip, laughter, sarcasm, insults, affection. People leaned forward on their chairs, gesturing vigorously and vociferously, accentuating their arguments, both about local politicians and national. Their battles were fueled by countless shots of schnapps and cups of Bokar Eight o'Clock Coffee.

Pesach Shabus, "Mr. Easter Saturday," the village blacksmith, always with his wide-brimmed cap on, and his pinochle cohorts, were relentless in their arguments and humorous in their good-natured put-downs accompanied by Yiddish curse words directed at one another. I most often sat next to Pop, not really understanding all the words from their colorful, musical, foreign language and their adopted version of English, but reveling in their camaraderie and loud, infectious laughter.

I watched him still shoeing horses in his later years. I pumped his forge and hammered on his anvil and wondered who Michael J. Quill was, that stern-faced, bald guy whose poster hung in Pop's blacksmith shop. Later on, I learned what a tough sonofabitch labor organizer he was for the TWU, Transport Workers Union, in New York. No wonder my grandfather liked him, a fellow tough sonofabitch Cossack escapee.

Raining Delusions is a work of fictionalized stories woven together about those who grew up in a tiny community in The Catskills, and how they related to families, friends, lovers, life's experiences, obstacles and fate.

Some of the events are based on memories, fragments of information, really of village life and the eccentric way people communicated with one another, the Borscht Belt way. They cover the gamut of raw obscenities, conflict, digs, spontaneous humor, passion, grief, revenge, war, politics, compassion, sarcasm, depression, celebration and love, spanning four generations of larger than life characters, of emotional cyclones, hurricanes, earthquakes, volcanoes, tornados, firestorms and tsunamis, all hitting you at once. It's not for the weak of heart.

— Noogie Ernstein

# 1. Sweet Solitude and Back to Once Was

1996

The sun at this time of year doesn't rise till 7:15-ish, but it's no longer dark, and as much as I hate getting out of bed early in the morning, there's always some problem I wake up to, real or imagined, that gets me up abruptly.

I don't know when happy dreams ended, but they are rarities now and the weight of life magnified in my twilight zone of sleep generally prevents them from helping start the day smiling. That is a bitch, but I have a dog who follows me downstairs and needs to be walked, and as cold as it is this early, as snowy or windy or rainy, I join him in my wellies, bathrobe, hooded down parka and scarf, and feel revived, wondering what the fuck I'm doing living in such a cold climate, but loving it nevertheless, when it's not too frigid. If it's not too miserable, I like opening my bathrobe to the woods in front of me to pee on the grass or snow too, and let the freezing early morning air freeze and shrink my pecker while I make Jackson Pollocks at my feet. I should've been a urine painter. What a MoMA show that would make!

I'm always the first one up, long before Sophie and the girls. I like the solitude. I like making freshly ground French Roast. I like sitting alone. It's my only time to take a breath. I love reading The Times, editorials first, Op-Ed Page next, sports, Home, the Science section—Tuesday, my favorite Times day, Wednesday, restaurant reviews and food recipes we'll mostly never use, movie reviews, shows, cars, fascinated and incredulous by all the varieties of meshuger killers around the world, each with their own meshuger agendas: machete-toting Tutsis killing Hutus and visa versa, Catholic and Protestant bombers, Palestinian suicide car bombers, Serb and Croat rapist-killers, Algerian throat slitters, Iraqi poison gassers, Cambodia — if-you-wear-glasses, you're-dead—killers, Congo hackers, Vietnam leftover landmines, abortion clinic bombers, and the usual serial killers here in the U.S..

I cannot breathe until I get The Times every day, and travel a minimum of fourteen miles round trip to the nearest convenience store just to buy it. This morning is no exception. It's a connection. I like the solitary quietude in the kitchen. I like the sun coming up over the hill and exploding in my face through a semi-clean kitchen bay window from where I can look through to our overgrown wisteria-covered arbor and part of the front lawn. I like the way it glows through a newsprint page, rendering it translucent and difficult to read. I like the mist of the frost and the sugary granules of snow blinding my eyes, causing them to tear. I like the look of my oversized Crate and Barrel coffee mug next to my bagel and organic creamed honey. I like mornings. I like the white ghost of a moon in the deep Prussian blue early morning sky.

And this morning was a nice way to think about the adventure and mystery of the new year ahead in just a few days.

While everyone was asleep, I decided I was going to

take a quick trip to Woodridge and visit my late grandparents' and parents' home. I quickly dressed, grabbed a screwdriver and pliers, in case they might be needed, wrote a note and quietly tiptoed out the door.

It was the first time I had visited the house in twenty years. It was easier not seeing it. The ghost of the house, at first glance, looked almost exactly as it had looked when it was still occupied many years earlier. But then I noticed a broken window on the gable on top, and the unpainted French front door, the twisted wrought iron gate, missing bricks and exposed cement of the supports holding the gate and steps, the missing decorative planters from which the vibrant red geraniums grew, the weeds behind the gate where once the small flower garden and crimson peonies announced spring and summer. The sloping driveway had been filled in so that the woodworking and blacksmith shops and the two-room living quarters were now inaccessible. The tomato garden, chicken coops and the two barns that had all been demolished, exposing the guts of the steel beams, now bent over, that once supported the blacksmith shop's ceiling.

All that was still standing was the apple tree, now much larger, on Yushka's next-door property, the tree under which, many lifetimes ago, he urinated every morning. His buildings, butcher shop, home and barn, were long gone as well, and the morning chorus of roosters and hens was also silent and invisible amongst the high weeds emerging from the snow cover of a tough winter. The tree in front of his butcher shop still stood, now with a sign nailed on, advertising a "Ritualarium," both in English and Hebrew, and phone number. A "ritualarium" is a *mikvah*, the religious bath for orthodox women to cleanse themselves after menstruation or childbirth. "Ritualarium" is one of those crazy, made up words. Never saw that one before.

Maple Avenue looked deserted when I pulled up. Many of the majestic maple trees up and down the street had disappeared. I walked up the broken, brick steps to the front door, the same door my grandmother opened when Max returned home from the army at the end of World War II, and noticed a sheet taped across a window pane condemning the house. The porch was emptied of all furniture except a solitary, white, plastic chair in the corner. Although I knew no one was there, I knocked anyhow. I tried the other front door to the left and there was no answer. I then knocked on the porch door and got no answer there either.

I tried the front door and it was sealed shut, came around to the porch door, and although it was locked, I took a chance and reached for our old secret spot between bricks near the door where we used to hide a key...

## 2. Full Power and Authority

1925

The movie theater smelled like *dreck*. It smelled like an old bar, but without the beer smell. It smelled of cigarettes and cigars and other shit left on the floor from past showings. It smelled of perfume and cologne, the lingering cheap shit kind. It smelled of stale and crumbled popcorn stuck to that filthy, gum-stuck floor and seats. And it smelled of disgusting three-day underarm sweat, not even fresh sweat. The disinfectant they used made things even worse.

That was the Lyceum in Woodridge in 1925. The marquee had many missing and burned out bulbs. The white stucco was cracked. It needed a paint job to replace the brown, peeling trim around the doors and windows.

Hildie Schluffen was the ticket taker. Her skin was whiter than the stucco. The veins in her hands and forehead were accentuated blue. She had a false green-teeth smile. Her glasses made her look older than her eighty-two years. She had a heavy smoker's voice, almost manlike in its female baritone timbre. She knew everybody, even the kids. She observed careless secrets that only occurred in the darkness of the theater. She chain-smoked Camels while selling tickets and her little booth seemed to always be filled with a cigarette haze. It sometimes looked like she blew smoke rings through the small, round, hole in the hazy, unwiped glass, perhaps from all her coughing and hacking.

The lobby's red carpeting had seen better days and worn areas were pronounced near the doors and snack counter. Black gum and cigarette burns were embedded in the threadbare areas. Behind the counter were the popcorn machine and the pot of butter. The aroma was intoxicating and the bags sold for five cents or ten, butter included.

It wasn't a large theater, perhaps seating three hundred people. The screen took up most of the small stage and the old upright was placed in the right corner. It was scratched and had names dug into it by people who could not care less, when no one was around. The ivory on a number of the keys had been chipped off, exposing the bare wood. They looked like five day-old manicures. The ivory was yellowish from age. The piano was chronically out of tune, but that didn't stop the local pianists from playing in local concerts and recitals held on stage during the weekdays when movies weren't played. The National Anthem never quite hit the perfect high notes. Mrs. Schmear was the most prominent of the local pianists and she played valiantly, despite her handicaps. She sat bent over, leaning toward the music sheets, as if she had a terrible case of arthritis. She was also very nearsighted and crinkled her nose, both in concentration and in effort to read the notes. Her glasses inched downward in Ben Franklin style.

The brown velvet seats of the theater were worn and ripped. Besides gum, there were all kinds of stains; from soda pop to cum from young guys getting jacked off under the cover of lettered jackets in the darkness by country girls with wet panties and groping hands.

One could write the history of social life in

Woodridge just by analyzing those movie theater seats. Weekends belonged to teenagers nearest the screen. Families as well as the more mature-looking couples sat toward the rear. Dave Malisoff, the manager, patrolled the aisles. He kicked more kids out than one-legged from the war, Mr. Balducci, ever did in the South Fallsburg Rivoli Theater.

The stairway led upstairs to the projection room where Moishie Schnopz threaded the film every night for the double features, newsreels, cartoons, short subjects and coming attractions of little consequence. Every night he sat there in darkness, except for the projection bulb lighting the room enough for him to read the latest paper or Police Gazette. He often fell asleep and it wasn't until the yelling of moviegoers woke him to change reels, or to stop snoring. How often he heard, "So Schnopzie, I hear you was schnoring again?" It became a village joke, but Schnopz was a lighthearted guy and he laughed heartily with them.

Adjoining the projection room was the room used for the village board members. It was a large, unadorned, modest room with a couple of bare lightbulbs hanging down from the ceiling, furnished with a long table and an assortment of mismatched chairs. The walls were painted medium beige, with brown trim. The door was painted brown and was covered with assorted tape and torn corners of papers that had been ripped off from the hanging posters, orders and announcements. An American flag of forty-eight states was tacked to the far wall and formal, sepia-toned photographs, in five and dime store black frames, of past members and dead volunteer fire chiefs, hung crookedly on a long hallway wall. Firemen, yes; policemen, no. Policemen weren't necessary.

No one thought about that. Nothing was ever stolen. A bulletin board was opposite, covered with notices and pronouncements of village events and necessary public projects. A window looking out onto the main street was covered with dark, deep, red curtains, probably sewn by one of the ladies in town in order to save village money.

There were four board members and the mayor, and they met upstairs at least once a week and often more so when necessary, to solve the problems of a village of three hundred thirty-seven people. It was just as much a social meeting as the whiskey and shot glasses were always at hand...and liberally used. The room smelled of cigarette and cigar smoke and the ashtrays overflowed with the remainders of bent, extinguished, mostly smoked, leftover butts. The room was foggy and stinky from the smoke. Here was the room for democracy in action and every board member was given a certain responsibility for the running of village affairs, and responsibilities were always assigned with a certain sense of good-natured humor.

Yussie Chazah, a kosher butcher, was the unofficial mayor. He was "five foot wide by five feet high" and spoke in a loud, nasal voice. He often complained that already there were too many people working for the village, but he didn't have the heart to let any of them go. He was asked how then he might cut down on workers and he said that, "Don't worry, we'll get rid of them by nutrition."

The board members were Pesach Shabus, the village blacksmith, Yussel Schlepper, a garage mechanic, Herman Schnittesvogel, the barber, Hymie Titzkowitz, the baker, and Tillie Schmear, the secretary/bookkeeper who took meticulous notes in English. Yiddish was the spoken language among board members, although they all spoke a certain version of English as well. Mr. Chazah, the mayor, would say to board members, " Schlepper, I give you full power and authority to clean the toilets. It's a perfect job for you. Schnitzelman, I give you full power and authority to sweep the floor. Titzkovitz, I give you full power and authority to bring a coffee cake mit you next time. We'll pay, don't worry, but don't sneak a two-day stale one on us again.

Pesach Shabus, 'Mr. Easter Saturday,' I give you full power and authority to choose a new piano for the social hall. The one we have in the movie is a *schtick dreck* and we need a new one to play in the theater. It sounds even worse when Mrs. Schmear over here plays on it. Tillie, since you play the piano so good, like a boid, I tell you, like a boid, I give you full power and authority to... wash the dishes. It's safer then listening to you playing 'The Schtar Schpengled Benner'."

"I should wash dishes and Mr. Shabus he should choose a piano? What he knows about a piano? He knows from nothing, pianos." I studied music. I play piano and Shabus chooses? What are you crazy? Him, a *maven*?"

"Shabus will be the piano chooser. You can help. He knows pianos better then you think. Right, Shabus?"

"Yeh," said Shabus. "I know pianos as good like I know a good *tuchus*."

"Yeh, Shabus is an export with both!"

" Mr. Chazah, mit all due respect, I think there are two chozzers in this room," said Tillie.

Mr. Chazah says, "Yeh, Shabus, but no one knows good quality like you, so you will be the one to choose a piano. You have full power and authority. Tillie will sit and play, oy vey, hold your ears, but youuuu, you make the final choice. You'll make an appointment with Izzy Schmockel in Monticello and go choose a piano. He got used ones we should buy, but cheap, Shabus, cheap. Too good, we don't need."

With that, they all had a drink. Tillie said, " I know how to play a piano! Mr. Shabus, mit all respect due, do you think you could choose *besser* then me?"

If Chazah says for me to choose, he's the mayor, but we'll make the choice together," making her feel immediately better. "Zayeh good," she said.

The next day Mr. Shabus called Mr. Schmockel and made an appointment for him and Mrs. Schmear to go to Monticello to Schmockel's Music Shop in the middle of the town. Compared to Woodridge, it felt like a big city. In those days, leaving one's village for Monticello was both thrilling and anxiety-filled. It was like going to a big city from a tiny village, even though it was no more than twenty minutes away by rail.

Two days later, at the O&W Railroad station, they boarded the train that came through the village daily, first to South Fallsburg and then to Monticello. The steam engine, at the command of the train's engineer, whooshed white steam between their feet at the station, and off they went. They sat on oak seats covered with either green or red velvet. The fare was twenty-five cents each. The route took them through the woods and over hills and trestles, over the Neversink River, through the richly lush Catskills.

Mrs. Schmear wore a black dress that ended at her pencil-thin ankles. Her shoes always appeared to be too large for her thin legs, perhaps because she had overly long feet. Her black velvet hat was set at a forty-five degree angle on her substantial hair, and stuck into the brim was a long exotic feather, probably pheasant.

Mr. Shabus *kibitzed*, " Is that feather from one of mine leghorns?"

"Are you serious, Mr. Shabus? You know your leghorns are too good for mine hat."

Mr. Shabus was wearing his only suit. It was black, double breasted, a bit tight around the arms and shoulders and a little short at the wrists. He wore it for funerals, weddings, bar mitzvahs and *shiva* visits. He cleaned his work shoes for the visit. His tie was two shades of red in a diamond pattern. It was very wide.

They finally arrived in Monticello and walked along Broadway, past the thriving stores to Schmockel's Music Shop. There were many people on the street, window shopping and deliberating, conferring, weighing, discussing, bickering, laughing, checking purses and wallets considering the possibilities of possibly buying, but maybe next time.

The sign above the store was gold leaf engraved,

"Schmockel's Music Shop" on a black background in elaborate script. It was an expensive sign. The window was spotlessly clean and through it, one could see a number of uprights and three baby grands. They were crowded together and meticulously dusted in a room of flowery wallpaper, velvet navy blue curtains with gold trim and assorted Persian rugs to deaden the sound. A bust of Beethoven, looking very stern and in need of a haircut, was placed in the middle of the room.

Above was a large brass and crystal chandelier. Mr. Schmockel wore a black suit and matching tie. His gold watch chain hung from his vest pocket. He was a slight man with stooped shoulders, a kind smile and a monocle over his right eye. He scrunched his nose to hold the monocle, He looked like he was perpetually about to sneeze. He spoke in a nasal voice. One could see the numerous hairs up his nose, some sticking out, untrimmed.

His fingers were long and delicate, fingernails perfectly manicured in contrast to the huge Shabus hands of callouses, burns and thick, black and yellow-stained fingers. His nails were cracked, scarred and disfigured. He had tried to clean them.

## It's The Steinway!

Mr. Schmockel welcomed Mr. Shabus and Mrs. Schmear effusively and began asking questions about the type of piano they would need. Mrs. Schmear did most of the talking, explaining the general use of the piano for events and movies in the community of Woodridge, running her hands caressingly over the pianos as she walked about the room, examining each one carefully. She looked at prices, as did Mr. Shabus.

She sat down in front of a few and played bits of classical music from memory, eyes closed, some Bach and Brahms, Chopin and Mozart. It was all very beautiful, as she had been a trained musician, long before she became a secretary/bookkeeper. As was so often the case, money guided lives and she had to help support her family. Dreams were put aside for the practicality of economic survival. She played Jewish and community events to earn a few extra pennies.

"You play very good, Mrs. Schmear," said Mr. Schmockel. "Who learned you?"

"Thank you so much, Mr. Schmockel. When I was a young girl, mine parents got me lessons and I loved every second. I was like a moth drawn to a candle, and so, now I play wheneveh I can, for movies, for the village, for weddings, parties, whateveh and wheneveh."

"And you, Mr. Shabus? You play, also?"

"I wish I could, but mine daughter, Sophie, she plays. I bought her a piano and she plays for the family. To tell you the truth, though, I wish sometimes I could cover mine ears. But she tries and I give her a smile and I encouragerate her."

"So what I can do for you? What kind piano you like? Upright or grand? New or used?"

"We would like a good used one. An upright," said Mrs. Schmear.

"Aha!" exclaimed Mr. Schmockel. "We have a few real beauties; a Steinway, an Albrecht, a Schafer and a good Schumann."

Mrs. Schmear went from one to the other, playing on each, sampling the action of the keyboard, the quality of sound, the resonance, ease of foot pedals. Mr. Shabus followed her to each piano and listened carefully for the richness of the sound. He ran his hands over each piano, inspected the legs and the finish, the quality of construction, the wood.

She, without saying a word, secretly preferred the quality of the Steinway, although all the other pianos were varnished and finished to perfection, not one speck of dust on any of them, thanks to Mr. Schmockel's back pocket handkerchief. But, too, the Steinway was available for the right price. To her, it was the best of the group... and it was, after all, a "Steinway." She knew, though, that if she said "Steinway," he might prefer another, knowing his contrarian personality, just for the sake of making a decision of his own. She took a chance.

Mr. Shabus asked, "So Mrs. Schmear, what do you think? Which one do you like?"

She answered, "Well, Mr. Shabus, I think I like the Albrecht. It plays beeudelful. It's perfect for Woodridge."

Mr. Shabus examined the Albrecht again. He pushed down on the keys with his huge, thick fingers, rubbed his hands over the finish, smelled it, examined the legs, the back, opened the top, the hinges, inspected the strings.

He walked over to the others and repeated his examination, carefully and meticulously inspecting every part of each piano.

On all pianos, he gave a loud and final *klop* with the side of his oversized fist onto the tops of each, startling everyone, and at last, with that one test, made his final, educated decision: It came as no surprise. "It is with full power and authority that we buy the Steinway! Mrs. Schmear, you might know pianos, but I know pianos better! I like the wood and legs of the Steinvay and dat's the one it has to be. Besides, Steinway is Jewish. Who knows from Albrecht and the others? A chance we cannot take. "

So Mr. Pesach Shabus, the village blacksmith, with one good klop and Mayor Chazah's blessing and with his full power and authority, became the Village of Woodridge's piano maven. Who ever said he only knew from good horseshoes and good tuchus?

That, to the ears of Mrs. Schmear, you should only know from, was music, even with a final Shabus *klop*.

# 3. Raining Delusions

1932 – 1952

He made horseshoes and chose pianos, if you can call giving a piano a *klop*, and Laya Shabus attended to all the household necessities, including plucking Pesach's chickens in the middle of the yard, between the chicken coop and barn.

Her real name was Lena. He called her "Laya." The feathers stuck to her dress and apron and hair and hands. They fluttered and swirled like butterflies or maple tree seeds all around her. She spit some from her mouth. "Feh!" The chicken coop to the left and the connected gray barns behind her were used to store chicken crates, the truck, old furniture, marble counters, deli cases, a decorative full-length mirror given to her and Pesach for a wedding present, metal signs, tools, boxes of newspapers and an A&P coffee grinder. The pigeons made the barns their homes in numerous nests, and everything was covered with their whiteish-gray droppings. The barns and coop were all painted a light battleship gray with dark blue trim. Pesach's blacksmith and woodworking shops, sharing bottom and top floors, were behind the house, but in front of the coop. Connecting the blacksmith shop to the coop was a three room, very small, unfinished, one-story wooden building that was their home before the handsome brick house was built and finished by Pesach himself in 1932. There was a little vegetable garden in front, about fifteen square feet. All the kids, except Minnie, were born in that tiny building and later grew up in the brick home. There were five in all, the first of whom was born when Laya was sixteen.

Yushka, the butcher, who also raised chickens, and his miserable, hateful, scary wife lived next door on the right. His butcher shop was in the front, the house and barn behind. On the left of their property was a little rooming house owned by Mr. and Mrs. Haber. It was always Mr. and Mrs. Haber. Never first names with them. They rented mostly to the seasonal workers, mostly alcoholics; shickers, as they were called. Mr. Haber always gave all the neighboring kids pieces of brightly colored candy.

The Malisoffs, Perlmutters and Kulbitskys lived across the street up a few houses and beyond the Caulters's grey two story house, which was always draped with drying underwear and work clothes for Charlie, the highway superintendent, and country dresses for Vera. Their underwear was overly large, especially her white panties and large brasieres and his boxer shorts. Vera worked across the street in the Bell Telephone Company office as a switchboard operator. She knew everyone's number by heart. You could ask for anyone by name and she would automatically know which cords to plug in. Strangers used numbers when calling. If only they knew Vera.

The large orange and red tomatoes were hyper-fueled by Pesach's chickens' smelly manure. They could've been a well-endowed size double D, easily, and weighed a pound or considerably more. The driveway sloped downhill, until it leveled out where Yushka's apple tree's heavy branches hovered over Pesach's black truck in the driveway, until the next load of chickens was either delivered or shipped out. In autumn, the ripe apples fell on both adjoining properties and made for good pies baked by Laya. In winter, the driveway's steep slope was perfect for sleight riding. Yushka kept his chickens on the other side of the common fenc

When feeding them, Yushka usually first *pished* under his side of the apple tree, by reaching under and pulling his dirty, stained, white butcher's apron to the side of his pants, where he was always surrounded by expectant, hungry chickens who welcomed him with their loud clucking, waiting till after he re-buttoned his stained pants, waiting for him to toss them corn and rotting vegetables collected from Proyect's fish and produce store in the village.

Yushka made loud, high-pitched, falsetto "Here, chick, chick," noises they easily recognized and to which they responded. One could hear his occasional farts as well. He huffed when he walked, stooped over, supported by an old, rusty baby carriage that he salvaged, the one with which he used to collect Proyect's and Gerson's vegetables. He had a white goatee like Buffalo Bill and short, swollen fingers. Did Yushka ever wash his hands?

Lena Shabus called her husband Pesa. Laya, he called her, would sit under the apple tree on a stump with a big pot of hot woter, heated by her son Max's propane burner, holding the chickens' carcasses by the two feet and dipping them into the boiling water to soften the feathers and skin, in order to pluck them out more easily. She methodically and patiently pulled the white leghorn feathers out and tried to place them in a pail, but many floated like weightless milkweed, landing at her feet, on her dress and dark brown hair and silver-rimmed glasses.

She usually wore a dress buttoned in the front, a

schmatta. Her stockings were rolled down neatly to her fat, white, somewhat purplish, shapeless ankles that looked as if ringed by bagels. It was more comfortable for her that way. Her shoes were black grandmother laced up shoes with two inch, thick, practical heels. Piano leg ankles would have been a compliment. Sturdy harvest table legs was more accurate. She was five one. The undersides of her arms, even when she was a young lady, were mushy and quivered in movement like Jello. But in her own way, she was beautiful and her smile brighter than any sun. Her blue eyes matched the color of a clear, country Catskills sky. She *kibitzed* with the best of her husband's "professional" *kibitzers* and gave as good as she got. It was a spontaneous Woodridge vaudeville show night after night. She laughed readily and heartily, throwing her head back when the jokes or observations were especially humorous. The words "I love you" were never spoken to one another, but there was never a question of their love for one another.

Plucking the freshly butchered chickens was her job. Pesach did the killing in the back of one of the barns. He had a special place there, behind stacked wooden chicken crates, with galvanized triangular receptacles that looked like long upside down megaphones, only about two feet long. He did it like a rabbi, a shoychit, pulling the head backwards and quickly slitting the bird's throat with a very sharp knife, and then dropping the chicken into a megaphone until it swiftly bled to death and stopped helplessly shaking its legs and wings. Sometimes he chopped a chicken's head off in the yard, perhaps for childrens' amusement, and it ran all over the yard, squirting blood, until it dropped to the ground, dead. That vaudeville show lasted a minute or two. It was something that happened just for entertainment and was both fascinatingly gruesome, but most mesmerizing, nevertheless. Who knew better? It was just a fact of life. It was fun but it gave one nightmares for a long while and vivid memories to this day.

I'm their grandson, Noogie. When I was ten years old and old enough to shoot a BB gun, I found it fun to shoot the windows out of my grandfather's barn and woodworking shop and the pigeons that landed and roosted on and in the barns as well. They were very pretty and some tame from my handling, but thinking back, there were lots of hero cowboy sharpshooters on the radio and they would've done the same thing. I was too insensitive a cowboy myself to feel too guilty. I got the shit kicked out of me for breaking the windows and whacked on my ass by both my grandfather's gigantic hands and trusty auxiliary punishing belt. I guess I didn't realize the consequences at the time I was target shooting; had too good a time playing sharpshooter cowboy. I learned, though. My red, black and blue ass learned even better. It got an A+ in life's lessons.

My grandfather never hit me again, though. Not his nature. The only other time he ever yelled at me was when I, at the age of twelve, drove my uncle Max's new orange pickup truck from my grandparents' house up the street on Maple Avenue to my parents' house. I backed out of the driveway, engaging a steel pole I met along the way, on one side, denting the left fender. I was new at driving trucks alone at the time, only used to my mother's car, which I drove regularly at night through the village environs. Kids started driving early in those days, I didn't see the metal pole. Didn't realize I was supposed to look out the side mirror. Surprisingly, my grandfather never learned to drive, so he depended on me for that one and only time until I got a license five years later.

Once was enough. He called me a "sommanabitch" and scared the hell out of me to have to face the consequences of that fiasco to Max. I had never heard him use that kind of language, much less in his own particular interpretation. He preferred Yiddish when he cursed, which would've understood, but for effect Pop spontaneously thought his English version, at that moment, was preferable. I was spared any further pain for the courage I'd shown in attempting to drive the truck myself, despite the dent.

Laya and Pesach had five children. She married Pesach at fifteen and they didn't waste any time having a brood. Her kids were Sam, Nainie, Max, Charlotte, aka "Shandie" and Minnie. I was named after Minnie, whose name seemed to be fairly common in those days, before a certain Mr. Disney named his mouse after my late aunt years later. Noogie was a nickname, but that's how I was known. M, N, what's the difference? I was happy I wasn't born female. I'd have been cursed for life. Judging from an old sepia-toned, frayed photo in which Minnie's standing, smiling, next to charlotte, my mother, she was very pretty, prettier than Charlotte, and sort of resembled her father. She had Pesach's sweet, wry, humorous smile, prominent nose, but not as wide, and straight black hair. If I were her age and not related, I'd be her hound dog.

It was 1934, two years after my grandfather built his handsome three story brick house that replaced the little three-room oversized, uninsulated closet of their living quarters. Their son, Max, had scribed into the drying concrete in the basement, "Max Shabus 1932", so I knew that was when the house was built.

It was a lifetime's distance from the pogroms of Minsk, where my grandmother was born, and somewhere in Russia from where my grandfather escaped, to eventually come to America. I never knew the whole story. We never asked those questions; too wrapped up in growing up. They were just here, and all I knew was that they came from over there and spoke with Jewish-Yiddish accents and phrases mixed with their deliciously colorful interpretations of the English language. There was no discussion of the past, other than the most important story of my grandfather choking a Cossack border guard to death with one hand to facilitate his escape from the Russian army. He never elaborated when asked and was never asked enough, to my great regret.

Besides being Max's resident genius, I also helped my grandfather in his blacksmith shop by pulling the handle on his forge, forcing more air onto the coals, getting them much hotter, to get the iron light-yellow hot and soft in order to form horseshoes and other shapes for gates, fences, carriages, tools, utensils, fishing spears and truck bodies. I loved the reverberating, rhythmic, clanging music of hammer on anvil, and the hissing of red-hot iron dipped into a pail of water, causing clouds of steam to fill the small shop. It sounded like an angry cat in a fight.

I'd also buy the ultra-lefty Freiheit for him and the Forward secretly for my grandmother, who hid it under the couch pillow. They disagreed politically. Pop smoked Chesterfields, no filters in those days, for twenty cents a pack. I bought them at Abe's, where I always enjoyed going in order to read the latest Superman or Batman "jokebooks," which is what we called comicbooks. When Pesach finished smoking his Chesterfields, he put them out with his thumb and side of his pinky, which were consequently yellowed and extra-calloused. I tried to do it once myself and burned and blistered both uncalloused fingers; a *schmuck* for even trying.

Pesach's thick fingernails were all broken and ragged from work. Even with careful washing, they were embedded with the schmutz of grease, coal, oil, rust. And when he needed to have his fingernails and toenails clipped, he used tinsmith shears. Clippers, even toenail clippers, were much too small. Many years later, when I returned home from my freshman year at college, when my Pop was dying of throat cancer, I used those same tinsmith shears to give my Pop his last clipping. He was only seventry-three at the time, but was so bent over from arthritis and cancer, that he looked like a ninety year old, a shriveled shadow, a Giacometti, but with the same giant oversized hands, only no longer calloused. The wrinkled skin on his fingertips made them look like they just emerged from a long swin, now missing the calluses. To have seen his hands when he was in his prime was to know his strength, One could never squeeze hard enough, even with two hands, to force his pinky to move out of the perfect row of fingers he held stiffly. They were the hands that made horseshoes for five cents a hoof, hands that held my hand when I was a little boy.

Summertime. Hot July. Humid. Woodridge in the Catskills. What's air conditioning? Ice in front of a fan? They did that then. For three feet in front of the fan, you were fine.

At five feet, you still schvitzed. On the second and third floors of the house, you could die from the heat and thick, soupy, musty air. The nights are cooler in the Catskills, but humidity is humidity and summer is summer and all the fans at three feet in the world, even in the elevated mountains, are useless.

The plaster and brick walls radiated heat. Perhaps because it was so unbearably hot, dresses were more revealing and most often, men wore sleeveless undershirts. One coped. Folding hand fans fanning faces helped. You just had to bear the schvitzing and move as little and as slowly as possible on the unlit porch until the evenings cooled and then seriously kibitz the nights away with friends and neighbors, laughing and arguing and making your points and disagreeing, debating, counter-arguing, sweating, reminiscing, smoking, and drinking cold water, iced tea, Coca Cola, homemade lemonade, or a Canadian Club or two or three in schnapps shot glasses, getting *a bissel schickered*. Inside, the pinochle and gin rummy wars started the evenings until darkness, then everyone moved to the porch and the recognizable faces became the voices of silhouetted ghosts, from whom emanated the curling, undulating, writhing, dancing, cigarette and cigar smoke.

Most people smoked. Not Lena. When I was old enough to smoke, ten, I smoked Max's Hava Tampas. Max got me started at three to show me off, right after he returned home from the war. I wasn't given the opportunity to smoke my grandfather's Chesterfields. But when I was thirteen, I went into my mother's purse and stole one of her Pell Mells, as we called them, and smoked it in the woods. It was the first time I inhaled, I was so nauseated and woozy that I could hardly hear my uncle yelling at me at work in his propanegas plant. It affected my hearing.

My kid brother, Burt, smoked Hava Tampas too, to everyone's delight, when he was five. My clever uncle was showing me and my younger brother off. They tasted sweet and had wooden tips and the smell wasn't offensive, very sweet, actually. We held them like the adults, with paper rings on etended pinkies. Max proudly exclaimed, "Look at the little bastids! It's like rats thriving on rat poison," proudly watching us trying to blow smoke rings like the adults. He also taught me how to spell "psychoanalyst" and to say "You fucking whore," to my aunts, uncles, cousins, male or female.

Who knew what all that meant? All I knew was that it made my uncle proud of me. "Ha!" he exclaimed. He liked the laughter. He didn't realize it was the embarrassed type. He was the same uncle who spit in cousin Shirley's face while saying "Hello, you fucking whore," and thought that was funny too. It was humorous to him, not malicious. Many years later, she told me how disgusting it was, and she never forgave him his idiocy. She had no sense of humor.

The unbearably sweltering days and nights were like that. "Very, very swelterous," my grandmother said. She kept a handkerchief up her short sleeve. One coped. But summer nights in the dark, surrounded by the kibitzers on the front porch, was what summer was all about.

Television was World's Fair fantasy and radio was rare. Catskills Jews talked and laughed. The put-downs flew from one to the next, all in good fun. They were the first two generations in America: The generations of wounded, broken, persecuted families escaping the *shtetyls* and ghettos of "antisemitten bestids," as they pronounced it, of Eastern Europe, of World War I and the Great Depression. World War II would come later. These were the nights in their tiny, mostly Jewish, village in America, though, where the world's problems were always solved on that dark porch by some of the most renowned, international politicians and philosophical lefty thinkers; the blacksmith, hotel owner, barber, deli owner, car dealership owner, steam laundry worker, farmer, bungalow colony owner, butcher and other leftie rabble rousers who came to make mischief and solve the world's problems nightly.

## What's a Carcimona?

On one of those mid-July days, Laya developed an eye condition, not very noticeable at first, but one that within a day or so, became much worse; very red, a swollen, pus-filled lump, and extremely painful between her brows. She was not the type to complain. Pesach took her to Malisoff's office in the village. Malisoff had the white house with columns on our street, and lived with his wife and daughter, Elsie, which had to be a worse name than Minnie. Elsie the cow, the kids cruelly called her when she was not in hearing distance. She was almost totally blind. She lisped. Homely, too, and aloof and dignified as one would expect of a doctor's daughter in Woodridge. Compassion, shamefully though, was not in the kids' vocabulary.

Malisoff was the only doctor in town and was loved. He

was known to be ice, emotionally, but smart and dedicated. He was never seen without a tie and white shirt, even when called out for a house call to one's home in the middle of the night.

He recognized Lena's problem as being severe, and immediately insisted she see an eye specialist in the Bronx, and she was taken to see him after much reluctance to leave her house, family and duties at home. She had no chouce, her eyes were steadily getting more red and swollen from the lump, and they were almost closed. The specialist in a white lab coat said she absolutely had to have surgery to correct her condition, which in 1932 was incredibly risky. It was before antibiotics.

## Cousin Ray, The Medical Expoit

Lena was a country woman living in a little village of just a few hundred people. In 1932, the roads had not yet been paved. Going into a city hospital in the Bronx, leaving home, being amongst strangers, was disorienting, frightening and traumatic. Pesach had to work and take care of the chickens, blacksmith shop and family, and had to remain in Woodridge after the operation.

Their only link was Cousin Ray Fess from the Bronx by way of England, and she was a practical nurse. Ray was Laya's closest cousin. She talked fancy with that accent, nothing like Lena and Pesach's Yiddish—English. It wasn't anything like the Woodridge people spoke. Cousin Ray helped with the home deliveries and was the medical expoit. If you had something to worry about, you called cousin Ray.

If you had a "hunkus of the bunkus," you called cousin Ray.

Her daughter Shirley, "Shoiley" they all called her, and hunchback son Bernard, were like sister and brother to Laya and Pesach's kids, and stayed in the Shabus home often for extended periods of time in the summers.

Sam and Charlotte, in turn, stayed in cousin Ray's apartment while he attended New York University and she, secretarial school in Manhattan. Shoiley and Charlotte were like sisters. Bernard died the year before after a botched operation on his back to remedy the bone deformity from TB of the spine. An assistant surgeon fucked it up, and Bernard died soon afterward at twenty-one from, of all things, a heart attack, probably caused by the strain on his heart from all his post-operative difficulties. Maybe it was that, as well as the strain of the TB and pain of being so bent over, that put enormous pressure on his heart. Go figure. His death was a terrible event for the entire extended family.

He was a brilliant kid, high-spirited, well loved by everyone. Cousin Ray stayed with my grandparents for a long period of mourning. She cooked and plucked chickens with Laya. They picked huckleberries together and made pies and huckleberry kreplach. It was therapeutic. She was consoled by the only people she could turn to. Her husband Isaac, "Yitzy," was of no help. In between working as a tailor making overcoats seven days a week, he somehow found a few minutes here and there for other women. He made Ray's life miserable and was of little comfort at the death of their son. He was an icebox, everyone said, "Except when he gave his overcoat to a someone who was a little cold, when she was undressed." "He was a miserable bastard," said

Ray. "He's the one who should've dropped dead, that mamzur. G-d willing, they should only cut his *schmeckel* off, as small as it is!" It was the curse of curses.

## Doctor's Orders

Lena saw the eye surgeon and the decision to operate was confirmed, to be done immediately, as her eyes were growing worse by the day. The doctor used a medical term. He said it was carcinoma. "What's a carcimona?" she asked, and he told her it was a growth in a nerve, being as vague as he could, without trying to scare her any more than she already was. He said it was very small and she shouldn't worry. He would fix it. It was a relief. She was told that she had to remain in the hospital for two weeks and could get out of bed only to go the the bathroom the third day after surgery. In the old days, people stayed in hospitals for long periods. Her eyes would be covered for that time. They could not be exposed to light. She received a strict warning too, as did Persach and cousin Ray, who was at her side, that she was not to cry under any circimstances. She had to heal first, had to remain calm, stoic. She was a country woman struggling with life and bills and caring for five children, although Sam and Charlotte were already out of the house. "No crying, Mr.s Shabus. You should only think happy thoughts," the doctor told her. That would be the worst of it. Cousin Ray would be the one to visit every day. Pesach, after the operation, had to return home. All the news would come from Cousin Ray. After all the appropriate tests and results, the surgeon successfully performed the delicate, five hour operation.

When she was wheeled back to her room, she smelled of the strong odor of ether. It permeated the room. He eyes were bandaged and her intense pain managed with morphine. Cousin Ray took her battle station and was Lena's constant companion and eyes. Like Shirley and Charlotte, they, too, were like sisters, and Ray was allowed to stay with her long after visiting hours were over. She fed Lena, gently bathed and changed her, held her hand, shared stories, traded gossip, like two yentas. Charlotte and Sam came when they could, as school responsibilities consumed their time. Ray gave the Woodridge daily news updates of Pesach, the kids, the goings on in the village. She provided Lena's medical updates to the family by using the phone at the corner candy store by her apartment building, "Cohen's Handy Candy and Soda Fountain."

Pesach called cousin Ray in the Bronx at Cohen's. Mr. Cohen, the sweetest of men, ran, wearing his apron, from store to street, yelling up to the fourth floor apartment time after time "Mrs. Fess, for you a call!" Mr. Cohen combed his hair in oily strands across the top of his head in an effort to hide his baldness. Someone had to run into the building and get Ray in her apartment and she had to call Pesach back. She didn't have a phone in her apartment. Shouldn't have one till 1937. Couldn't afford it. She was home and had to run down four flights to the corner and call him back on the two-piece black phone of which she held the receiver to her ear and spoke into the vertical mouthpiece. There were the usual hellos, how's by yous, the family. Short. Expensive.

"And mine Layinkeh?"

# Scarlet Fever

Two days after Lena's operation, Minnie, whose skin even in summer was almost white, suddenly acquired a sunburn. She turned very red and developed a severe rash all over her body. She developed tiny bumps, more like pimples, all over her face and neck and was compelled to scratch incessantly. It wasn't a sunburn. The rash spread quickly to her body. Her throat and glands swelled, her mouth too, when she opened it, was red with whitish, yellowish, pus-filled purulent pimples covering her tongue and inner cheeks. It was repulsive to look at and to hear when she tried to speak in a growling voice. Her breath was oppressively worse than garlic and onions. Speaking was difficult, at times impossible, beause of her strep-like throat.

She developed a fever, started throwing up without warning; first in the kitchen and later in bed, and within a day, was so weak she couldn't get out of bed. Her temperature skyrocketed up to 105 degrees and sweat flowed into her down pillows and soiled sheets. The room stank. She trembled under the covers. Pesach called Dr. Malisoff, and Minnie was diagnosed with scarlet fever. The house was quarantined with a large X painted on a sign next to the front door, and no one was allowed to enter. No one had seen scarlet fever before. The doctor said she must have lots of liquids, forced on her if necessary, and told Pesach to cover her eyes against bright daylight, both because of their sensitivity to light and for her comfort. "Cool washcloths would help," he said.

Cousin Ray, the family medical expoit, was immediately called. She knew scarlet fever. "Give her iced tea. Give her ice cream," she ordered, "as much as possible. Keep her cool. Put ice on her head and neck and body. Make her drink. She must drink. Wash your nands. Keep her dishes and towels separate. Make like *milchedik* and *fleishedik*, like when we celebrate *Pesach*. Make like kosher. Separate her dishes towels. Don't mix. Wear masks. Anything. Wash, wash, wash."

"I want Mama! I want Mama, she should come home! I want Mama! Why can't she" Papa? I want Mama. Please, Papa! Papa, please go get her. I want her!" The tears dripped down her pimpled, red, bloched face onto her upper lip, into her pimpled, yellow mouth and onto her tongue, into the agony of her anxiety. How could she ever know how much Pesach wanted and needed her as well, and had to keep silent?

Pesach sat on the edge of Minnie's bed in his blacksmith's work clothes, dirty, stained leather apron tied around his waist and neck, an oil and coal one stained black hand held hers, wiping her sweating forehead and cheeks with a damp washcloth with his other, a blackish, gnarled hand on a young daughter's cheek, a caress, really, as only a father can do. He rinsed the washcloth out in cold water and covered her teary, painful eyes for comfort.

The etched blackness of his hand on her forehead accentuated the scarlet redness of her young, frightened face. Her fear was silently spoken. "Minnileh, Mama's sill in the hospital, with cousin Ray. Home she can't come, mommileh. She can't be moved. The doctor says G-d forbid if she moves, she could go blind. They won't let her get out of bed even. Soon she'll come home. A week she'll come home in. She'll make you what you like. You want a *bissel* Mama's chicken soup? You need a little something. A *gluz* tea? What I can get for you? You should have."

"Papa, I miss her. Maybe some soup." He got up, went to the old black stove and heated the soup. She weakly sipped a bit from the spoon he put in her mouth She was too weak to hold the bowl. She threw up on his apron. A big heave. A yellow vomit. She couldn't hold it. She fell back into the drenched pillow, groaning from the throat and chest pains. She had no strength. She shone from drops of sweat, dripping slowly off her face and nose.

"Oy, Papa, I'm so sorry," she whispered. "I couldn't help it. Maybe later. Oy, I made such a mess for you. I feel so tired. Maybe...a...little...nap." He held her limp hand while she quickly fell asleep and slowly got up holding his apron so it wouldn't drip on to the floor. She was curled up under the covers, shivering in her sleep. Her mouth was open, breathing hard. She made noises you should only know from.

Ray said, "She's feeling a lot of pain in her eyes and she complains that the bandages are tight. They give her something for it. She had to lie there and be helped. She asks about you and the kinder and the chickens and the shops. I tell her the weather's good and everyone's helping, even Maxileh. She says, 'Maxileh? He helps in the house?"

"Mine Maxileh, a helper? To a machine he's a helper. A little vasser, he wouldn't know what to boil." "We laughed over that, even though she's not supposed to laugh, and it hurt. She wanted to know how Minnie is and if Maxie is bothering her, and Charlotte and her Samaleh, the college student, when they're not visiting." Pesach said to Ray, "She's worse, I think. A fever she got. Her *keppie* is like a hot *schvitz* pot, she's so wet. I try to give her soup and then she vomits. I try to give her a *bissel* ice cream and she vomits. A bissel tea? She vomited on mine apron. Then I vomited. You can help it? She can't eat a thing. She's getting redder and got pimples like in a pincushion.

She can hardly talk to me. She doities the sheets. We are with her full time. Me or Max. He's got a tough job that Max. I run back and forward. I cover her eyes from the sun and lamp mit a wet schmatta. They hurt. It helps a *bissel*. Malisoff says just keep doing. It'll break."


## No Tears for Minnie


"What we tell Laya? She should know."

"Pesach, sweetheart, she can't know! You can't tell her anything! If she finds out, she'll wanna rush home. She'll see Minnie like that and will start crying. That she'll do. Remember, Pesach, my dawlinck, if she cries, she could go blind, the doctor says. Home, she can't go yet. And she can't know. Not a word! Minnie will start to get better in a day or so, please G-d."

"Yeh. Better she's not. Maybe she should sleep more. I need Layinkeh more than her. She should only see Maxileh what he does for his sister, of all people. Mine son Max, a real menschadikeh. Laya, she wouldn't believe it. So, nu, just tell her that all's good here. I miss her cooking, tell her. Give her a *kibitz*. Tell her I'm *besseh* when she's not around, so I can make mine salami and eggs and a *schtickle* sour pickle for breakfast. The house only stinks a *bissel*. Tell her to worry, she shouldn't. I'll have Max wash the dishes for once in his life and clean the house for her."

"Pesach, dawlinck, I'm watching Lena. She'll be home soon. She's getting better. I should tell her you miss her, G-d forbid?"

"You should tell her I miss her?"

"Such a *schtunck* you are!"

"Awright, tell her we're all good. If you tell her I miss her, she'll *pish* from the eyes, so don't tell. Thanks Ray, for everything."

He went back into his bedroom, where Minnie slept, and covered her forehead and eyes with a fresh, cold washcloth. He straightened her cover and air-kissed her cheek, without response. Her mouth was open and breathing through it with difficulty. Then he washed his hands and mouth vigorously. Couldn't get his hands clean enough, and spent a long time washing the cuts and bruises and burns and scars from each finger, washing his lips and falling tears. Max shouldn't see. He needed a shave and noticed the few gray hairs in the stubble.

Just as Lena finally had her first peaceful night, Minnie died in her sleep, eyes and forehead still covered with Pesach's *schmatta*. No one was in the room with her. Cousin Ray was home at 951 Jennings Street in her tiny three-bedroom tenement apartment. The building and hallways smelled of tenement stench, a rancid smell and odors of cooking from many apartments. It wasn't a country smell anyone was familiar with, unless one grew up there. It crept up one's nose and invaded one's senses, a combination of disinfectant floor cleaner, cooking, garbage, dead mice or rats, onion, bagels, empty pickled herring jars without caps, maybe garlic as well. Charlotte and Sam stayed wih her.

Charlotte shared a bed with Cousin Shoiley in the six by nine bedroom. Sam slept in the dining room—living room next to the table and the dark green velvet couch. The armrests were frayed. They all shared the one bathroom. The brown-stained bathtub was in the kitchen. The walls were thin. What's privacy?

In Woodridge, Max was upstairs. Pesach slept on the couch in the living room adjoining his bedroom. Nainie was upstate on a chicken delivery. Sporty, Pesach's chicken-catching mutt shepherd, slept next to Minnie's bed on his back, legs up in the air, torso curled one way, head the other. It was his spot. He snored like a human and twitched when dreaming.

Pesach was the first up in the early morning. It was going to be a hot one. He quietly went to the bathroom to do the usual; removed his teeth from the overnight glass, brushed them in his hands, dried and glued them to his gums and pushed tight to make sure they were secure. He made a little smile in the mirror, securing his teeth, uppers and lowers, with his two thumbs. He walked to the bedroom softly. The dog stirred and yawned and was petted on his belly and behind the ears. Pesach realized — in that instant

— that Minnie was dead. Her skin was no longer the bright red it had been. It was much lighter, more greenish-grayish-pink. Her mouth was open, exposing her yellow, pimpled mouth, but it wasn't a grimace or pain; just tranquil. It looked like she was in a deep sleep. She resembled Pesach.

He took a deep breath, as if inhaling when smoking, and let out a deep moan, a growl so deep, from a volcano inside where sound never before emanated, and moaned more. Staccato moans, short breaths of moans, moans humming with pauses, helpless moans from a man of extreme physical power, resistant moans, moans that drew heavy breaths while on his knees beside the dog, left hand on his child's face, the other unconsciously stroking the dog, caressing Minnie's face, petting Sporty's head, ears, muzzle. Crying so loudly, he exploded in the lava of grief cascading over his beautiful sixteen year old daughter, lying on his pillows, who was gone.

"Oy yoy yoy yoy yoy yoyyyyyyyy yoyyyyyyy yoyy yoy yoy yoyyyyyyyyyyyy..."

It woke Max, who ran downstairs and he too lost control upon seeing her, crying and sobbing uncontrollably. He was just a year and a half older than Minnie. He jumped on the bed and hugged her tightly, but her now stiff body was of little solace, as he and Pesach held her and cried. Men in the Shabus family didn't cry. Max, at seventeen, was the toughest of the Shabus kids. He loved to fight and was encouraged by Pesach. It wasn't the same Max on that bed. They couldn't look at each other in embarrassment. Sporty was up, front feet on the the bed. Shepherds howl in packs or when goaded on by people who imitate wolves. He was howling in concert, head up to the ceiling. He thought it was the howling game they played so often.

"Call Malisoff." Max ran to the phone in the kitchen, a wooden box on the wall. He cranked the hamdle and asked Vera, the operator and neighbor two houses down the street, to ring Dr. Malisoff.

"What's wrong?" Vera asked.

"Minnie….. She died."

"Oh, no!" and started crying over the phone. Choking up, Max abruptly hung up, not wanting to reveal his grief.

Dr. Malisoff hurried over and officially pronounced Minnie dead. To Pesach's reluctance, she was covered, but the washcloth was left on her face, for comfort.

"Max, call cousin Ray for me. Ask the operator to ring Cohen's."

In five minutes Ray called back. Pesach answered, voice shaky, "Ray, mine Minnileh….."

Long, interminable pause. "Nooooooooo!" Silence. At last, "Yeh, I woke up this morgn and she… was lying the way I left her last night. She died while we was sleeping. Quiet, she was. Who could know?"

Oh, noooooooo! Oy yoy yoy yoy yoy…" She started crying with big, heavy, heaving breaths and sobs. It sounded like a Jewish song. "Oy, Pesach, I'm so sick. My heart is pulminating. Was there any sign? Anything?" "No. Nothing. She was so weak last night, but this…? Oyyyyyyyy, min Layinkeh. *Ich gayst* to New York to tell Layinkeh. I'll have

Max drive me. We have to tell the *kinder*, Charlotte, Nainie and Sam." They were both sobbing.

"Oy, Pesach, oy what a thing. What to do? Pesach, wait before you come in." Ray was crying, but trying to think through it in that brief moment. "If you come in and tell Lena, remember what the doctor said; she could go blind if she cried and ruin the operation. If you tell her now, it could be more terrible *tsouris*. Oy, Pesach, how is this possible?" A lond pause...

"What a decision."

"Pesach... I'm supposed to go see her in two hours. I have to get ready and wash my crying out. How, I don't know. My eyes, what they much look like. Thank G-d I don't have to worry about. To see, she can't. Charlotte and Sam are already out of the house for school I'll arrange for them to come home with Shirley. I'll call the schools. I can't come to the funeral. I'll stay with Lena. I'll make like nothing, I promise. Somehow, please G-d, I'll make like nothing. I don't know how. I'll tell the family about it tomorrow. NO talking from any of them. Oy veyyyyyyyyyyyyy." She cried with the longest, trembling sigh. "And I can't even come to Minnie's funeral. I'm nauseous. I'm sick, the right thing, I don't know if I'm doing."

"You was right. Blind we don't need. Laya, oy. We'll have to have Minnie's funeral tomorrow. I will call the rabbi and arrange. They won't want to wash her body mit the scarlet fever, I know. We're quarantined, but we'll have it outside the shul by the Woikman's Circle Cemetery in Glen Wild. Call me later and I'll let you know."

"Okay, Pesach, I'm so sick. Shirley will have a broken heart. I'm glad Charlotte is with us. They're like *shvesters*, they're so close, those girls. Give my love to Maxileh and Nainie. I love you, dawlinck Pesakel. I feel so terrible. Minnie, sheshouldonlyrestinpeace."

"Yeh. I will make the calls. I'll make her box in the shop. I have oak. Ray, I want mine Layinkeh in one piece. Be an actress and don't tell a woid. You was right, you shouldn't worry, but she... I don't know what she'll do."

"Oy, what can I say? I did a terrible thing, I did the right thing, a wrong thing. I did, that's all I know. Oy, did I do, did I do," said Ray.

He called Rabbi Goodman, who came right over to console. He was the respected and much-loved rebbe, not one of the meshugeners, as Lena and Pesach and their friends talked about on the those porch nights about some of the other rabbis in the area. A real mensch. He was kind and gentle, thoughtful and organized. Her body was not religiously washed. He was a good consoler. He said the right things. Max tried to prove his young manhood by holding back, but he and Minnie were the closest of all the brothers and sisters. The funeral was arranged for the late afternoon to give the Bronxites, the whole family elsewhere, time to get to Woodridge.

Pesach took Max into the woodworking shop above the blacksmith shop, and picked out a number of strong, heavy oak boards, also used to make truck bodies for the farmers and other haulers in the area. They measured, cut, shaved, sanded and bolted a sturdy coffin together. It took hours. It was a time to release. Max helped with the bolting and finish work, cut out a Jewish star in the large band saw and screwed it onto the top. There was no time for shellac, but it looked beautifully constructed and finished without shellac. A professional coffin maker would have done less. He and Max carried it up to the living room and then wrapped Minnie, after last caresses and kisses and more tears from Pesach and Max, in a sheet and tenderly placed her now-stiff body into the open box, but not before placing a bottom sheet inside it. Her pillow was placed under her head and then her favorite knitted throw was placed over her. It was pink. She made it herself. Lena taught her how to knit. Minnie was an excellent knitter and learned the complicated stitches easily. In the box they placed a picture of Sporty and a few of her favorite rag dolls she kept on her bed. She and Lena made those as well.

They closed the coffin reluctantly and walked into the kitchen to have a late lunch of Kessler's salami on Al Schwartz's rye, which they bought from Zeldie and Sam Karschmer's Deli in town the day before. They added a couple of Lena's sour tomatoes from the large crock in the adjoining pantry. They were hungry. Max always ate with his eyebrows moving up and down with each bite. The kitchen smelled like a good deli. They drank from the blue seltzer bottle. Sporty always got his piece of salami or two. The meshugener dog loved Lena's sour pickles and got one of those for his treat. Only a good Jewish dog could love a sour pickle. He liked gefilte fish too, with a little horseradish, believe it or not. He liked his sips of coffee too.

"Max, *gayn* and wash the truck. Make it clean." It was a used 1929 1.5 ton Chevy. Black. They bought it used. It had dents and rust spots, but a strong oak body Pesach had made. "Abraham Shabus, Blacksmith and Chickens, Woodrodge, NY Tel. 71," was painted on the doors by Charlie Miller, the sign painter from up the road. Charlie had a painting on the side of his house of a cow stepping on one of its outstretched udders. Sporty followed Max to the yard. He liked being splashed. Abraham was a Yankee name no one ever used. He was also called "Honest Abe," like Lincoln, and "Mr. Easter Saturday" by the gentile salesmen who came to town once looking for him because of his Jewish Pesach Shabus name. All his Jewish pinochle friends gave him the "Helloooooo, Mr. Easter Saturday," treatment when they met him on the street.

Pesach was alone with Minnie's coffin. He sat down next to it on a kitchen chair he brought in and smoked one of his Chesterfields. The late sun poured into the room. The thick white-blue lazy, hovering smoke enveloped the room. Sunlight from the front window next to Pesach's brown easy chair illuminated the haze. The portrait of a lady with big breasts under her dress hung behind the chair. It was a 100% authentic reproduction they once bought on the Lower East Side in an art store.

He leaned over, resting his forearms on his thighs, facing Minnie's coffin, his neck bent toward the front windows. He flicked his ashes onto his other palm with his pinkie. When he finished the slow deep inhales of his smoke, he put the cigarette out between his thumb and pinkie. There was no feeling of pain. He did it every day, twenty, thirty, forty times a day, with yellowed fingers, heavily calloused from work and endless other cigarette burns.

He opened the bedroom windows to cleanse the air in

the room, removed the remaining sheets, pillow, cover and towels, and burned them in the backyard. Yushka was already with his chickens, and he and Pesach talked briefly. The village would soon know about Minnie. He was called "Yushka the *yenta*." His wife, Malka the witch, was hated by the family; she was so nasty to the Shabus children. She shrieked in Yiddish when yelling, and had long, straight, white, witch-like hair.

Sam, Charlotte and Shoiley came home from the Bronx on the steam engine-driven train that stopped in the middle of town, steam pouring out top and bottom, and Nainie drove home from Greecne, near Binghamton, which was a five hour drive, in between fixing endless flat tires, which were then so common.

Later in the evening when all were together, they gathered around the coffin and remembered much about Minnie with stories that made them cry or had them guiltily laughing uncontrollably. It looked like they were crying, so it was okay, as long as they kept their heads down when laughing. The absence of their mother was acutely painful, and the conversation centered on the decision of telling her about Minnie or not. It was divided and heated, defensive and angry.

Late next morning Pesach and the boys, Max, Nainie and Sam, carried minnie's coffin and laid it onto the flatbed in the back of the truck. Max gave a wipe to remove the morning dew and accumulated dust. It looked as good as a utilitarian, used vehicle could look. Who could afford better?

The family arrived by train and by Ford, Chevy, Nash Ambassador, Plymouth and Studebaker cars. The street was crowded with unfamiliar vehicles. Everyone wore black or dark gray or navy blue. Pesach wore the only suit and tie he owned. It was a Kulbitsky suit, at least ten years old, but kept in good shape, although a little shiny from ironing. His Perlmutter dress shoes squeaked and hurt. They never got enough wear to have been broken in after he purchased them when he got the suit from Kulbitsky's. The women wore a menagerie of fox and mink furs and of hats with pheasant feathers and see-through black veils of decorative spider webs.

The neighbors and villages turned out and filled Maple Avenue surrounding the house. It was a large crowd, sweaty and hot. The pervasive aroma of fresh schvitz was evident through wet shirts and blouses and everyone's underarms. Women fanned themselves with paper fans, local advertising artwork on front and back.

Nainie drove the truck up the driveway on to the unpaved street, flanked by large, stately maples shading the mourners underneath with dappled sunlight piercing through. The trees made all the mosest homes seem majestic. He looked straight ahead.

The procession proceeded ever so slowly up the street, with Pesach and children walking immediately behind the truck and everyone else following. He held Charlotte's hand on one side and Lena's very frail stepmother, *Bubbe* Anna Fein's arm, on the other. She was brought over from the distant nursing home in which she lived with Lena's father, Jacob Fein, who held on to Anna's other arm. She was a large, very overweight woman who could hardly walk. He has a long beard and was short and also fat. They once had a boarding house in Woodridge.

All the Fein children were short, but still too young to become as fat as he was. Lena's brothers and sisters were all there. Sadie Fein Reinstein, whom everyone called Sadie Reinstone, wore her mink scarf around her neck. It had an open-mouthed head on one end at breast level, ready to pounce on one of her breasts and the tail on the other.

Mac, her little husband with thick glasses, raised minks, killed them and made coats. Rose Fein Landau, children Jackie and Anita, Julie, Abe, his son, Richard, Hymie and Sam Fein, all walked side by side behind Pesach and his children. Sam Fein was the oldest. He worked in the garment district and sported a diamond pinkie ring displayed prominently when smoking his long, fat, smelly cigars, whose wet ends he chewed on like worn pacifiers. He flashed a gold false tooth on the right side of his set of false teeth. Irene, his wife, thought he was shtupping evey woman he ever met. Looking at her, who could blame him. The family couldn't stand her. The named her "Aunt Urine."

Her under jaw jutted out belligerently, exposing her yellowish, greenish, ill-fitting false teeth that clicked when she talked. Her eye makeup and bright red lipstick were excessive, as was her stinky, cheap ship perfume. Her lipstick extended beyond her thick lips. The lipstick stained her teeth red when she occasionally smiled. Her plucked eyebrows were as thin as written letters and just as black. Everyone she kissed had residual lipstick impressions on lips and cheeks. She had skinny ankles and a flat, shapeless *tuchus*, not worth a pinch, even during younger and better days, probably even too difficult to find. Hers was the only *tuchus* her husband, Sam, never dared to pinch in public and certainly, never her sagging tits, even at family affairs.

They all walked to the *shul* two blocks away. The road dust lightly covered their clothes like a dusting of confectioners' sugar. Solemn Rabbi Goodman greeted them outside. He said his prayers of mourning. Charlotte, through sunglasses hiding her red-tinted eyes, read a poem she wrote about Minnie, and then everyone walked back to the house to get their cars to go to the cemetery. The poem hovered like the dust, embracing Minnie's memory. There were endless tears and long pat-on-the back hugs and the sweetest of words and many compliments for Charotte's poem and the casket pesach and Max made.

"It was a casket only Pesach Shabus could make," they said. "You couldn't get one made like that in the Bronx. Real wood," said Hymie. "I think it's hamogany," said Sadie. "No," said Mac, " think it's boich, if you aks me." "Vaaaaa? What do you know about wood," asked Sadie? "Pesach's mine brother-in-law. It's hamogany, without question." She got the last word. She always got the last word.

More tears and prayers in the Glen Wild cemetery. Minnie's brothers and a couple of cousins carried her overly heavy coffin to the grave, and after more mourning prayers, kaddish, and heartfelt eulogies, Minnie was lowered into the hole and everyone took turns shoveling dirt on the box, but not before Charlotte dropped a small bouquet of wildflowers and the copy of her poem on it.

No one wanted to shovel until the Rabbi explained that shoveling dirt by family and friends was, in fact, creating a warm blanket for her, protecting and comforting her forever, and that it was the final *mitzvah* that could never be repaid but that's what real *mitzvahs* were. It was a kind way to translate the gruesome, sad task of throwing dirt down a six foot hole in rocky Catskills soil. The rocks first made loud, clunky, hollow sounds against the coffin, but as it was covered, the sounds became muffled. Everyone participated. When Sam Fein started shoveling, he threw a few shovelfuls energetically, and his upper false teeth with gold crown somehow slipped out of his mouth and fell into the hole with the dirt. The shock was evident to everyone and they immediately began, resistantly but hysterically laughing as he stood there, cheeks and upper lip caved in, holding his hand with the fancy diamond pinkie ring over his shrunken mouth.

He couldn't get to his teeth with the shovel, as much as he tried, and in desperation, jumped in on top of the box, located them under some dirt and tried to get out by himself, slipping backwards and falling on Max's Jewish star. A bunch of arms reached down and pulled him out, but the fake, pink gums part of the false teeth were filled with dirt and no one had any water to wash them. So, there was Sam Fein in his garment district finest suit, dirty teeth in one hand and shovel in the other. He raised his false teeth in wry, victory salute, looked back at the grave, shrugged his shoulders and walked back to the car. His wife Irene gave him a hard zetz on the back of his head and angrily called him a "real *schlimazel*, as usual."

After a dairy buffet at the house, family and friends dispersed, leaving Pesach and children to sit *shiva* for the next two days. There was too much work to do to extend it for the week. The kids went back to school and work.


## Oy Yoy Yoy Yoy Yoy Yoy Yoyyyyyyyyy


Lena was told nothing. She came home a week later with Ray at her side, wearing sunglasses to protect her eyes from the white, hazy, late afternoon summer sky. The areas around her severely bloodshot eyes were already turning from deep navy blue to violet tinged with yellow ochre; healing colors. She was happy to be home, at long last. They entered the house and Pesach was there to greet her, and, so unlike him, put his arms around her and spontaneously started to cry, his body heaving, breath sobbing loud, haunting, painful moans, shaking, quivering, tears flowing in waterfalls onto her shoulders from cheeks, wetting her dress-up-only-for-the-Bronx-dress.

"What, Pesa what!?"

"Minnie."

"What, Minnie? Is she hurt? She's awright? What!!!?" desperate questions.

"No." He held her tighter, rocking her back and forth, mammoth blacksmith hands on her back and back of her head, rubbing, squeezing, kissing and kissing nd kissing and kissing. "No!" she screamed, "Not mine Minnie! No, NO, NO, NO, NO, NO! Mine Minnileh?"

"Yeh." He whispered, "our Minnileh." And she fainted, bloodshot eyes rolling up into her head. Pesach held her up from falling, and then lifted her to the besd with Ray at his side. In his arms, she weighed nothing, a reverse Pieta. The sheets and pillows were fresh. Ray ran to the kitchen, grabbed a wet washcloth and ice from the icebox, and rubbed Lena's forehead, face and neck. It took a long while to bring her out of her faint, but finally, Lena opened her eyes, in Ray's loving arms, a torrent of tears flooding her face, tears that had been forbidden to fall, tears and cries, and sobs, punches in Pesach's chest, screams, wails, that pierced the collective heart of the neighborhood where everyone had waited in quiet trepidation for the homecoming to unfathomable grief. They weren't disappointed. Those who heard cried with her. Their requiem was heard through the living room windows. It was the dirge of immigrants who knew all too well the misfortune of infinite pain and loss from the old country.

"Why you not tell me, Pesa? And you, mine cousin, why YOU didn't say a woid to me? Not a woid? Nothing? I shouldn't know? Mine Minnie? Mine Minnie she's dead and a woid I shouldn't know? I shouldn't hear a thing from you?" screaming at them, tears falling from all three of them. "Don't touch me Pesa!

"And you, you, Ray, you was with me every day. You take care of me. The news you give me, so happy, so good. Everyone's good. The chickens, the shop, the *kinder*, they're good, they're wondehful, school is good, the family, what's not to be good? Mine eyes see good under the *schmattas*. You give me good so I see good. Good, alright, I got good from you, *zayeh* good. I lay there and I think, enough they got what to eat? I think flanken and a *bissel* veal and mine *kreplach*, a little chopped liver they should have, and a good Shabus chicken, and I think *aliz* is good and to come home to mine house I *cennisht* come home soon enough to mine *kinder*, mine Pesa and mine stove, mine bed, and *aliz is gut*, you should only know from, mine cousin Ray. Mine cousin Ray. Like a sister, Ray, a sister. You?

"Where is mine Minnie? In glen Wild?" He nodded his head affirmatively. "I wanna go there now! Get Max. I wanna see my Minnie. Pesa, what happened to Minnie?" She sat in the chair where she always hid the paper, handkerchief from her sleeve in her hand on her cheek, wet.

"Scarlet fever, she got, Malisoff said."

"Oy, mine *Gut*! *Guttenyou*. *Gevalt*! *Oy, vey is mir*. How? When?" Her hands covered her mouth and cheeks, and squeezed.

"She got sick when they operated on you. When she got woise I called Malisoff and when he come over, he took one look and a stick in her mouth and said scarlet fever she has. Give her liquids, gonseh liquids. Lots of liquids I gave her. She stayed in our bed. I was on the couch."

"Oy, mine *Gut*, mine Minnie. When she died? What day?" The handkerchief she kept under her sleeve was in her hand, wiping the tears and snot. Ray handed her her own handkerchief.

"Six days ago. May 26th she died. The doctor said keep putting cold washcloths and ice on her for the fever and I gave her a *bisseleh* juice and mit the ice and a washcloth over her eyes and she fell asleep and me *aoyket*, and I woke up and went to the bed and she was *schluffin*, but wasn't. I knew. Max hoid me and ran down and we called Malisoff. He ran over and it was too late."

"Oy yoy yoy yoy yoy yoy yoy yoy yoyyyyyyyyyyyy," and she threw up onto the floor, gagging violently, holding her stomach until the spasms subsided. Ray held her head. Minutes passed.

"I have to see Minnie. Pesa, we're going to the cemetery. Get Max. We're going now! *Gay avek* and get Max from school. I have to wash and change."

"But Lena, you just got home from the hospital," said Ray.

"You are telling me I shouldn't go to see mine Minnie? You? You, who lied to me. You're telling me? Who are you to tell me the cemetery I shouldn't go? How you could do to me this? How you couldn't tell me? Every day you come, you hold mine hands, you give me news. Your voice smiles at me from under mine bandages. You wipe mine face. You comb mine hair. You help me wash. Some news! A liar you are! LIAR! *Shakren!*"

"Lena, Lena, Lena, I couldn't tell you. I made a decision after the doctors said you could go blind from the operation. I couldn't." She was crying, trying to hold Lena's hand, without success.

Lena swept it away with the back of her hand.

"You couldn't? You don't think for mineself I could make a decision? My Minnie is dying and I shouldn't know from it? What do you think, I would care if I went blind? So, I would go blind. So I would die? So she should die in bed mitout me? Mit no one? You lost your Bernard. You don't know what that means to lose a *zin*? You were with him when he died. He died alone without you? No, not alone. Mine Minnie died alone. Whattaya think, you're a god you should make such a decision? I would rip both mine eyes out to be mit her. Would I care? And now I lost mine Minnie. You don't have the pain I have. You were there mit him, your Bernard. You held his hand? You gave to him a kiss? You touched him? You covered him, your Boinie? And you worried I should go blind? Since when you become the boss? A god you are?" Ray stood there, frozen, hands over face, doubled over, sobbing.

"Now Pesach. Get Max from school to drive." There was no resistance. He quickly left to walk to the school, cigarette between lips, probably his twentieth or thirtieth even then, a heavy smoking day. She sat on the bed, gently, absently caressing the pillowcase between her fingers, smelling the pillow for any sign of Minnie, not knowing her pillows and sheets had been burned. She was drained and white, except for her yellow purple eyes.

"Lena, dawlinck, I couldn't tell you. I just couldn't tell you anything. Pesach also decided you should not know. Doctor's orders. It was a warning. Sweetheart, *momileh*, my boubeleh, we followed his orders."

"Don't you *momileh boubeleh* me! Orders you followed? You'll come to the Workman's Circle with me. I'll give you your orders when you see mine Minnie. You'll come, you'll see his orders. In your *tuchus*, you should see his orders!"

After a long, tearful reunion with Max, they all got into the truck, Pesach and Ray sitting on the floor in the back. The drive to the cemetery was without discussion, but noisy from the engine and bumps. Max drove up the steep hill, through the wrought iron gates Pesach had made for the cemetery, and parked near the far end where Minnie was buried next to other family members. It was a new cemetery. The hole had been back filled to overflowing and at the head was a paper sign tacked to a thin piece of wood, stuck in the fresh ground with Minnie's name, date of birth and death: "Shabus, Minnie." Next to her grave were large maple trees shading that part of the cemetery in the late afternoon. It was a pretty spot, very tranquil.

She got out of the truck and, assisted by Pesach and Max, slowly, hesitantly, walked to the grave. Everyone was crying. She kneeled down on the bare earth and cried hysterically, bending back and forth like davening in shul and mumbling to Minnie in words no one could understand. She smoothed the dirt until it was without lumps and smelled it deeply. "Pesa, you have to make a fence for her. Make something so no one can walk on."

"Yeh. I'll make tomorrow."

"What is she in?"

"I made for her mit Max a beaudelful box, a bed. Max made the Jewish star for the top. A clean sheet I put under her and wrapped her up in another and I put her pillow under her head. A picture of Sporty I put in and a doll, the one she likes and had on her bed. You know which one. I dressed her in her white graduation dress from school."

"And her funeral?" Lena asked.

"Everyone. Everyone from the village. The family. Goodman gave a *gonseh* speech, and we all covered her. I wouldn't let the woikers do it. The boys and me and the family made for her a blanket from the shovels of dirt. We finished the covering."

She stood motionless, staring blankly at the grave for the longest time. Her eyes didn't blink. They were glazed over. There was no sense of impatience. *"Zayeh gut.* Come, I'm tired. Tomorrow we'll come back to mine Minnileh." She knelt down and kissed the soil. Max pulled the truck out and Lena was asleep almost immediately. Her head rolled from side to side, up and down, seemingly detached from her slumping body.

It was almost dark when they arrived home. Sporty was there with a big greeting, jumping on everyone he could. Cousin Ray immediately went into the kitchen to heat up the chicken soup Pesach had made. She stayed with Lena overnight and then returned to the Bronx after being told to leave, and probably wished she could've left immediately from the cemetery. Through the tears, Lena would not let up nor forgive Ray for carrying out the secret conspiracy she and Pesach felt was necessary. It was Ray's fault, as far as Lena was concerned, and Ray did not stop hearing about it. Ray had expected a lesser reaction, considering how close the two of them were, and probably felt that time would eventually diminish the heartache and accusations. But it didn't, and every time Lena visited Minnie's grave, her anger toward Ray, the family's medical expoit, surfaced.

Forgiveness was not to be given.

But the years passed, many of them, and Lena kept her distance. The rift grew, despite Pesach's and Ray's attempts to heal the wounds of grief. Ray visited, as did Shoiley, many times, and together, they all went to the cemetery to place stones on Minnie's headstone, as well as on the headstones of other relatives buried there. Flowers were not allowed. Too fleeting. Lena tolerated the company. As in every community, the cycle of life and death, of grief and celebration, continued, and the intensity of pain, the scar of death, receded to some degree, only to surface again when moments of what ifs and only ifs reappeared.

## 4. A Marriage Made In Kulbitsky Wedding Night

### 1939

The marriage "made in Kulbitsky" was one of those events in 1939, seven years later, after Minnie's death. The Shabus family was invited to the Kulbitsky/Perlmutter wedding in New York, where the Kulbitskys lived, and it was the usual questions of how to go there, what to wear, can I borrow Sadie's mink stole and is Pesach's white shirt too tight around the collar? Endless concerns that were disruptions to the rhythm of life in Woodridge.

Nuchum Perlmutter had an English accent. He emigrated from London with his Polish-English parents. His advantage in moving to America was that he spoke English while most of the other immigrants spoke only Russian, Polish and Yiddish, and later, English with heavy Jewish accents. He, on the other hand, spoke Yiddish with an English accent. No one ever said that someone spoke Yiddish. Jewish. What Yiddish?

Nuchum's father was a shoemaker, too, but Nuchum learned his craft as an apprentice to another shoemaker. His father was very demanding, and it was better for Nuchum to learn from someone else. The Perlmutter family was originally neighbors of the Shabuses on Henry Street in The City, and it was at Pesach's urging that enticed them to move up to the Catskills after Pesach and Lena moved to Centreville Station from the Lower East Side.

They, like most of the new settlers, came by train, steam engine driven, loud, the sound of a hooting whistle and shooting white steam, "pshhhhhhhhhhhhhh," and exciting to see whenever it stopped at the train station in the middle of town at the beginning of the 1900s. Initially, many of the Jews were greeted by signs on trees that proclaimed, "No Jews or Dogs Alowded", as well as the prerequisite gentile welcoming party intent on beating them up to try to prevent them from settling in their gentile enclave. The Jews knew they were hated, but what did they have against those poor dogs? One wondered too, how many of those immigrants could actually read those "welcome signs" which had been written only in misspelled English.

My grandfather, with friends, organized a welcoming party of their own one night and beat the shit out of the gentile anti-Semites, or so the family story goes. But knowing what a fighter Pesach was, it's a good story to pass on. His eyes of gray steel were intense enough to alert any adversary with his potential for anger, but he was a gentle man, as strong as he was, and when I was a kid, that was all past history of Pesach. He only fought for valid reasons. He was too busy surviving, shoeing horses for five cents a hoof, to continue to fight.

And no one ever asked much about the past. To this day, nothing was known about his parents, great grandparents, and siblings. Centreville was more of the future than the past, and today, that memory is an empty cave whose entrance had been blocked. Centerville's name was changed to Woodridge in 1932, further pushing back the past even further.

Nuchum Perlmutter opened his shoe store in 1905. He ran it until 1932, when he unexpectedly and suddenly had a massive heart attack while fitting a black thick-heeled shoe onto Mrs. Leibowitz's purple-ankled foot. He keeled over into her lap with his head lodged between her thighs. By the time she stopped screaming, neighboring storekeepers had finally arrived to help. She had pushed him off her lap and he lay at her feet, eyes fixed and open, dead. Her urine dripped onto the black and white checkered linoleum floor that was supposed to look like marble.

There was nothing anyone could do. Nuchum's wife ran the store for a few years, and in 1936, when their son, Manny, was barely out of school himself, he took over, selling, repairing and handcrafting the finest English leather shoes in the Catskills, just like his father and grandfather, one generation to the next. He was a young master cobbler and Nuchum would have been proud of him. His fingers and nails were permanently stained black and never looked clean, just like his late father's.

Manny was a distinguished looking, slight, young man who always dressed impeccably and carried himself proudly. He wore a white shirt and tie to work. He met Molly Kulbitsky in New York on a visit to the Lower East Side while buying his English leather from the nearby supplier, Lefkowitz's Leather Goods and Remnants on Delancey Street. Molly worked in her parent's men's shop and Manny stopped in to buy an all-purpose suit. Black. Three piece. Wide tie with crests and little dragons. Very sophisticated. The store was well known: Kulbitsky's Clothing, "A Fit for a King. Free Alterations. Tailor inside."

They were attracted to each other immediately. She talked about the quality of her parent's clothes and he about the handmade shoes that he and his late father, heshouldrestinpeace, made. Whenever someone in a family died, he or she automatically was given the last name of "Heshouldrestinpeace." They had much in common and lots to talk about over the counter, one would guess about shoes and suits. What else? Through the course of being fitted and flirting, albeit subtly, she told him that her parents came up to the Catskills and rented a bungalow in Glen Wild near Woodridge every summer.

She accompanied her parents to the Catskills that summer. Her father stayed only for the weekends like most city husbands, and took the train back to New York late on Sundays. Manny courted her through the summer into late autumn, whereupon he asked her father for her hand. A great philosopher and a loving father, he looked into his daughter's eyes, asked her if this was what she really wanted, to move up to the Catskills, and proclaimed his approval to her when she nodded yes. He had gotten to know Manny throughout the course of the summer and proudly wore a handmade brown pair of Perlmutters, a gift from Manny. He said, "A better husband you'll never find, mine Mollinkeh, and if his shoes fit, you should wear them." It made sense. He liked those American expressions.

"Yes, Papa. Thank you, Papa. Thank you, Mama. Thank you! You'll come stay with us after we get married so you won't have to pay for a bungalow.

"Ahhhh, that suits me fine, too." Her father said.

"When do you make the knot to tie? We need to make a date for your *simcha*." A marriage was arranged shortly afterward.

She was barely five feet tall, perfect for his five foot four inch height. They married in 1938. It was a big wedding in the famous Cohen's Classic Catering on Houston Street, the best in New York. All of Mannie's Woodridge friends made the five hour trip to New York. The food was good. They had the Jewish works. It was worth the trip. He was twenty. She, eighteen. All the Woodridgites wore Perlmutter's shoes, including Lena and Pesach who, on a rare trip to New York, wore theirs. Manny pointed them out to his *machetunim*. After he gave his Molly a kiss to remember, he performed the final rite of the wedding ceremony: His own English leather shoe broke the glass soundly with a real *klop*. "Mazel tov" from everyone. His father would have been very proud to see and hear how well his shiny black shoe performed. That was THAT! That sealed the deal. It was the final gesture of their marriage ceremony. And then, of course, that quick, modest kiss not to be forgotten.

The men danced with the men. The women with women. That was the custom. They carried the bride and groom on chairs all around the catering hall as Manny and Molly held aloft a white napkin together in the middle of the frenzied swirl of relatives and friends, lifted and swaying up and down like swelling ocean waves at their peaks and valleys, guests and families stamping and clapping, frenetic and frantic, singing, yelling, kicking, crying, *schvitzing* and *kazatzkehing* in the ecstasy and joy and abandon of an old-fashioned Klezmer hoe-down of siren clarinets, screaming violins, pulsing drums and piano, playing the *horah* and other Yiddish classics faster and faster to a throbbing inner beat driven relentlessly by the bearded musicians whose yarmulkes bounced up and down aside their heads as they played, held to their hair with bobby pins. Never stopping, they danced arm in arm, hand in hand, balancing candles on foreheads, pretending to be bull and bullfighter, arms outstretched, children flying through the air held in maypole suspension, in a gloriously wonderful *simcha* of a Jewish wedding that began fifty-seven hundred years before.

The Kulbitskys and the Perlmutters. In America! Their children got married in America! THAT was a wedding, they said! Only in America. If only the Bubbes and Zaydehs could have lived to be here, theyshouldrestinpeace! *Vey iz mir*, would they *kvell*!

In their bridal suite above the catering hall, Manny

made love to Molly wearing his sweat-soaked Kulbitsky suit, pants down to his knees, suspenders hanging over his soggy, white, unbuttoned shirt, wearing his Perlmutter English leather shoes, in honor of the memory of his late father, Nuchum, and his father-in-law, Mr. Kulbitsky. On this first night of marriage, a better, well-dressed *shtup* they never had.

It was a welcome break for the Shabuses. Just a few years later, the war broke out and their sons, my uncles all enlisted, Max and Sam in the army, Nainie and Harry in the navy. Max, Sam, and Nainie were in Europe and in the Pacific, fighting, and Charlotte married Joe Ernstein, a pharmacist from the Bronx. Joe was needed at home to dispense prescriptions. They moved to South Fallsburgh over their drugstore in partnership with brother Harry, who was then a navy photographer in the Pacific. The family get togethers were as raucous as ever with whoever remained in the Catskills and city, tinged with the war, the rift and Jewish news. Everybody lost somebody to "that *mamzur* Nazi bestid." Lena and Pesach's home was the family magnet, and when the war ended, the family was drawn ever closer together. When they all came up from the various boroughs for the holidays and special occasions, the table was expanded into the living *room, and like those nights on the porch, the conversation* was loud, crude, sarcastic, funny, exuberant, loving, politically passionate and demonstrative.

Sam Fein was the dangerous one, the guy who greeted almost every female relative from behind with two hands over their tzitzkelehs, or a hand on one of their oversized, cellulite-dimpled *tuchuses*, a pinch here and a pinch there, wet kisses and the repulsive surprise of almost kissing but first dropping his top teeth next to their faces. At least he didn't spit. His loss of his teeth at Minnie's funeral was remembered. "Sam, you brought your glue with you?" Hymie asked. He was another of Lena's brothers, the little *schtunck*, was another of the Fein pinchers, an esteemed member of the *tuchus* patrol. He followed Sam around the table. As a joke, he thought, Max greeted cousin "Shoiley" by spitting in her face. Funny, he thought, not meaning to be malicious. Not funny to Shoiley. Some sense of humor he had, that Maxileh.

## 5.  Max, Maxie, Mockzie, Maxileh, Welcome Home

1945

On a Friday afternoon in August 1945, the doorbell rang, Sporty the dog snarled menacing, warning, ferocious growls. Lena opened the door, wearing a pale blue dress covered with little pastel-colored flowers and white apron. And there he was, unannounced, army green duffle bag on brick floor, in wrinkled uniform, needing a shave. He stood there, all five foot, seven inches, and she stood at the door staring at him, not moving, staring at a stranger she hadn't seen in over two years, a stranger, thin and balding, a soldier… from a Jewish town of five hundred people who went to war, the son of a blacksmith and chicken dealer, a country kid who could speak English hardly at all until he went to kindergarten in the little, yellow ochre brick, Woodridge school for all grades. He was twenty-five years old two years ago and now standing at the front door, an apparition in khaki. He kept his combat medals in his duffel.

Her hands went to her mouth and her eyes flooded. She slowly, slow motion slowly, reached for his neck and wrapped her arms around him and he put his arms around her waist and lifted her little, plump five foot, one inch body up in the air and rocked her back and forth, set her down and rocked and swayed her cheek to cheek, wordlessly both trembling and sobbing, shaking with the intensity only a mother and child could express without embarrassment, without words. She kissed his cheeks, his hands, his forehead, ran her somewhat swollen fingers over his stubbled face and felt his taut forearms and upper arm muscles and looked into his hollow, bloodshot, changed, distant steel-gray eyes, now spider-lined on the outside corners of his eye sockets, studying them, clutched him tightly again. It was a mother's unyielding hug. The tears fell on his uniform and on her flowered dress.

He was a Shabus, Pesach's son; tough as a blacksmith's son could be when he left. Shabus men didn't cry...except today. Two years in France, Germany, Belgium and the Battle of The Bulge, where he lost the hearing in his right ear. Their dog, Sporty, a mutt shepherd, his muzzle now gray, insistently dug his head and nose into Max's pants, whining, impatiently demanding to be petted, frantically jumping on Max from behind until noticed, leaving dirty paw marks on

Max's tan shirt, scratching his back.

From a distance, the two of them could hear the harsh, rhythmical clanging of hammer against steel, a musical beat to a silent song. He listened to that metallic music and she gave him a look, nodding and turning her face toward the blacksmith shop. He slowly walked through the black wrought iron gate fabricated in that shop by his blacksmith father and walked down, observing the maples and apple trees that had significantly grown, the cracks in the concrete driveway, the faded gray paint on the coop and barns, listening to the clucking of white leghorns and the happy barking of the dog following along. The black chicken truck was in the yard, a 1931 GMC Model T-18 that still ran like new. The doors read "Pesach Shabus, Blacksmith & Chickens, Klop & Cluck, Woodridge, NY, Phone 71." It was covered with dust. It was a truck. Who washed trucks? It was the engine that counted.

His pop was working in Caravaggio darkness, the top of his head illuminated by the only dim, yellowish bulb and the white-yellow hot coals in his forge. He wore a blackened, thick, stained leather apron, dark blue short-sleeved work shirt, gray pants and heavy dark brown work shoes. He was six feet tall and lean, his arms, pronounced muscle, sinewy. On his head was his wide-brimmed, gray cap. It hadn't changed. It was just dirtier and frayed. It tilted to one side, jauntily, but without a vain or flirtatious reason. It was just the way he wore it. His moustache was now speckled gray as was his hair that protruded through the sides of his cap. He looked like he hadn't shaved in two or three days.

In deep concentration, he worked the yellow-hot horseshoe on his large anvil, which rested on a wide two-foot slab of an old oak tree, solid and unmoving against the barrage of his powerfully rhythmical, effortless blows. The rest of the blacksmith shop was filled with various tools, many of which were crafted by him. The forge had to be pumped with air with one arm while the horseshoe was either held with his other hand or inserted in the coals to heat and soften for shaping on the anvil. The waiting workhorse stood next to Pop, a black Percheron, beautifully groomed. Shabus gave him a sugar cube. He doused the hot horseshoe in a pail of water, hissing and steaming while it tempered. It fogged the rays of sunlight and gave it shape, briefly outlining the horse and the blacksmith's face.

He turned his back to the horse's body away from the front door, and lifted its front leg between his own legs, aside his apron and held it securely while filing the hoof and then nailing the new shoe. He was careful. Two years before he got kicked just above his eye on top of the socket. Luckily, it only required ten stitches, but there was a pronounced line dividing his eyebrow. His back was to the door.

Max stood in between the open double doors silhouetted against the intense sunlight illuminating the doorway. He stood there patiently attentively watching the familiar pose, as if time stood still. His army cap was on his head and he waited silently. He watched. He wasn't noticed. He didn't yet want to be, not quite yet.

Then quietly, "Pop..."

Pesach looked up but found it hard to see, yet he instantly knew it was Max. He had just finished nailing the new shoe and released the horse's leg. They rushed each other and hugged. Pesach crushed his son, hammer still in his hand. They started crying, sobbing, emotions that were never shown so overtly, but were so deep, uncontrolled, spontaneous. His youngest son returned and in one piece.

Pesach pulled away to arm's length to observe his Max, in uniform. He put his muscular arm around Max's neck, pulling him to his face and kissing his forehead. They never kissed before. Pesach didn't kiss. It was the age of handshakes. Today, they kissed. Fifty years before, Pesach escaped Russia by strangling a Cossack at the border. He ran, not knowing to where, and somehow, ended up on Henry Street in New York City's Lower East Side until moving up to the Catskills and settling in Woodridge. The story ends there. He had told others that he didn't even know what that big green statue of the woman was in the New York harbor. And now his son returned home to Pesach's home in America far away from the War. Max was home, away from that land in Europe where that statue was made. It was time to have a glass or two or three of schnapps and eat.

The horse was tied up and they went into the kitchen by way of the back door, through the pantry, with its crocks of sour and half sour pickles and tomatoes on shelves, rationed cans of food, home preserved vegetables in jars, bags of flour and a small tin of rationed sugar. The kitchen hadn't changed: The porcelain sink and green and cream Universal gas stove, white hand painted cabinets, wallpaper with little children dancing in the woods, flowered oilcloth on table, flowered plates, Lena's best but some chipped, fresh baked chollie with schmaltz from Pesach's chickens, well-used flatware, tinted blue glasses and a couple of shot glasses for Max and Pesach.

Shabus dinner at the Shabuses: Chopped liver, meat *kreplach* in the clear chicken soup with little, unhatched hard boiled eggs from their butchered chicken, *lokshen*, roast chicken, string beans, carrots, homegrown tomatoes, pie from the rhubarb also grown in the well-fertilized garden nourished by their own chickens' manure. A typical Friday night dinner. The men took turns at the kitchen sink washing their hands. Max lingered over the sink, allowing the hot water to run through his fingers long after the soap had washed away. Washing hands was the Friday ritual before Lena covered her head, lit the candles, held her hands over her face and recited the Shabus prayers.

Time for dinner.

## The First Supper

The meal began with a schnapps and a "Welcome home, Maxileh! You're the foist to come home. *L'chaim!*" and down the hatch went the schnapps. "Laya, you got nothing to feed him? Look at him, he's stahrvink, mine soldier. We can't eat awready?"

"Sha, Pesa, food you don't see?"

"Here, mommeleh, *nem a bissel* chopped liver. I got *kreplach.* I just made it. Take with some *chollie.* You ate

79

like this in the army, I ask you?" The aroma of the chopped liver and fresh-baked braided bread overwhelmed the kitchen. Max helped himself, took a large knife-full and *schmeared* it on a ripped piece of the chollie, his eyebrows jumping up and down with each bite. He closed his eyes, slowly savoring every morsel, and burst out crying long sobbing, loud, intense sobs, gasping, unable to catch his breath. He covered his eyes and face and sat there crying, his elbows on the table, forearms upright and clasped, chin and bottom lip cradled on his hands, unable to look up, tears dripping down his fingers, chest heaving rapidly from the intensity of his crying, as if one were driving on a very bumpy road, from the effort of trying to catch his breath and long intervals of being unable to take a breath. Lena, too, started crying, as did Pesach, the three of them unreservedly crying. She got up and put her fleshy arms around Max, clutching him, kissing his hands and head and eyes, wiping his eyes, squeezing his fingers. He put an arm around her waist in recognition, looking up at her eyes with his wet, red eyes.

He finally, after minutes, softly said in Yiddish, "I see you and this food, our house, Pop's shop, and you have no idea what I've seen, where I've been, what I had to do to stay alive. No idea. You don't ever want to know. You don't want to know about my tank destroyers and the other brave guys I fought along with, and those fucking Nazi sonofabitch antasemitten bastids. We could never kill enough of them. Sorry for the language, ma. And here I am eating your chopped liver and *kreplach*. Did I ever think I'd ever eat your chopped liver ever again?"

They sat, more in silence, at the green enameled table and drank coffee, never hot enough for Lena, as scalding hot as it always was, and finished the meal with fried in the pan huckleberry *kreplach*, sprinkled with precious, scarce sugar. Max kissed her forehead and each cheek and walked out to the porch to sit with Pesach on the rocking couch and chairs. They smoked together and they talked about the local guys who had been killed and if any of the others had made it home yet. They talked about the guys who were wounded. The dog lay down on the cool cement between them. Max idly ran his hand under the dog's ears, scratching gently.

"Did ya hear from Sam and Nainie?" His brothers.

"Yeh," said Pop, Sam's still in Joimany with UNRRA. He's a major. He's working with the DP's, helping them get food and finding missing families and putting on plays and concerts in the DP camps. Make a little life for them. Nainie, he's stuck in Guadalcanal, but he's good. He wrote he'll come home soon, but what's soon? A week, a month? As long as he comes home. Mama will make them suffer, too, at the table. You saw the floor mat when you came into the house, "For Mom, From Guam?" He got some natives to make them and he sold them to his sailor friends and makes a *bissel gelt*, my businessman sailor. He's in the Pacific on a supply ship, somewhere by Gaudalcanal. When we last saw him, he says that bastid Red Cross: Our men, he says, are eating crap and the officers, only the best they got of everyting. That's the Red Cross, they should only drop dead."

"Pop, maybe you call Charlotte for me and tell her to

come home from Fallsburgh? Ma needs her help, tell her. Don't tell her I'm here. I can't believe she got that little boy I haven't seen since he was a little baby! What's Noogie now, three?"

"Yeh, I'll call now. He's a real *vance*, that Noogileh! He got a mouth on him, a *kup* on those shoulders. You want anaddeh schnappsle?" Max nodded "Yes."

He returned with two glasses and Canadian Club, this time regular glasses, and filled them half way. A *l'chaim* to each other and long, burning sips. And then another. "So, you killed those basstids?"

"What do YOU think, Pop, those Aryan sons a bitches? We only recently heard about concentration camps all over Poland and Germany, mostly Poland, killing Jews from all over Europe. I loved killing those muthehfuckers. I loved blowing up their fucking tanks and watching 'em explode and waited for them trying to get out. We all popped 'em, shot 'em in the dicks and balls first when we could, and sometimes afterwards. Give all those fuckers a *bris* on the battlefield. Make Jews outa them. All I thought about was them or us, and I thought about those poor bastids, our people, Jews, murdered in the camps. Fuckin' war made us into animals, Pop, just tryin' to stay alive.

I got one SS Nazi officer, badly wounded, and took his dagger, and while the blood was running out of his ugly fuckin' mouth, told him in Yiddish I have a little present for him from Buchenwald, and I stabbed him with his own dagger in his throat and held it, giving it a little extra *zetz* while he choked to death. '*Auf Wiedersehen,* you motherfuck,'

I smiled at him, like I smile at girls! I have the dagger here in my bag. I have it in the house to show you. One less Nazi *mamzur* to kill Jews, besides our own army guys. Got a Nazi flag too, I took from one of the tanks we hit, after we shot 'em all, and that inspiring book by Mr. Hitler, *Mein Kampf*, I saved just for you. It's this version that is entirely in Yiddish, you believe that?"

"Nooooo, you mean it, Maxeleh?"

" ….Kidding, Pop. You think he'd ever write it in Yiddish for us? It's like when you strangled that Cossack when you escaped Russia. Him or you. You really strangled him with one hand?"

"Yeh, It was fast. I had mine little suitcase in mine other hand. I lifted him up in the air and squeezed his throat, the *mamzur,* and watched him squoim a *bissel*, not too long. Then he stopped and I threw him in the woods, he should rot for the birds to eat. When I think back at that time, I don't know how I escaped, but I had to get out, mit what they was doing to the Jews in all the *shtetyls*. It was a long time ago. He stood in mine way."

"So a Cossack you killed by squeezing his throat and I killed a Nazi in the throat with his own dagger."

"*Nu, boychickel*? Like papa, like son." After a long, inner thoughtful pause, he softly placed his hand on Max's wrist. Max placed his on top.

He took a long, deep drag on the Chesterfield, and the smoke, like a sunset fog, hovered between them on a warm, windless, humid August evening. Max was on his chain third. Third drink, too. The orange sky was turning purple green and deep navy blue. They stared out onto Maple Avenue, over the wrought iron fence Pesach made and red geraniums in the cement planters on top, across to the Kriegers and tree-lined street into the fading horizon, their gray eyes hardly blinking, watching, staring, getting very drunk.


## Get Over Here, You Little Bastid

His younger sister, Charlotte, arrived in her 1940 Black Plymouth, screaming, and helped me l out of the front seat next to her. I was three years old. Max rushed down the brick steps and they grabbed each other and she and he started crying, heaving, in their intense embrace. His cheeks and lips were covered in bright red lipstick. I started crying too, thinking something was wrong. She picked me up and said, "It's OKAY, Noogie! It's OKAY! It's your Uncle Max. Give him a salute, just like I taught you. How do you hold your hand and fingers? That's right! Good! Now give Uncle Max a huggie kissie. Don't be shy, sweetie, he's Uncle Max from the army."

"I scared, Mommy. What's a uncle?" He's wearing funny clothes. He smells!"

"SHHHHHHH, Noogie, that's not nice to say!"

"But he smells, Mommy."

Max grabbed me away from Charlotte, "Smells, huh? C'mere, you little bastid, I'm gonna make you fly," and he threw me up into the air and then threw him again and them again, and I started screaming with laughter, "Dowwwwwwn!" and Max buried his lips onto my neck and gave me fartsy kisses behind my ear, forcing my neck sideways and squeezed me tight to his chest so I couldn't squirm away from those noisy, slurpy fartsies. "Now I'm GONNA GET YOU AGAIN," and Max planted more kisses on my neck and cheeks. I squeezed my eyes shut and scrunched my lips, trying to escape.

Lena had come out by this time and they were all crying, watching Uncle Max and me, together for the first time. Then Max turned me upside down and hung me from his ankles and swung me back and forth as I yelled, "More, more, more!" Max cradled me in his arms, and with his mouth, pushed my shirt up, exposing my belly and belly button, and planted more noisy kisses all over my tummy as I tried to get away, squirming as best I could. He lowered me to the floor, and then he had a boxing match with me and I got him to the floor and jumped on top of Max as Max lifted me up in the air by the midrift, letting me dangle my puppet legs and kick and scream, laughing a kid's infectious, high-pitched laugh, hardly able to catch my breath. He lowered me numerous times to nuzzle me with those kisses and then raised me again, threatening to GET ME AGAIN!!! "Down! I wanna go down!" I screamed.

"Hold my hands. Okay, put your shoes on my shoes. Awright, hold on, I'm gonna give you a ride." He held my hands tightly and walked me all over the porch, high stepping, small stepping, left, right, back, forth. I was yelling, "More, more!"

"Not until you salute me again! Show me how." Max bellowed, "Ten HUT! That means stand like this, straight up," Max demonstrated and Noogie came to attention and saluted with his left hand. "Ahhhhhh, good! But first one more time! I'm gonna get youuuuuuuuuuuuu," and he fartsied me one more time on the back of my neck, before finally releasing me.

"How'd ya eveh get such an ugly kid?" he asked Charlotte. "I had to come home to see this ugly little bastid? What the hell is wrong with you? This is what we're fighting for? Where's your fuckin' husband? Did you take some of his ugly pills from the drugstore to make such an embarrassment? Jesus Christ almighty! Get over here, you little bastid." I came over and snuggled between Max's knees as Max put his arms around me and squeezed tighter and tighter until I gasped for breath.

"Say, 'Uncle,' or I can't let you go! Say 'Uncle.'"

"Uncle!" and Max let me go, but grabbed me quickly again and squeezed tighter. "UNCLE!" and Max said, "Nope, you can't get out until you press the button, and held out his hand for me to press, which I did, and Max then released me, and then repeated the game a number of times, making a buzzing, button-sounding noise each time. "Go give Grandma and Pop a big kiss. Hurry up, you little *mamzur!*" as I ran over to kiss each of them, and then ran back to Max.

I held Max's fingers while Charlotte asked him about the war and told him how skinny he got. "You need to eat. I can't believe you're home, that you're here. That you're in one piece. Novogrodsky, heshouldrestinpeace. The others made it: Schwartz, Kaplan, Davis, Smith, Krieger, Rachmelovitz. Schlammy was badly wounded in the Pacific. How was it for you? Did you fight? Did you kill any Nazis? Was it terrible?"

"No, I didn't kill any Nazis. I wasn't anywhere near them. I was lucky, very fuckin' lucky. They put me far behind the front lines and had me repairing vehicles and equipment, and making sure the guys were well-supplied with some of the shit that was mailed over, like salamis, chocolates, cigs. I never fought. Never killed anyone. But I happened to buy a Nazi dagger, Hitler's *meshugener* book and a Nazi flag from a gift shop in a small town near Poland. I have them here." He showed her.

She took the dagger from him and examined the beautiful workmanship and asked, incredulously, "Do you really expect me to believe you bought this in a gift shop? Do you think I'm that much of an idiot? But I really don't wanna know. It's bad enough I can imagine it." He quickly glanced over to his Pop for an instant eye-to-eye recognition that she didn't notice.

"But I'm here, genius, and do me a favor…save your, what is called cooking, for your other brothers when they get home. Even the Army food is better than the crap you put on the table, even after all these years. Lucky they got army and navy cooks."

"And…did you learn that "f" language in Germany? Do you HAVE to use it here, and in front of the kinde? Come, Noogie, time for night, night."

"Noooo, only if Uncle Max comes up and weads to me."

"Awright, c'mere. Turn around. Ready? Up we go." Max hoisted me onto his shoulders and swung me back and forth. I grabbed Max's substantial ears to hold on, and to the door and up the stairs we galloped.

His bedroom, at the left top of the stairs, was the same, except for the toys and children's pictures taped to the walls, some reproductions and others of my creations. The cherry wood double bed and dresser were in the same position and the quilt was the patchwork hand-stitched by Grandma Lena with cutout animals, red barn, red house, white trim, sky and clouds. The beige walls looked drab and darker as the oil paint had aged, but no one noticed. Charlotte had placed an animal throw rug next to the bed. My crib and changing table were long gone. I was toilet-trained! My stuffed animals had been placed on his play table against the wall.

## His Bazooka Blew Up The Silhouetted Tank

"Okay," said Max, after I was dressed for bed, "Hop in and I'm gonna read a wonderful children's book I brought home with me. It's called Mein Kampf, and it's story of a funny-looking man with a little moustache. Can you say, *Mein Kampf?* That's hair over here," showing him where the moustache went.

'My Kamp," I repeated. "Good." I was placed in Max's bed.

"This is funny to you? asked Charlotte, incredulously. "This is what you wanna read to a three year old? You need to go back to Germany to read to the little Nazi children there and then have your head examined. This, you think is humorous? Oh, very funny, very, very funny. You're still an idiot. So funny, she said sarcastically, "I can't wait to tell the girls in the office my *meshugener* brother came home from Germany with a children's book he wanted to read to Noogie. What was the name of it? How 'bout that adorable children's book, *Mein Kampf*? I'm sure they'd all want to read it to their kids too, don't ya think?"

"Of course, that's why I wanna read it to Noogie," he said, straining to remain straight-faced.

"Awright, enough with the joke, awready! Read him that Golden Nursery Rhymes book. He loves that one."

Max opened the book to the Mother Goose nursery rhyme, lay down next to me and started reading, with me cradled in the crook of his arm. "I yike dat one," I exclaimed, and Max read on for about two minutes, tears dripping down his cheeks and nose. I reached up to wipe Max's cheek and said, " Don't cwy, Uncle Max. I'll hold you." Max squeezed me tight, heaving, "It's awl wight. I'll hold your hand, Uncle Max," until Max fell into a deep sleep, snoring loudly, holding Noogie protectively. "Mommmmmmmyyyyy, Uncle Max is sleeping loud and he was cwying."

"Shhhhhhh, Noogie, you go to sleep too, like Uncle Max. You can hold him. Gimme a kissie good night. Mwah!" she whispered. *Gayn schluffin*. I love you, sweetie puppy dog. Sweet dreams, sweet thoughts, two minutes."

"I wuv you, Mommy. I wuv my Uncle Max. He's funny, but he smells."

"He'll smell better tomorrow, Sweetie. Maybe you can take a shower with him. Ask him when you wake up in the morning. Love you a million billion dollars."

I was soon sound asleep in a tush up position. When kids are overly tired, nothing ever disturbs them, not even a newly discovered uncle spending his first night at home from the war zone and battlefields of Germany, Belgium and France.

After a night that never seemed to end; a night of nightmares and cold sweats, of walking around the house, opening the fridge, 4am coffee, back to bed, lying motionless, up again and again, of eyes that wouldn't close, Max finally fell asleep. His bazooka blew up the silhouetted tank. The cadmium orange sun set behind it and the ammo inside exploded into a display worthy of a Macy's July 4th, a garden salad of reds, oranges, yellows, purple and pink, of black and gray smoke and scraps of burnt uniforms and bloody remnants of the screaming crew within. It was beautiful. While in his foxhole he reached in his pocket for the final slice of kosher salami from the care package sent to him from Woodridge, took a bite while breathing in the sweet sounds of the last, desperate cries of those broken, burning men, and thought how delicious Pop's breakfast used to be of fried eggs, lox, onions, homemade sour pickles and Eight O'Clock Bokar coffee.

I jumped on top of him and woke him up from his fitful sleep on the floor, huddled in fetal, protective, foxhole position, sweating and trembling after his first night home after two years on the front lines somewhere in France, Belgium and Germany. He had rolled off the bed in the middle of the night, unable to feel secure enough to sleep "above ground." "Wake up, Uncle Max, we can get the eggs together in poppa's chicken coop and I'll let you hold my favowit chicken."

He twitched awake, looked around, gently squeezed me, lip farted in my ear and a kiss, and jumped up to go into the shower. "Go say hello to poppa, Noogie. I'll come down soon and eat you up for breakfast!" I ran downstairs.

The shower had a big head above and six small heads on the walls that sprayed him all over at the same time. He lingered in the shower for almost a half hour, soaping with Ivory Soap; soaping and crying, soaping and crying, soaping and crying, and crying, ridding himself of the blood he remembered. He soaped himself repeatedly, compulsively, every part of himself and then sat down on the shower floor with his knees up and arms held tightly around them, head into his arms, without motion, allowing the very hot water from the top and sides spray him with needle-like intensity, cleansing himself of the Nazi officer's blood that squirted in his face and lips when he inserted the dagger into that bastard's throat. The imagined blood flowed into the drain with his salty tears until, at long last, the hot water began to run cold, forcing him into the realization that the grotesqueness of war was now momentarily put aside, at least, before he was to fall asleep in the foxhole of his bedroom.

His Pop was already up and dressed in his work clothes, making breakfast for the two of them. "You want coffee, Max? Take. The percolator's hot. *Zetz zich avek*, I'm making eggs with onions and lox. Take some pickled herring I got from Karschmer's. Homemade. Make some toast with momma's chollie," Max sat down with his Eight O Clock Bokar coffee. "Wait, I get for us some sour pickles." He walked over to the crock in the pantry, lifted the stone holding down the round, wooden cover he had made in the woodworking shop and pulled out two pickles that came from the victory garden next to the blacksmith shop and placed them on each plate.

"Here Noogileh, take a bite of pickle." I took a small bite and gave a sour puss look, eyes scrunched shut, but took another bite and then jumped onto Max's lap for a bite of egg from Max's fork.

Max closed his red eyes, remembering his nightmare, and took a chomp on one. He paused before chewing. Sour, like he liked. "Ya know, Pop, to get even a cup of coffee sometimes, you could stand on your head. Too busy killing them and trying to save your own ass. Coffee? You could dream about. Sugar? Milk? What sugar?" The lox, and eggs from the chicken coop, were wolfed down while they smoked in between bites, the smoke mixing with the aroma of breakfast. The orange to yellow sun's light came through the small kitchen window onto the kitchen table, morning moisture still on the glass, illuminating the residue in the frying pan, plates, rye bread, chipped coffee cups and old souvenir ashtrays from the Grahamsville Fair.

Pesach hacked and coughed his morning cigarette

cough. You could wake the neighborhood with that cough, but who noticed him bent over, coughing his guts out? He wasn't the only one on Maple Avenue.

After the salami and fried eggs and sour pickle breakfast with his pop, Max got dressed in his uniform, just a khaki shirt, no medals, khaki pants, and walked down to the blacksmith shop.

The shop was filled with tools for shaping, punching holes and cutting iron. They were hanging on walls and strewn about his long worktable. His anvil rested on a large, wide chunk of maple, and his vise was bolted to the thick, worktable, hardwood boards, at least three inches thick. There was just enough room for a horse.

They started the fire in the forge with the wood shavings pushed down from the overhead hole in the floor above from the woodworking shop and he pumped the forge the same way he did when he was just a small boy. His father waited till it got white hot and, with tongs, placed a raw piece of iron in amongst the coals till it too got white-hot. He removed the iron and began the rhythmic hammering on his anvil, shaping it into the rough shape of a horseshoe, placing it back into the forge to keep it white hot and malleable. All blacksmiths have their own personal anvil rhythms. Yushka's rooster next door welcomed the morning disturbance with a loud crow, repeating it numerous times. The hens responded. They always twitched their heads when the rooster crowed.

Max grabbed a mallet and hammered too, to an inner musical beat, not perfected. There was little talk. The pre-war familiarity returned; the smell of the coals in the forge, the smoke, Chesterfields, sizzling steam of iron in water, oil, grease, chicken manure from the adjoining coop, dumped out just outside, providing high test fertilizer for the tomatoes and cukes.

"Pop, Pop, POP! I'm gonna take a walk." He was hardly heard in opposition to the clanging of the mallet.

"Yeh, go and say hello to everyone." Pop put his huge hand on Max's shoulder, squeezing and leaving a small black smudge on his shirt. They shook a long handshake. Max tried to squeeze his father's calloused fingers together.

Could not, still.

## Home From Joimany

Max walked out of the shop, picked a large tomato from the adjoining garden, and took a detour into the chicken coop, scaring the leghorns into a frenzied chorus of hundreds of shrieking clucks. Out again, observing the two attached barns, home to numerous pigeons and the old, black truck, looking like it hadn't been washed in those last two years, streaked with grime, dust and pigeon shit all over the hood and windshield. It apparently hadn't been too important to clean all that shit off. Walking up the driveway, he opened the basement door, the handle and hinges of which his father had fashioned, and walked in. It had changed little: assorted shovels and rakes leaning against the same wall, old cans of brick-red and battleship gray oil paint piled in a far corner, old wooden chairs on top of one another to save space, laundry table piled high with towels, underwear and blacksmith's clothes, exposed asbestos insulation peeling from the overhead pipes, and the valentine scribed into the concrete that he made when the house was built and the cement was still not quite dry in 1932. "Max Shabus 1932" inside the heart.

Through the door into another section of the basement was an old hutch, covered in peeling, yellowed, white paint, with old family photos too numerous to keep in the house, and endless spider webs attached, vibrating with the jitterbug dances of daddy longlegs and captured fruitflies. Although the basement was dry, it retained its familiar musty odor. He felt like their dog rushing from room to room to familiarize himself.

Yushka, the next-door neighbor, hadn't yet noticed him, and Max caught him *pishing* onto his apple tree in the middle of his own chicken yard. He was still doing it. "I pissed and crapped in foxholes," he thought, "and Yushka? Yushka got his fuckin' tree." He always wore a stained white apron. Who knew when it was last washed? Maybe before Max left for the army. Yushka pushed the apron aside to pee, not noticing Max. Soon he would trudge his old baby carriage to the village to the back of Proyect's produce store to collect the rotten lettuce and other vegetables being thrown out, to feed his chickens. It was his version of a wheelbarrow. He was always out of breath and walked bent over in his heavy work shoes, making him look even smaller than his short size. His daughter, Devorah, was class valedictorian in the Woodridge High School. Brains, she had. Like Max, first generation American. She was later married to a guy named Claude, AKA "Buster." Buster loved to loudly blow his nose into cloth napkins in restaurants. It sounded like a loud foghorn with snot. Make ya want to vomit. He could give a shit.

Yushka had a butcher shop next to the Shabus's home with his window proclaiming that his meat and chickens were kosher. Behind his shop was a storage area for his junk underneath the store, overloaded after two years, and his home, a dilapidated, sloping structure covered with roof shingles as siding, and Malka, his white-haired ever-shrieking wife who was still screaming at him, the same as two years ago, demanding he come up, there was a customer. Children were frightened by her and her angry face. Jews would say she had a *farbissiner punim*. She never combed her wiry hair. Disney would've loved her, had he only known. Yushka took a daily nap in an old, metal, navy blue, outdoor chair outside his door. He was able to escape some of her shrieking. Kids called her a witch.

"Maxileh!!!!," he yelled out, "Maxileh!!!! That's you?"

"Yeh! Yushkileh, it's me! Who else?"

"You're home from Joimany? When you get home, boychickel?"

"Yesterday afternoon." He went over and they gave each other a big handshake. Yushka's hands were dirty and his fingers puffy, but he had a strong handshake. "Welcome home, Maxileh, welcome home! It's been a long time I haven't seen your *punim*. You're okay? Not hurt, not shot? You look skinny, boychick. They don't feed you?"

"They fed me *dreck*, but you get used to it. You ever hear of Spam? It's a mushed up can of ham. Crap I never want to see or smell again. Worse than your chickens and shit I wouldn't feed even YOUR chickens. And coming home on the ship, I puked my guts out for a week straight from the ocean. Food, I couldn't look at for a second."

"*Oy vey*!!! So your mother, she'll make for you, you should eat. It's good that you got home. Some of the other boychicks in the village they weren't so lucky. You heard?"

"Yeh, I heard about some. Nainie, though, is still okay in the Pacific and Sam they sent to Germany for UNRRA, the United Nations Relief and Rehabilition Admistration, to help settle the DPs. It's a long way from Washington and Walter Reed. You knew he was a food inspector there? What he would've done to you!!!"

"What, mine chickens? Look at them. I love them, mine beaudelful boids! He'd give me a metal, that Sammileh!"

"Yeh, yeh. I gotta run and see the village, Yushka. I hope I don't get lost. It's good to see you. How's your wife? She treating you okay?"

"Yeh, the same. What can I tell you? She cooks mine food and sticks her *tuchus* against me when we go to sleep and she *schreis* like she always did. They tell me you can hear her in Fallsboig. I don't hear it anymore. Mine ears she took avay. I'm almost deaf. What can I tell you? I married a meshugenim, but I got me a very smart daughter, that Devorah. Brains, she got. And she got a little boy now, mine Richileh, the same as Noogie. I think he got something in his head, too."

"I'll see her later. Say hello. See you. Go kill a chicken, why doncha?"

"For you, Maxileh, I'll *shoichit* a boid and pretend it's a Nazi, and do it the kosher way," gesturing slitting a throat.

"YOU deserve a medal! *Zei gezunt.*"

"Yeh, you too, boychick. Welcome home!"

The Krieger's tan stucco, art deco home was across the street. The wealthy Kosors lived upstairs. It was the fanciest house on Maple Avenue and certainly the largest. All others were modest in comparison, except the three story Shabus's brick house that Pesach built himself with some construction workers. All the decorative wrought iron fencing and window ledges were fabricated in the blacksmith shop. Near the corner was Elliott's dealership and garage, selling Studebakers and tractors and parts. Elliott was another big deal guy. Next to that was Penchansky's Dairy. And then, on the corner, was The Kentucky Club, owned by Max Kurtz. He was known as "Mr. Koitz," the way the first generation Jews pronounced it. His son, "Shepsie Koitz," was always by his side. Shepsie probably weighed three hundred fifty pounds or more, a young guy who tended bar for his father. They said he had a glandular condition, "fridgeritis," or some similar disease that kept him inflated. His father was of normal size, about five foot seven inches, one hundred seventy pounds or so. Shepsy was rejected from the military, most likely from "fridgeritis" disease.

Across the street was Sam Prager's grocery store, dreary but convenient for milk and eggs. The Pragers loved geraniums and their entire store's window ledge had large, red clay pots filled with his healthy plants, always in bloom with brilliant, red flowers, in contrast to the haphazard, drab and disorganized food displays, mostly absent of color. The Pragers lived above the store. When the weather was warm and business was slow, Sam or the missus sat outside the front door on a kitchen chair on guard for random customers while watching the various trains stop at the train station, while one of them tended the store within.

Opposite was Jack Hechtman's hardware store alongside a shoe store and Katzowitz's printing shop to the right of it. Down the Main Street slope was Oppenheimer's clothing store, Weisbord Insurance, Moe's Barbershop and Doctor Kaplan's dental practice. His wife Anne, was the nurse-secretary and she also taught tap dancing on the side. Then Kaplan's Butcher Shop, a different family, Karschmer's Groceries & Deli, Abe Krutman's Candy Store, where Max bought a carton of Chesterfields for his father and read a few of the comics on the shelf to the right of the front door, Proyect and Gerson's fish store and fresh produce store where Yushka got the discarded vegetables for his chickens. He probably kept some of them for himself and family. Unlike Shabus, he didn't have his own victory garden. On the corner was the Rexall Pharmacy, shoe store, Kessler's Butcher Shop, a bar and grill, Kagan's Butchers and Podhurst's Custom Mattress store in an old, downward slanting, about to fall over manufacturing barn. Across the street, was Sam Horowitz's Fruit and Produce market.

On the other side of Main Street and across the O&W

train tracks was train station for the trains that ran through Woodridge, South Fallsburg, Monticello and beyond, God knows where. The steam engine chugged and belched and whooshed white steam and woo wooed its arrival numerous times of the day. It was a busy station.

Across the tracks was the baking aroma of Schwartz's Bakery, a luncheonette, Fox's Barbershop, René the hairdresser for the toilet paper ladies, Doctor Immerman's house and office, Temes's Law Offices, Woodridge National Bank. Next to the theater was Bushkie Cohen's luncheonette where Pussy Ruderman the truck driver hung out. If Pussy wasn't there on his days off, Bushky always wondered, "Where's Pussy?"

And no, Pussy wasn't at Slater's Garage, which was across from Hymie Balbirer's Garage, Dr. Malisoff's office, Dr. Fernhoff's office, Rittner's grocery store, Cooperative Federal Insurance office, Woodridge School, all grades, Chim Krieger's Law Office and Pittie Ruderman's accountant's office. The Krieger Chevy dealership was further down the street, before Al Kaplan's car dealership. Saperstein's oil company was next to Kaplan's dealership. Pussy was sometimes elusive and mysterious in Woodridge. Everyone always looked for Pussy. You'd never know where to find him, though.

These were the names of storekeepers and professionals in all their local color. It didn't mean shit to outsiders, but they were the lyrics of a village business and social chorus that grew to six hundred or so from a tiny number of locals and immigrants many years before, along the time Pesach Shabus was given full power and authority to help select the Steinway piano for the Lyceum Theater.

Max walked through the village at a very slow pace, greeted by all who saw him. "Mockzie, hello Mockzie!" "Maxie, welcome home!!!" "Max, you son of bitch, get in here!!! Here, a chunk of salami." "Maxileh, come boubileh, let me give you a hug." "Hey Shabus, you're back? Good! Some of the guys didn't make it. Those dirty, fuckin' *mamzurs*. You hoid about the camps, yeh?" "Yeh, we were right near some of them. Our guys were stringin' the bestids up, I heard. Some of them were kind enough to let us bake them in one of the many ovens. Charcoal broiled. Delicious."

"Maxie, you fought in Joimany?"

"Maybe a little. Not too much. A *bissel* here, a *bissel* there. France and Belgium, too. Not like Mike Davis on Iwo. I heard he kicked a lot of Jap ass and was highly decorated. A miracle he lived through it."

He bumped into Bill Kaplan, and they hugged long and hard. He was a little guy who strutted around to make up for his short height, but a tough motherfucker and he also survived, having also been stationed somewhere in France. He didn't give a shit about punching anyone in the face for a wrong word or misunderstanding. His family owned one of the butcher shops. They were pals before the war and hadn't seen each other in a couple of years. He wore his army cap at a jaunty angle. "Shabus, meet me later for a drink at Kurtz's?"

"The Kentucky Club? Yeah, Kaplan. Eight o'clock, after dinner with the family. You think they still have strippers and girlie boys?"

"What do you think, pinhead? How could Kurtz not

101

have strippers?"

"Good," said Max, "You can have a girlie boy and I'll take the stripper. Strippers would want a real soldier, not a private with little fingers like yours."

"Little fingers, huh?" Kaplan held up his hands. "You think I don't have the goods down here? You're crazy."

"Yeah, right. Probably, maybe a good two and half inches. I don't know how they ever let you in the army. They shoulda failed you on your fingers and *petzeleh* alone. Besides that, they say you're one of those secret girlie boys yourself. Tell me the truth. Is that true? Are you one of them?"

"Maxileh, I am, and go fuck yourself. I'll see you at eight, schmeckel."

"Good, we'll catch up."

"Sounds like a good deal, Kaplan. More pussy you've ever seen. Don't forget to rub some *schmaltz* on your *tuchus* before you walk in."

"And you, Shabus? Wash your *petzeleh* with your mother's pickle juice!!!! See ya later." He threw Max a kiss.

"Fuck you! Don't forget to wear your WAC-off uniform."

"Is that a Joiman woid, moron?" asked Kaplan.

"No, boychick. Your mother taught it to me. See you at eight. Fuckin' strange being home. Not real. It's like normal here. Was there ever a fuckin' war? They could never imagine. I could never talk about it, except a *bissel* to Pop. My sister asked me if I killed any Nazis. I told 'No, I was repairing vehicles far behind the front lines. You think I'm gonna tell her or anyone except my father I was in the Battle of The Bulge? I got my own nightmares. She can do without."

"Got that right. I got back a week ago and I'm still totally fucked up. Can't fuckin' sleep. Don't wanna talk to anyone. What's a bed? I've been on the floor every fuckin' night, waiting for the flares and mortars incoming."

"Last night, I slept. Couldn't move. Had the worst nightmares. I had Charlotte's Noogie curled up on me. Fuckin' ugly kid, always *pishin'* from his eyes and nose. Looks like her fuckin' husband, Joe, who I haven't seen yet. I finally moved the little bastid away and ended up on the floor, next to the bed. Much more comfortable, if ya know what I mean?" He's a sweet kid, though, the little bastid. Three years old. Tomorrow, I'm gonna teach him how to smoke cigars. See you later. Wear a pretty dress tonight. Some lipstick, too, and nylons."

"Fuck you, Maxileh, fuuuuuuck you! I'm gonna wear my best nylons for The Kentucky Club and for you. Should be some scene tonight!" Kaplan placed two fingers to his lips, closed his eyes and threw Max a tender kiss.

"And you, you *mamzur* bastid. Ten hut!" They jumped to attention, saluted each other, shook hands up and down and separated, Kaplan into the family butcher shop and Max down the street for more meeting and greeting with shopkeepers and people he knew and hadn't seen in years.

In a town of approximately five hundred people, it was easy to know almost everybody. Down the street, he walked past Oppenheimer's clothing store, Weisbord's insurance agency and Moe's Barbershop, which smelled of cologne from five feet away from the front of the shop. The red, white and blue barber pole was lit up and turning round and round and the various Police Gazette magazines were strewn on a ledge just inside the window. Moe already had a customer he was shaving. Then into Karschmer's grocery and deli. Sam was behind the counter and Zeldie was straightening shelves. The homemade sour and half-sour pickles and sour tomatoes were in the same tall wooden barrels as when he went away; the farmer's cheese, cream cheeses, plain and pickled herring, egg salad, tuna salad, knishes, salami and hot dogs in the trays behind glass, the breads; bialys and bagels in wooden bins, neatly stacked up. He walked into the store and stood still there for an extra couple of seconds, breathing in the intoxicating perfume of Jewish delicacies. It didn't smell like Moe's and Fox's oppressive hair tonic and aftershave aromas.

When they saw Max, they both ran to him and all embraced. Zeldie was one of Charlotte's close mah jong friends. It was like her own kid had returned home. Servicemen and women were the husbands, wives, brothers, sisters, children of the entire village. Small town America embraced their own, suffering their losses and celebrating their return; some less than whole.

One store after another, old friends, parents' friends, people he didn't know. His smelly uniform was no deterrent. The war in Europe was over.

He stopped into Kessler's Butcher shop. The brothers, Doudy, Label and Moishe, were already back home and back at work, all in their red-stained white aprons over white shirts. They looked like a group of three comedians, "Ladies and gentlemen, the Kessler Brothers!" "Maxie!!!!! Maxie!!!!! Maxie!!!! They let you back in America? Are they crazy, a *nudnick* like you!!!??? Here, come 'ere, Shabus. Here, take a chunk of this tongue. You get tongue like that in Germany. Maybe a bissel pussy, but tongue????" They all went at him. "Was it kosher?"

"Better than this *dreck* you have the nerve to give me. Jesus Christ, what shit! I wouldn't serve it to Hitler. Actually, I shoulda served it to Hitler. Would've ended the war a lot sooner. And your family stayed in business these last two years selling that crap?"

Doudy said, "*Schmuck*, that's why we won the war. We snuck this shit overseas to the SS to poison them. We are like the rats we have running all over the place, surviving on kosher rat poison, but the fuckin' Nazis? One bite of the Hebrew National Salami and they're dead. You know how many of those bastids died from Jewish salami poisoning??? Maybe twenty-five thousand. Maybe more. That's why you're here, moron. Here, take a piece of this salami home to your mother with the tongue. It's from one of Kasofsky's cows. Get the hell outa here and go take a shower, you smelly bastid. You don't wanna smell up the rest of the town. They'll accuse you of moider."

"I took one already, idiot."

"So go take another. Wear your shirt and wash it in the shower. You stink from krauts. Sour krauts. Maybe dead krauts?"

"Yeh, dead, fuckin' sour krauts, I got. I killed 'em with this shirt."

"Maxie, you done okay over there?" Asked Label. "It's good you're home. My brother's an idiot." He walked over and put his arms around Max. Moishe and Doudy, too. All tough guys who stood in the middle of the butcher shop, crying, trying not to, and laughing at each other in embarrassment, tears flowing and dripping onto the wood shavings covering the floor, laughing tears.

"Yeah, done okay. Even with those fuckin' southern antisemitten bastids who never saw a Jew before. I go into the army to fight the Nazis and I came this close to blowing the fuckin' head off my sergeant from Mississippi, with his Jewboy shit with their fuckin' southern draaaawl, day after fuckin' day. Until one of those days, my sergeant went too far with his crap. I grabbed my rifle, pointed it at the middle of his southern, ugly, scarred face, and told him, 'You say one more fuckin' word and I'll blow your fuckin' southern head off, cocksucker.' Luckily, the captain walked into the barracks right at that moment, a West Pointer, saw what was happening and gave the sergeant fair warning that he'd put him up for court martial if it ever happened again. These are guys who thought we had our horns cut off from all the Christian shit they had seen in paintings and sculptures. You ever hear of Michelangelo and that Moses thing he made outa marble? It shows Moses with horns, in Italy, for some fuckin' popes. You believe that shit? But THEY were serious. I told a couple of 'em that I really did have mine cut off just like they cut the horns off cattle. Good plastic surgeons so you couldn't tell. I still had a little hair left to cover the scars.'"

Moishe said, in his rapid fire voice, "You ever see the signs in the backwoods here 'No Jews or dogs allowed?'

Those *mamzur*, backwoods 'scoopers' are still all over the place. I hoid that your father, years ago, met those bastids at the train station one day with some of his friends and beat the livin' shit outa them for beating up the Jews who were coming up from The City. They called themselves *The Klopping Minyan* and fucked them over pretty good then and that was the end of it, those *goyisheh* bastids. That true?"

"True. My Pop is a tough guy, but I never heard him yell at anyone, other than when they all talked on the porch about politics. Then it was warfare, but they all had a good time yelling at each other and drinking schnaps. When I got home and shook his hand, I tried to squeeze his fingers together and couldn't. He still puts his cigarettes out with his fingers. Powerful."

"Awright, Maxileh, go awready. Take the salami. Take the tongue, Even for an idiot like you, welcome back," said Doudy, "welcome back."

"Why did I bother coming in here to see a bunch of moron Stooge brothers? I shoulda stayed in Germany. I'm gonna feed your salami to the dog. You think anyone in my family would touch that shit? I had to come home to this, you worthless idiots? It's good to see you assholes. Oh, I'm sorry: *putzes*." They shook hands again and pretended to kick him in the ass as he left the store, clutching the tongue and salami wrapped up in white butcher paper.

# BuhBuhBenny

The train station across the street was the center of commerce for the villagers, shipping goods, passengers, oil, propane and farm supplies for the Co-op, the largest farm supplier in the entire region. It was built in 1917. Like many train stations, it had a large overhang to protect people and goods from getting wet. The dark wood supports were wide and decoratively curved, giving the dark building a stately look. In the Co-op, one would find every bit of equipment for farmers, seed for large farms and vegetable seeds for victory gardens and huge storage buildings to store corn and locally grown grain. Next to it was the Best Natural Gas Company, owned by BuhBuhBenny Breslick. He didn't stutter. He just repeated words and phrases, but everyone called him "BuhBuhBenny."

He was the Brooklyn millionaire who built a house with a "magnificent" view that overlooked his propane gas plant, pickup and bulk trucks and giant propane storage tank. On the hill immediately behind the storage tank were the railroad tracks and the large black, cylindrical tanks that stored the gas. One had to walk to the top of the hill to get to the railroad cars that contained the propane. Workers hooked up hoses and unloaded the gas into Breslick's big tank. The plant was an old, wooden building in need of new gray paint with a large platform for trucks to load and unload cylinders of all sizes and where the residential and commercial tanks were sprayed with shiny aluminum paint, filled with LP gas and had valves repaired. The office was in a back room, desk on one side and propane parts on the other three sides. The desk was strewn with pens, pencils, notepads and an ashtray over-filled with non-filter cigarette and cigar butts. The office and filling room of scales and cylinders exuded the oppressive warning smell of almost empty propane tanks.

Benny, too old to serve in the armed forces, drove his older model Red Cadillac convertible appointed with light cream, leather seats and white top down whenever the weather allowed. He was a strutter, both in his Caddy and the way he walked like a wrestler, stomach out, back bent a bit backwards and shoes pointed at forty-five degree angles, like a walking duck. His smile was strained, not an easy smiler, more like Mussolini. Chin up, but not quite as belligerent. He knew Max and recognized him as he exited Kessler's, and pulled up.

"Shabus, hey Shabus! Welcome home, Shabus, welcome home!"

"Mr. Breslick, hello! Good to be home. Good to be home. I see you still got the same car."

"Yeah, can't get anything new, you can't. Maybe in a year or two when all this settles down. But Slater's Garage keeps it going, they keep it going, the Slaters. A good bunch of boys, a good bunch. When'd you get home, Maxie, when'd you get?"

"Yesterday. This is my first day to see the village. Hasn't changed much. Europe is bombed out. Germany, too. Most of everything we did to those bastids, so it's good Woodridge we still have. Was it tough getting gas for the plant?"

"Yeah, it was tough, it was tough, but I got what I

could. I got friends, I got. A *bissel gelt*, too, a *bissel*, to *schtup* some of them with a few bucks, a few. And we got by, we got.

"Come, get in. I'll give you a ride, I'll show you the plant and the town, I'll show you."

"Awright, not too long. I gotta get back to the family. I haven't even seen Charlotte's Joe or my *bubbe* behind the school."

Into the Caddy he went with its white sour cream leather upholstery. Benny gave him the "royal tour" of Woodridge, of everything so familiar, yet changed: the window displays, patriotic posters, some peeling and faded paint, a couple of new potholes and cracks in familiar streets, new American flags on telephone poles, in front of homes and numerous small businesses, the old Lyceum theater.

"You know, Mr. Breslick, my father, twenty years ago, was on the village board, upstairs in the theater, above the stage. He told us he was the one who chose a piano. He got full power and authority from the mayor.

We asked him how come he was the one and he said, 'Why not? You think I don't know wood? I gave it a *klop* and it sounded good.'" My father, who can't play a note, became the piano expert for The Village of Woodridge. Go figgah." They had a good laugh over that one.

BuhBuhBenny showed Max his new house, painted dark green, with a magnificent view overlooking the propane gas plant, and then down the hill into the plant property. A couple of his men were rolling tanks onto trucks and one could see the pumps and scales and empty tanks through open barn doors. The smell of propane permeated the air. Max found it to be pleasant, for whatever reason. Most people are nauseated by that aroma. "Very impressive, Mr. Breslick. Looks like the war hasn't slowed you down at all."

"Not for a minute, Maxie, not for a minute. Business is good. A little black market doesn't hurt. Maybe when you settle in we can talk. Maybe a job for you here at the plant, maybe a job. The war in Europe is over and a lot of people will need gas, they'll need."

"Mr. Breslick, I appreciate the offer, but I gotta get settled in. This is my first day home. Woodridge has been another past lifetime, and I gotta figure things out. Where and what, you know. First, the family, my pop, the chickens. You don't even know anything about me, either."

"Shabus, you're not gonna make a life with the chickens, you're not. Chickens you can eat, but gas you need to cook the chickens, you need. Everyone needs gas. Gas smells better than chickens, it smells. You wanna smell from chicken shit the rest of your life, you wanna? You get settled and maybe get in touch with me. I know all about you, I know. You come from a good family, you're a hard worker, and your father, he's an honest man. Everybody loves the Shabuses. Get settled, come talk to me. We'll work something out, we'll work. You do that? Maxie, wait a second. Here's a little something for your mother," handing over a few valuable wartime food ration stamps. "You tell her hello from me."

They were back at the Shabus home, shook hands and

said their goodbyes. Max ran his hand over the back of the leather seat, thanked him for the stamps and ride, and before he went into the house, said, "You'll be the first I'll call. Thanks for the private tour, Mr. Breslick. It's good to see you and be back in Woodridge. How I made it, I'll never know."

"Shabus, do me a favor. Call me Benny, call me."

"Will do," and gave BuhBuhBenny a stiff salute as he pulled away.

He walked down the yard to the blacksmith shop and his Pop was still making horseshoes. The shop had gotten sweaty hot, even hotter than the humid, hot August morning. The sweat was dripping down the tip of Pesach's nose, some of the droplets falling onto the horseshoes and transformed into instant clouds of sizzling, staccato steam. His arms were glossy, as if baby oil had been rubbed on them. "Maxileh!" He held out his hand, now black, and shook hands with his son, who again tried to squeeze his father's fingers. It was their game, the older man prevailing, still. "So, nu? You took a walk to the village?"

"Yeah, Pop, like old times. Nothing much changed. I saw a lot of everyone. Here, I got you a carton and salami and tongue from Kessler. I met Karschmer, Krutman, Kaplan, Kesslers, the *meshugeners*, and then I bumped into BuhBuhBenny, and he gave mom some food ration stamps, a little gift."

"Yeh, BuhBuh, you bumped into, you bumped?"

"Yeah, I buhbuhbumped into BuhBuhBenny, I bumped into," laughing. He said to get in and he showed me the village, he showed me."

"He showed you his new manshkin he builted over the gas plant, he showed you? Quite a view he got of that place, quite a view. It's beeudelful, you think, looking at the gas tanks from the kitchen windah? Who's *meshuger* enough to build a house above a gas plant? He don't have the gelt to build maybe next to an oil tank? Maybe next to a garage? Maybe next to the railroad tracks? Did he show you his wife too, Rosaleh? She's a fancy lady, that Rosaleh, from Brooklyn, a fancy lady. She wears poil neckelces all the time." They were laughing with every sentence.

"No, I didn't meet her. What can I tell ya, Pop? He thinks next to the gas tank is a beautiful location, he thinks. He'll make a garden maybe. Maybe put a little flowerpot on the windowsill. I'm home one day and he asked me to work for him, he asked. You believe that?"

"Well, now I know he's crazy. But, what can I say? He knows a good one when he sees one, he knows. Go work for him and help grow a gas garden for him."

"Pop, three weeks ago I was in France killing Nazis. I didn't take a shower in weeks, my ass was so raw, still is, and I was in combat till the news came that the Nazi bastids surrendered. Now I'm here. Go figgah. Who can even think of anything? I walked into town looking for snipers on every roof and instead, I got sniped at by BuhBuh Breslick in his red Cadillac tank."

## *Latkes* You Should Choke On

"Go see mama. She's cooking for you already. She wants she should fatten you up a *bissel*. She thinks you're too skinny. Thanks for the cigarettes, mine soldier boy. Go."

" Maxileh, you was up oily mit Pop and out so oily?" He walked over and gave her a tight hug, bending her neck and gave her a big kiss on the cheek. Then the other cheek. "That's how they do it in France, Ma, both cheeks. If they really like ya, they do it twice."

"What, one isn't good enough for them?"

"They do two, Ma. What can I tell ya? Shows how much they love ya, I guess. The men kiss the men, too, with two kisses. I got salami and tongue for you from Kessler's, and BuhBuh Breslick gave you a present of some ration stamps. He already wants me to work for him. I'm home one day, and I get offered a job. He's says I come from a good family. If he only knew, if he only? If he only knew what kind of cooking, he woulda never offered me the job. He drove me around to see the town in his big, red Caddy. I forgot how he talked, I forgot," slyly smiling.

"Maybe you should go back to Joimany and get some real food? I should waste mine time and make a lunch for you? They feed you *latkes* over there and chicken soup with eggs?"

"Much better, Ma. The K Rations can beat your cooking any day. They serve it on beautiful English china on the front lines with beautiful salads and bread called baguettes, long skinny loaves, *goyisheh wines*, like you can't

114

find here, with funny names you should only know from. Not sweet. They didn't have Mogen David or Manischewitz in Germany or in France. I looked all over for them."

"Go wash up and call Poppa."

"Where's my Noogie, the little bastid? With Charlotte in the drugstore?"

"Yeh. They're in Fallsboig with Joe."

"I'll go over there after you poison me, ma. I'll get Pop. What stinks in here? Those *latkes*?"

"I'll give you *latkes*! *Latkes* you should choke on." She raised her arm and hand across her face, as if to smack him. "Hurry, before they get cold."

Lunch was all questions back and forth: The war in Europe and Japan, Sam in UNRRA, Bubbe Fein, "I'll go see her after," concentration camps, families who lost family members, including their own, the war in the Pacific with Nainie, Woodridge soldiers who were killed and wounded and others from the other local towns, Joe's brother, Harry, who's in the Pacific in the navy, and local stories of hardships and shortages and deaths. "Denks G-d when Sam was the food inspector in Walter Reed and he brings us some of the hard-to-get foods."

The *latkes* went quickly and conversation was animated and non-stop. Max and his Pop smoked during the meal. Max pretended he was deathly sick, cluthing his stomach. Off he went to get the truck to go Joe's drugstore in South Fallsburgh.

# The Son of a Bitch Lullaby

He pulled the truck out of the barn, grabbed a hose and large sponge and washed all the grime and pigeon crap off the hood and fenders from all the pigeons that made their home in the barns. It was caked on the windshield, too, completely obscuring one's vision. "Pop, such a clean windshield you got! I think you need an experienced driver to even get it out of the barn, no?" His father never drove the truck and always had a neighbor, a young guy named "Buckshot Natelson" or a hired hand drive for him, so it wasn't used much. Other than delivering or picking up chickens, the truck remained in the barn. Grain for the chickens was delivered and the village was self-sufficient. He checked the gas, oil and tires, and off he went on a country road on which he had traveled endless times while growing up. The waterfalls in Old Falls was serenely beautiful, although much drier now in August than in the springtime.

When he arrived at the corner drugstore, I was helping my mother arrange items on a shelf. She was showing and telling me that the names and pictures of the items have to be facing outward so everyone could see what they were. I learned quickly and she made it into a game. She was teaching me to count the little boxes and bottles. Charlotte's husband, Joe the pharmacist, was behind the counter in his white pharmacist's jacket. With its high, tight collar, he looked like a priest. He was in the middle of pouring some dark, purple liquid from a big bottle into a small one, the size of a cough syrup bottle. He held the bottles far apart as he poured, a feat that would take anyone lots of practice to perfect without dripping or spilling. For him it was effortless.

He finished pouring and immediately saw Max and rushed out from behind the pharmacy counter and the two of them hugged and shook hands and Charlotte joined with the hug. I ran over, too, screaming, "Unkie Max!!! Unkie Max!!! Max lifted me up and threw him high above, my little body arching, arms and legs spread apart. It was repeated a number of times and I begged for more. " Do it again, do it again!"

"Enough!" said Max, squeezing me. I clutched Max's thighs and Max dragged me through the aisle on his perfectly shined shoes, dropping me off in front of one of the shelves that needed arranging and said, "Get to work, you little bastid! Go help your mother fix the shelves."

"Can you help me, Unkie Max?"

"Yeah, in a second, Noogie, I'll help you. Okay?"

"Do you HAVE to talk to him that way and teach him those bad words? Do you really have to show off your new army vocabulary? That's what you learned in the army?"

"Of course!!! That's why I came home. Everyone should learn a foreign language, and the younger they start, the easier for them to learn. Bastid is the same as bastard. It makes it very simple for kids who don't know who their fathers are."

"Home one day and you became a pig with the words. Go back to Germany, awready, and teach THEIR kids proper English. I'll buy you a ticket."

"Maxileh, it's good to have you home!" exclaimed Joe. "It's been a long time, a long, long time. You look good," as they gave each other a big hug and handshake. "We'll be home for dinner around five and have a few schnappsels. I have to get back to these few customers. Hey, folks, my brother-in-law, Maxie Shabus from Woodridge, yesterday just got home from the army in Europe!!!" They all came up to Max, shook hands, hugged him, not caring that he was a perfect stranger, applauded, saluted, congratulated. A couple of the people started crying. Max, too. "I wuv you, Unkie Max," as Max kneeled down, "I wuv you a million billion chickens. Daddy says tell you you're a bastid. What's a bastid?"

"A bastid is the best kid in the whole, wide world, and that's you, you little bastid. Me too. I wuv you, too. Some day, you'll become a wonderful, big bastid and I'll be sooo proud of you! Let's go get you some toys at Trudy's Toy Store. What kind of toys would you like?"

"A big fruck!" I yelled.

"A big fruck?"

"Uh huh, a big one, like Poppa's. Wed, not bwack."

"Okay, let's hurry up, you little bastid. Go fix the shelves. And then we'll get you a big fruck. I could use a big fruck too, you should only know from."

"Max!!!! Go back to Germany!!!!! Enough awready!!! Enough!!!"

I soon got off the floor and we left for Trudy's to find me my new toy, and returning, I screamed out, "See my new wed fruck!?" and showed it to my mother and father and whoever else was in the store at the time. I pushed it all around the drugstore floor. It was a big dumptruck.

"Maxileh, you're teaching him new words, Maxileh? Give him a day or two."

Dinner began with a whisky toast to Max, Canadian Club, and then another to Sam and another to Nainie and another to their late daughter, Minnie, who was always remembered, and to the end of the War in Europe. "Noogie, can you say "*L'chaim*?"

"L 'haiman!" I said, and everyone applauded and laughed and told him to say it again.

"Loochiman!" I exclaimed and everyone clicked glasses, including me, and applauded again, and the meal began, of veal chops breaded in matzoh meal and cooked in a big frying pan in vegetable oil. The string beans were perfectly cooked, having been started boiling at 1pm so that they'd be tender by 5:30. When they turned gray, you'd know they were done. A wedge of iceberg lettuce and Shabus-grown tomatoes with a homemade mayo and ketchup dressing was passed around, along with fresh homemade chollie.

The dog sat next to me, expectant, waiting for his daily treat that would inevitably fall from my high chair. He would lick my hand when he could.

A million questions were asked of Max: about the war, where he was, did he bump into anyone from Woodridge, what was it like, what was the weather like, did he meet any Jewish goils? "Are you an idiot"? he asked Charlotte. Any good friends, how many Nazis did he kill, what about the camps they heard about? I came over and sat on his lap. "Will you please stop grabbing the veal from my plate?" Charlotte to Max. "Max, do you have to take string beans from me? You don't have any of your own? Didn't any of your Nazi friends teach you proper table manners in Germany?" "Pass the pickles, please. Who wants a sour tomato?" "Ma, they're like lead." "Maxileh, stones you should have. Lead is for company, too good for you."

"I'm finished. Going up to shower and meeting Bill Kaplan at 8 o'clock. Come Noogie, wanna take a shower with me before you go to bed?"

"Yea! I never tooked a shower. What it does?"

"It squirts you ALL over, Noogie."

The shower squirted me from head to toe all at once and I squealed and screamed and peed, just like my uncle did. Max dried me off, wrapped a towel around me and then himself and called for his sister to take me from him.

"Unkie Max, can you sing me a song in bed?'

"Yeah. Hurry and get into bed and I'll sing you a lullaby."

"What wullaby?" I jumped all over the bed while Max held my hands.

"A special song just for you. It's called The Artillery Lullaby.

*Over hill, over dale,*
*As we hit the dusty trail,*
*And the caissons go rolling along.*
*In and out, hear them shout,*
*Counter march and right about,*
*And the caissons go rolling along.*

*Then it's hi! hi! hee!*
*In the field artillery,*
*Shout out your numbers loud and strong,*
*For where e'er you go,*
*You will always know,*
*That the caissons go rolling along."*

"I yike dat!!! Sing it again!"

"Can you sing another one, Unkie Max?"

"This one is called 'The Son of a Bitch Lullaby.' Can you say son of a bitch lullaby?"

"Max!!!!! NO! No, Noogie, he's fooling!"

Max started singing

*'You're in the army now,*
*You're not behind a plow;*
*You'll never get rich,*
*You son of a bitch,*
*You're in the army now.*

"I wuv dat song too, Unkie Max. Pwease, sing it again."

Charlotte, in exasperation, asked, "Did you HAVE to sing that song to the kid? Are you completely outa your mind from the war with those words? Is your feeble brain fried? Maybe from Belgium? A moron, you are, teaching those words!"

"Okay," said Max, "but then you close your eyes and go night-night." He sang it again.
"Can you say 'sonofabitch,' Noogie?"

I said, "Funabitch," closed my sleepy eyes and was fast asleep before the end.

"Out of my mind? He's asleep, no?"

"You are disgusting!" He grabbed her around the waist and gave her a giant squeeze and held her for what seemed forever. They started crying and she touched his cheeks with both hands and kissed him on each cheek, wiped each of their tears, before running into her own bedroom, handkerchief to eyes, head down, sobbing, sitting on her bed. He grabbed my shirt to wipe his eyes and tears yet again. There were no other words. Max never cried? Never. Of course, he never cried; he was a tough sonofabitch, a combat veteran, Tank destroyers. Bazookas, bullets. Grenades. Motherfuckin' tears.

## Madame Coq Au Vin!

Later that evening, he got dressed in his uniform: his mother had already washed one shirt, and out he went to Kurtz's Kentucky Club on the corner, not even a block away. In front of the bar and grill was a large poster on the sidewalk that proclaimed, "TONIGHT, Direct from New

York City, the Incompantable Songstress, KATE SMITH! Also featuring the beautiful French Dancer, MADAME COQ AU VIN!"

There were glossy photos of the two entertainers on the sidewalk billboard display. Kaplan was already there, waiting for Max at the bar, already with a whiskey in hand. A lot of other people also sat the bar and tables, men and women, happily drinking in an intimate smoky haze. The joint was buzzing! Mr. Kurtz was near the front door and Shepsie was sitting on a stool at the far end.

"Mockzie Shabus! Hello, Mockzie!!! Welcome home! Welcome, *boychickel,* welcome, welcome, welcome! Come, have a drink. You don't mind sitting next to this guy. He says he knows you fro somewhere."

"Hello, Mr. Kurtz!!! Thank you and a pleasure it is to be back in America...and in Woodridge! And Shepsie? Hello, Shepsie!!!" He walked over to Shepsie and they heartily and warmly shook hands and also hugged. It's not like Max and Shepsie were friends, but when people who know each other and who haven't seen one another for the longest time, reunions are that much more passionately expressive and genuinely emotional, even if people had only peripheral ties. "It's good to see you on the front line guarding your father's bar."

The bar was made of dark, shiny oak and above it was the Kentucky Club theme of a frieze of low relief of jockeys racing their thoroughbreds, one behind another. If it were in Greco-Roman times, those jockeys would've been riding on chariots. There were photos of winning horses held and owners alongside jockeys, and of reproductions of race horse paintings of Man O War, Seabiscuit and War Admiral and others hanging throughout the bar and restaurant. Also blue ribbons in between photos and paintings and glasses filled with beer, the Pabst Blue Ribbon logo painted on, the beer of choice. The room smelled like beer, and the bar, glistening like a fine patina on a valuable piece of antique furniture.

Moickzie, come, *zetz zich avek* right nest to this fellow. Not too close. He looks to me to be a *bissel*... you know what I mean, Mockzie? What's your name, soldier."

"Kaplan."

"Kaplan? You're the guy whose father owns the butcher shop across the street, the one who poisons my customers every week with his steaks and hamburgers? Come, have another schnapps. Enid, give this guy the special poison whiskey I save for the *schtunks* and give Shabus one, too. One for me too. A drink of anything for everybody. Welcome back, boychicks! I needed more customers."

Max said, "Mr. Kurtz, it's bad enough I had to eat my mother's version of poison earlier for dinner, but this? This should finish me. I dreamed of her poison every fucking day and night I was stuck in my luxury foxholes. Waddaya think, Bill, is he gonna kill us with this shit, after surviving the war?"

"No doubt, Maxi. Thank you, Mr. Kurtz. You first."

"Boys, I'm happy you made it back. Too many other sad stories I hear. Everybody, listen; *L'Chaim* to Shabus and Kaplan! They made it home from the war! And just for you two *schmendricks*, I got something very, very special behind the stage curtain." Shepsie was snickering. Handshakes all around. Glasses clicking. Other customers welcoming and congratulating Max and Kaplan.

"Bivens, you got some music, maybe, for once in your life? We got a show back there?"

"Yes sir, Mr. Kurtz!" He was the good-natured leader of a five-piece combo; piano, also sax-clarinet, bass, guitar and drums. "Gimme that beat, mama!" and the drummer, bent over, started pounding on his set, low and slow, and the bass popped in and then the soft wail of the sax and a few notes off the keys and that cryin' guitar, and Bivens shouted into the mic, "Ladies and gentlemen, direct from Paris, here's the siren that captured every soldier's heart in France, MADAME COQ AU VIN! Let's give her the clap, a BIG clap!" and then that beautiful, sexy, big-boobed "French" blonde stuck her luscious face out from behind the blood-red velvet curtain, half-hidden by yellow curls over one eye, a spotlight on her face only. The lights were dimmed almost all the way down by Shepsie.

Then he and the drummer intensified the beat but kept it ever sooooo slowwwww on the bass drum and out she emerged, gyrating to that relentless beat, one exaggerated step in stiletto spikes at a time, hips up, down, side to side, ass rolling like a coiled spring back and forth and up and down and round and round, breasts unable to be contained, delicate, expressive, ballet dancer's fingers caressing them, titillating the men and women as well, inviting them to come closer as she slow motion opened her black silky blouse, button by button, exposing teasingly half breasts, as she placed her red-lipped mouith to the mic and whispered, *"Welcome home, soldats. Bonne soir, mes amis.* I really, really, reeeeeeaaaaaalllly meeeeeeeesed you. Come over here and let me showwww you my beaucoup appreciation." The sax trebled the scream and wail and that deep bass hit the low notes as Max and Kaplan were summoned up to the small stage, not daring to look at the forbidden fruit too overtly, but she pulled them both close to her and she kissed Max hard and long, tonguing him, and placed his hand inside her blouse on to her breast, tweaking her arousing nipple, and Kaplan got the same treatment, hard and long, while placing her ass in his little hand, and they slow danced to the music while assisting her in the removal, to the beat, of that silk blouse as the crowd cheered.

One of the women, around forty-ish, jumped on the stage and moved in on them and the two women kissed each other, sloppy, hard tongue kisses, and simultaneously moved their hands down to caress each other's pussies over their dresses, and then kissed Max and Kaplan and the four of them moved almost imperceptibly.

"Ooooooooooooooo laaaaaaaaaaaaa la," the "French" lady exclaimed. "Ooooooooooooooo laaaaaaaaaaaa la, mes amis." You could tell that Max and Kaplan had miniature Eiffel Towers in their khaki pants. She grabbed them both, exclaiming *"Vive la France!"* Who cared? She ambled up to the mic, holding each Eiffel Tower next to her, and began her song, in a faux French accent, Julie Stein and Sammy Cahn's It's Been a Long, Long Time, and she made every note hang in the air of the smoky bar in deep shadow and orange light like heavy fog at twilight, slithering across a misty, purple field of fragrant lavender, guitar and piano fueling every kiss on her neck and ears and now, breasts and nipples, and the song surreptitiously emerged, whispered, half hidden, from that fog of an orgiastic dream to an orgasmic end. "Welcome home, *soldats*," she whispered in a voice of sensual longing.

"Got any food stamps? We've been hungry, too, for much too long, baby. I'm… especially… hungry." Her face looked down, the music slowly died and lights went to dark and they kissed again, very long and very hard.

## Ladies and Hard Ons, Miss Kate Smith!

"And now, ladies and hard ons, I mean, gentlemen, direct from New York and Broadway, the one and only, the great, the incompantable, the beautiful, MISSSSSSSSSS KATE SSSSSSSSSMITH! Let's hear it. Let's show her what a Woodridge welcome can be!" The place erupted in cheers, whistles, screams, stamping feet and non-stop applause. Shepsie's innocent face was covered in sweat as he emerged from backstage, dressed in a long, black gown, with ever so red, glossy lipstick and wearing a softly curled, brunette, Kate Smith wig, arms outstretched and kisses thrown to the audience. They cheered even that much more upon realizing who it was.

He waddled over to the microphone, grasped it in his small, pudgy hand and bent to it till his mouth almost soul-kissed it, and with his other hand that held a little American flag, signaled a stagehand to play the Victrola music, closes his eyes and began to precisely lip synch "God Bless America" in Kate Smith's powerful, operatic voice and gestures. Everyone rose and stood still, placed their hands over heir hearts and Kaplan's hand over the stripper's bare breast and joined in in a semi-drunken, uninhibited chorus. She placed her hand over his. The speakers were turned to full volume. Shepsie gyrated his inflated belly, in the same way he and observed the strippers and female impersonators undulate their bodies. It was grotesquely patriotic. Everyone saluted him and whistled their appreciation when he pulled off his wig and lifted it high in the air, hoisting the little flag like the eternal flame of the Statue of Liberty and then attempted to escape backstage as the men and women rushed him and playfully grabbed and pinched his flabby ass and oversized, real breasts under a pointed, stuffed cream-colored brassiere.

Fat Shepsie was… loved!

Mr. Kurtz walked out on stage, dashing and elegant, on might say, in a mink stole wrapped over his shoulders he removed from one of the chairs of a female patron, and quickly whispered to Bivens, who immediately had his drummer strike up a riff: da da dot dot, da da dot dot, da da da da da da da dot dot! The piano duplicated the sound and in came the bass and clarinet, and Mr. Kurtz yelled into the mic, " 'tenHUT!" Everyone stood and came to attention while the music repeated, and he shouted out for everyone to sing a tribute to 'Mockzie' and Kaplan, "You're in the army now!" Everyone shouted out with him as loud as could be, "You're NOT behind a plow! You're diggin' a ditch, you sonsofbitchs! You're NOT behind a plow!" The joint erupted and everyone sang it again, "You're in the army now! You're NOT behind a plow! You're diggin' a ditch, You sonsofbitches!!! You're in the army now!"

Shepsie marched out onto the middle of the stage, stuck his wig on the flag stick, raised the flag and saluted the cheering crowd, and out went the lights, except for the candles on the bar room tables.

"Max, Maxie, Mockzie, Maxileh, you sonofabitch, welcome home! You too, Kaplan!" They threw Max high in the air, neck bent backwards, legs and arms spread apart, the women grabbing his crotch from on top and underneath, a glass of booze in his hand, spilling all over everyone, his fifth, on this, his first Saturday night at the end of the war, back home in Woodridge.

Triumphant!

# 6.  Come Cook. Help I Could Use.

1957

Pesach pleaded with Lena to "maybe the hatchet they should bury. It's time, Laya. Ray is a good cousin to us, the best. You can't blame her forever. *Macht* peace. Make nice. It's time awready. Give her a call. Invite her oily to come up. *Genug*."

She knew he was right. Life was short and what was the point anyhow? She got on the phone and called Ray. After the wary greetings, she said, "Ray, I would like you should come up to Woodridge, if you can, a couple of days oily, and maybe help me cook a *bissel* for mine Fiftieth Annivoisary party. A hand I could use."

A prolonged silence...muffled cries, deep, loud breaths, and after a long pause, Ray answered, "Lena, dawlinck, it'll be my pleasure to give you a hand. I'll come up tomorrow on the train. What else does an old lady have to do? We'll cook. I have some special recipes for *rugeluch* and chopped lentils that taste, you won't believe, just like chopped chicken livers. We'll make *kreplach*, too, like in the old days. You'll swear that the lentils are chopped liver. It'll be such a pleasure to see you, dawlinck. And what, *boubileh*, can I bring for you?"

"Nothing, nothing at all. Just come. You'll bring yourself and we'll cook. Come oily. Tomorrow is *Shabus* and we'll have a *Shabus* dinner before the party Sunday."

The next day, Friday, they prepared both the usual Shabus meal of roast chicken, as well as all the wonderful special Jewish-Polish-Russian dishes for Sunday's Anniversary dinner. It was a happy day in the kitchen. The combined aromas of all the special dishes enveloped and embraced the house.

At sundown, Lena brought out the candelabra on to the kitchen table where Pesach was already sitting, waiting for dinner, and the women placed shawls on their heads. They lit the candles and slowly twirled their hands toward the candlelight, drawing the warm, yellow light and smoke into them in a slow, circular motion. In prayer, they gently covered their eyes with their hands, turned away from the candles, and wished each other a good *Shabus*.

In 1957 on the afternoon of May 19th, Lena and Pesach celebrated their 50th Anniversary. I, now thirteen, took pictures of my grandparents with Joe's Brownie camera. The whole extended family attended, having grown larger with spouses and grandchildren. The *tuchus* patrol, let by Sam Fein and followed by Hymie, went into action. No one was safe. Oy such a family!

Cousin Ray and Lena, at the end of the party, found a private moment, hugged ever so tightly, weaving back and forth, kissed and cried, and would not let go. An eternity had passed.

But the same?


It wasn't.

# 7. The "Ph" Word and Superman

I, from Kindergarten on, and now a fifth grade wiseass, was one of the most aggressive guys on the field, an outspoken mouth in school, and had visited the principal's office more often than any other student in my class, which had to be absolutely the most scary, embarrassing moment any Woodridge student had to face, particularly when that principal happened to be Mr. Blumberg. Parents were notified by phone and letter when summoned to appear with children. The whole village knew. The telephone operators blabbed and nothing was sacred to the people sorting the mail. Those particular letters had their own special appearance. It was a dreaded delivery. Mr. Blumberg and Mr. Weiss, the Superintendent, were omnipotent gods. Most of the parents were first generation children of immigrants who escaped the pogroms of Eastern Europe, and it was a time in a rural community when authority was taken very, very, very seriously. A letter from them could make a parent *schvitz*. Poor me! My father *schvitzed* more than anyone, and promised more often than not, to keep mefrom getting in trouble and that he would get his son to behave in order to avoid the ultimate embarrassment of being thrown out of school.

Had I not been such an exceptional student, Blumberg would have been less forgiving. And he only gave me short suspensions. A "scooper," backwoods kid would have been thrown out for a week or more at a time. When I wrote the "F" word in chalk, spelled "Phuck", on the side wall of the school, someone ratted, one of the girls, and I got two days for that one. Did I ever get it from my father for that! I was beaten more often than not with the tried and proven scientific, understanding, progressive method by the heels of my father's best Perlmutter shoes. If you needed a pair of shoes already broken in, the ones used on my ass and thighs and arms were the softest. Okay, you're not supposed to hit your kids. So I got hit. So those unlucky parts of my body were black, blue, red, purple, yellow and green for the better part of two weeks.

Everyone got whacked for something or other. It was called "parental understanding." Seemed like, in conversations with my friends, that all of them had understanding parents as well, at one time or another. "You wrote 'Phuck' on the school? I'll give you a 'phuck'. I'll break your goddamn head and I'll break your hands you go to Blumberg's office again! I swear to God, I'll break'em. I'll give you such a *zetz* across your mouth you'll fit in a shoe box. I'll give you a 'phuck' on your ass you won't be able to sit for a week. You know what you did to your mother? A word like that! Do you think I need the whole village to know what a *mamzur* you are? I have to face them because of a son who goes to Blumberg? You think they'll ever go into my drugstore again? *Nu!?*" He asked a question and God forbid I should answer, I'd get another whack for talking back, no matter what the answer. I was a wiseguy in school, but a pussy in front of my father. Sometimes Joe used his belt, sometimes a rolled up very liberal New York Post or a lefty Daily Compass.

"Get the hell in your room and don't come out until you're ready to go back to school, and make sure you sweep the store after I close, and straighten the shelves. No TV at

133

Fishkill's house for a week. No dinner. Veal chops. Charlotte, let's eat. And next time, goddammit, spell it right!"

## 8. Hey, Kids, It's Howdy Shitty Time!

When the Fishkills got the first TV on the street and one of the first in Woodridge, my friends on the street all tried to conveniently join them in their living room when our favorite programs were on once or twice a week. Of course, we all became best friends with Seymour, who was a year younger than us. (I really liked him anyhow), and got to watch Howdy Doody, Perry Como and the news whenever we could, or whenever Seymour decided to let us watch. He had the power. And we let him play ball with us on the street any time he wanted to join in, which was always. He was a fuckin' good ballplayer too, for a younger kid, and we competed to have him on our side.

I could never figure out who made up the name, "Howdy Doody." I thought 'Doody' meant doody and how could they ever use the word "doody" on TV? Did Howdy make doodies in his pants? Manny asked why they didn't call him "Howdy Shit". So from then on whenever we went over to Seymour's, we mimicked Buffalo Bob and yelled out with him, "Hey kids! It's Howdy Shitty Time!" and laughed our asses off at Seymour's special interpretation. Television; what a miracle to come out of a five inch screen! The

Novicks bought a magnifier to go in front of their screen to make the picture bigger, but it was easier to see the shows without it. With a magnifier, you had to sit directly in front of the screen. Everyone seemed to be on each other's laps competing for a better view.

Our family, on the other hand, did not get a TV until 1951, a 9" or 10" Dumont. Leibel, everyone called him Label, Wishinsky climbed a big, tall maple in the back of our then new house and installed the antenna. Label, in later years, bacame the inventor of the Wishinsky Bagelmaking Machine and the Borschtmobile, having converted his Mercedes to run on borscht. It had a pipe coming out of the hood. What difference did it make that it was a Mercedes? It became the Borscht Belt Grand Touring Borschtmobile. It ran either on Manichewitz Borscht or the homemade version. My mother said, "I'm gonna waste my borscht and put it into that Nazi car? Whatareyoucrazy? He should put Hitler's blood in it, the *meshuggener*. Maybe then he could burn the engine out. It'll serve him right!"

Prior to TV sets and never knowing they existed, me and Burt sat at the large mahogany radio every evening at 5:30 pm to listen to our favorite radio programs: Superman, The Lone Ranger, Sergeant Preston of the Yukon and Hopalong Cassidy. They came alive in our imagination, and we had to compete with Pop for the listening time. He wanted to listen to his news programs, but my kid brother and I HAD to listen to ours, and he let us win.

We were given the hour. Not many years later, we could not hide our immense disappointment when Superman came on TV. He didn't look at all like what we imagined him to be, from the "jokebooks" and our image of him from the radio program. He hardly had any muscles and his Superman suit had wrinkles in it. What kind of Superman doesn't have muscles? Batman looked like he could beat the shit out of him and we all knew that that was impossible. Nobody could beat Superman. When we were much older and George Reeves killed himself, we knew then that he was a phony and could never have been the real Superman. But we were too old then to care, even though it brought us back to the mornings we walked to school arguing who could beat whom and who was the King of the Cowboys, Roy Rogers or Gene Autry. And did Lois Lane know the true identity of Clark Kent, and did they ever make out? And if not, how could she be so stupid? We all could tell who he really was.

I miss all those days when imagination was unencumbered and arguments with Butch and Seymour, my walking-to-school-companions, were serious and passionate. So passionate that one day, after school on the way home, Butch jumped me from behind and punched me in the back of the head because I told him that Roy Rogers, his favorite cowboy, was a fairy. I flipped him over my back and he got me again in the eye. It hurt like hell, but I punched him in the belly and whacked him with a left to his jaw. We fought a bit longer until he ran off, surprised at his defeat. I couldn't wait to tell Pop and Uncle Max. They saw my half-closed black eye and had to hear about every punch, and couldn't be prouder of me. My mother, on the other hand, yelled, "If I ever catch you fighting again, I'll yank every hair out of your head! Do you hear me? Every hair!"

I said, "Ma, I just had a haircut. You can't yank it. It's

too short."    That was the wrong thing to say. "Are you talking back to me? Don't you dare talk back to me! If I want to yank your hair, I'll yank it!" and with that, she gave me a good I said, "Ma, I just had a haircut. You can't yank it. It's too short."    That was the wrong thing to say. "Are you talking back to me? Don't you dare talk back to me! If I want to yank your hair, I'll yank it!" and with that, she gave me a good slap on my face and tried to yank my hair, but couldn't, and gave me another slap to the side of my head. All I could do was laugh, and that fueled the fire. "Papa, you should not encourage him. He'll only fight more. You think I need this? I don't need to go to Blumberg's office. That's all I have to do is go to Blumberg's office." My Pop and Max just laughed and that pissed her off that much more. So much for Jewish mothers. They just don't understand. But the word spread about my fight around to my friends, and most of them would no longer try to mess with me. Butch and I ultimately became best friends again, closer than ever.

## 9. Noogie's Hemingway Moment: The Young Boy And The Pond

We fished all the time together for sunnies, perch, lox, pickerel and suckers, which we speared. None of us was ever able to land an elusive gefilte. We didn't even know what they looked like. We also gently lifted the suckers, hiding under rocks, out of the water with our bare hands.

When I had my ninth birthday, my grandparents gave me a rod and spinning reel and a few lures, one of which was named a "Red Devil." They knew how much I loved to fish and it was the best present I could've ever received. The day after my birthday, I took my bike and rode about three miles to the Cantor's pond on their egg farm property. The pond was more like an oversized bathtub, about a foot or so deep. I always wanted to fish there. It was such a pretty spot, and now that I had that shiny new rod and reel, I placed it in my bike's basket, told my grandparents where I was going, and off I went.

I dropped my bike on the unmowed grass and weeds and walked slowly through the mosquitos, crouching so as to not disturb any possible fish, to the far side of the pond. I had already tied my favorite lure, that beautiful red and white "Red Devil," onto my line. I had always used floating, red dobbers attached about two to three feet above a small hook, baited with a worm, but never before had I thought of using a lure. I never knew the word, much less knew what one was, until I read the package.

Standing next to the edge of the water, I freed the line and red devil, pulled the rod all the way back and cast the line toward the middle of the pond, perhaps as much as eight feet away.

Before the lure ever reached the water, something exploded upward exactly like the cherry bombs I'd thrown into an old, unused well behind my house, other than the loud fireworks boom. It looked like it flew up at least two feet and splashed down, immediately pulling strongly on my line. My rod was rapidly being pulled into the pond and I had to lunge into the water to retrieve it, fearful of losing it forever.

I grabbed the line and pulled it toward me, completely oblivious of the handle on the reel. The monster fish was fighting, jumping, swerving left and right, fiercely resisting my every tug. The line got entwined around my sneaker and I almost lost my balance while pulling, but immediately realized I was pulling my own foot and tripping all over myself while trying to keep my balance.

I was sweating and desperate, but I finally yanked the fish out of the water into the air and it hit me on the side of my face and scared the crap out of me. BUT… I got him!

I never saw a fish like that before, silvery and very big and heavy but slimy like most other fish I knew and it had small, sharp teeth. I held it up as best as I could, sloshed through the high undergrowth, placed it into my bike's basket headfirst, tail sticking out along with my tangled line, rod and reel, and rode my bike as fast as I could to show off my catch to my grandparents. It seemed like forever till I arrived home and yelled to my Gram and Pop to come look. Hearing my screaming, out they ran, alarmed.

"Noogileh, oy vey, the fish you got at Cantor's? In that mudhole? Such a fishmen you are!!! A monster you catched!!!" My Pop grabbed my shoulder with one hand and squeezed my arm muscle with his two giant fingers to feel how strong I was and nodded his approval. My grandmother gave me a big kiss on my forehead, a pinch on my cheek and a tight hug.

"Mine Noogie, so proud of you I am!!!! Poo, poo poo!" exclaimed Pop.

"What do you think the kind of fish I caught, Gram? I never saw one like this before!"

"You don't know what you caught, mine big fisherman? You caught a giant *gefilte* and I'm going to make him into a *gefilte* fish dinneh for everyone to eat. And for you, mine big Noogileh, a special treat for the fish you catched; I got five M&Ms I saved, just for you being mine best gefilte fish fisherman king! You oined mine reward!"

A *gefilte*?!!!!! I was the first one of my friends to have ever caught a *gefilte*. I couldn't wait to tell them!!! It was the best birthday I ever had, even though I hated the taste of *gefilte* fish!

Then we shot woodchucks a few years later when his father got him a small shotgun for his fourteenth birthday. It practically knocked my shoulder off the first time I shot it. I was used to my 22 single shot rifle. My uncle, who fought all over Europe in the tank destroyers division, taught me how to shoot. Move slowly and silently. Take aim. Quietly take a deep breath through the nose and breathe out through the mouth and ever so gently so that the rifle remains rock-steady, pull the trigger. I was deadly. I shoulda been in the movies. I was as good as Gene Autry. I relished sharing those moments with my pop and uncle.

## 10. "Yes, Mrs. Walkowitz" and Pointy Bras

Emanuel Perlmutter, Manny the *nudnick*, Fancy Manny, owned the only shoe store in Woodridge. It started as his father's business. "A Better Shoe You'll Never Wear" was his slogan under the store's official name, "Perlmutter's Shoe-ery, The Greatest Shoe on Earth." I often wondered how many customers he had with only one foot. He also made shoes from imported English leathers — imported from the lower East Side you should know. Only the best. And he repaired all of the shoes of the local villagers, including my grandfather's, who was a real fanatic when it came to his shoes, especially his work shoes for the blacksmith shop.

Pesach's shoes had to be big and thick around the toes so that they wouldn't be crushed by a horse's stray hoof as he changed its horseshoes. We kidded him every time he needed a shoe fixed. "So Pop, a better horseshoe you'll never wear?" we asked. Everyone went to Manny's. Who could afford to buy the fancy new English shoes that were sold in his Monticello shoe store for $4.00? Besides, he made the used ones as good as new. And if he or Lena wanted new ones at those rare times, they bought the Monticello shoes and worked the stiffness out of them sooner or later, most likely during a wedding or bar mitzvah, and lived with the blisters for the following week.

Actually, though, there were a few who could afford to indulge themselves besides the limited number of locals who earned considerably more than our family did. Included on the English leather handmade shoe list were

Louie Lepke, "Waxie" Gordon, Jake Shapiro and Phil Strauss. Believe it or not, they were customers.

So what if Mr. Lepke was Public Enemy #1 and the others, real life members of Murder Incorporated. Only a few ever knew who they were anyway, and those who did would not dare breathe a word. (A hero there wasn't in Woodridge.) Let the *mamzurs* buy their shoes and get the hell out. They either had homes in the Catskills or stayed at places like Grossinger's or Brown's. They could make you nervous. They wore expensive suits and big hats. And Manny's shoes. When they came into Woodridge for an egg cream at Willie's Luncheonette or Bushky Cohen's or Abe Krutman's Candy Store, their presence was felt. They always stopped at Manny's to buy shoes. Lepke would come into town from New York. He was seen there often through the window, with an entourage, making sure his tough guys all bought Manny's shoes. Mr. Lepke, ever a realist, told Manny that if he had to go, he wanted to be killed with his Perlmutter shoes on. It was classier that way to wear Jew shoes, not Italian, like those other *goyim* wore. Later on, thinking back, after hearing all those scary stories about Mr. Lepke, I wondered how bad he really could have been, particularly after giving Manny an extra twenty dollars after every visit, a fortune in those days.

Sid Caesar hung out at Bushkie's too, to play poker and pinochle. He, too, wore his Perlmutters and spent as much time in the shoe store *kibitzing*, it seemed, as he did at The Avon Lodge, Maj Neukrug's hotel a few miles out of the village. What a maniac and what fun he was. He used our kind of words, too, in front of everyone. If he could do it, we could do it too, and more often than not, we tested the verbal waters from behind bushes by yelling those special words as loud as we could at older people and running our asses off before anyone could identify us. We all gathered around him while he did his *schtick* hilariously, particularly his Hitler routine. He was our favorite, and when he later had his own TV show, we all felt terrifically proud that we knew him from Woodridge and that he cursed in Yiddish, like my grandfather, uncles and all their friends. Everyone grew up cursing in Yiddish.

We all worked as kids. Arnie Perlmutter worked at his father's store, stacking shoes, cleaning shelves, waiting on customers and in the summer, shining shoes for ten cents a shine. He was ambitious and always trying to hustle a few cents for himself. Arnie, that little prick, was two years younger than me and always tried to hang out with us, but we couldn't stand the little bastid and threatened more than once to beat the shit out of him if he didn't leave us alone. But Manny was pretty protective of his son and succeeded in convincing us to let Arnie join us once in a while on the sidelines when we played ball and marbles and baseball card flipping, and ass and tit grabbing of our female schoolmates behind the school during lunch hours and after school, before we all went home. Arnie liked that. He played the mascot role. He was in fourth grade and these were lessons he didn't learn in Mrs. Walkowtz's class.

He got the Mrs. Walkowitz treatment just like the rest of us. Mrs. Walkowitz made everyone say "Yes, Mrs. Walkowitz" or "No, Mrs. Walkowitz" when answering her questions. She would get extremely pissed off if we forgot. "Yes, who?" she would demand, not ask. "Yes, Mrs. Walkowitz" and THEN a response to her intimidating question. She was tough and she scared the shit out of all of us. "No, Mrs. Walkowitz, I would not like to suck your tit, Mrs. Walkowitz."

We were in sixth grade and learning, after hating and making fun of girls for so long, what it was like to look at our female classmates' bodies and emerging projectiles, without seeming to look, instead of the big tits of Mrs. Walkowitz, Miss Turner and Mrs. Engelhardt, the tittiest of our teachers, causing us frequent hard ons during spelling bees and science lessons or whenever they bent over a bit too much, especially in warmer weather when their prissy dresses were a bit more revealing. Mention the word "sex" in a science lesson and our minds were off and running.

Some of the girls were now wearing bras. The girls with bigger tits wore pointy bras like paper soda cups that looked like funnels without holes in the bottom. Jane Russell wore my favorite bras when I went to see her in cowboy movies. She wore double scoop ice cream cones. She was always good for a two-hour stiff one in the dark. But that little cocksucker Arnie, constantly tried to weasel his way into our group just to listen to us sizing up the girls and their boobs, and who was prettier and who was the ugliest. He was also panhandling us to borrow a nickel or a couple of pennies for ice cream or candy, until I told him if he came near me again, I would break his fuckin' arm, and I didn't give a shit what his brother felt about it, 'cause I'd beat the crap out of him, too. It's not that I was tough. I wasn't, but that little bastid was one of those kid brothers you would just like to murder. It made me think of asking one of his dad's special Murder, Inc. customers how much it would cost.

And those, too, were the days when we were testing the verbal waters on the ball fields as we learned more and more choice Yiddish words, the selection of which our grandparents and parents used extensively; words like *mamzur* and *schmeckel* and *putz* and *schmuck* and dickface and *gonnif* and *schnorrer* and *shtup*. Words that had a certain ring to them. Awright, so dickface isn't Yiddish.

Big deal. We used it interchangeably. Nobody ever used *schmeckelpunim*. It didn't have the same ring as did dickface but, mostly Yiddish expressions were much more expressive.

Arnie was just the most annoying, pesty little schnorrerfuck any serious sixth grader ever had to endure. He learned to stay away from me and finally got the message from my fellow friends as well. Everyone would noogie him to torture him and punch him in the shoulder right on the bone for extra measure. We also heard that, occasionally, he would take money out of his father's register when his father was in the back room, sorting shoes. We may have felt up some of the girls, and probably would've gotten killed if our parents ever heard about it or if their parents ever heard about it, but we didn't steal. I just had a feeling that Arnie wasn't entirely innocent. I don't know why. Maybe because he was always trying to prove himself because he was the shortest kid in our crowd, or maybe he always seemed to have more money than any of the rest of us.

If my parents or grandparents or uncles ever caught me stealing, I'd be totally dead. That sort of thing happened in other families somewhere else in the world, but not by us.

Not in Woodridge. Not in the village where doors were never locked, and refrigerators were opened by unannounced but welcomed visitors looking for a nosh and where keys never left a car's ignition. That changed in our household, though, when my seven year old brother Burt, decided to copy the way I was able to take my mother's car to the village alone. I was twelve. So that little kid drove the car down the very steep Deutsch's Hill and subsequently, into a ditch. He couldn't reach the brake pedal to stop it. My brother had big balls from the time he was a little kid, bigger knadles than those in our mother's chicken soup.

## 11. Yitchy, The Plum Ber

1959

"Oy, the rain, the rain! Kets and dogs, dogs and kets!" exclaimed Mrs. Ruderman, "And the wind, you should only know from."

That roaring sound, squeezing through the pines and oaks and maples like an oversized body trying to fit into a narrow kitchen chair with arms, gasping for breath and schpritzing against the windows and house and blowing leaves and branches, large and small, in a cacophony of threatening music, made everyone worry about trees falling on the house and bungalow in the rear. It was a real *mamzur* of a storm. The candles were on the table, just in case, and the tub was already filled for toilet flushing water. No electric, no well pump. Cooking, yes. The stoves and water heaters were on gas, filled and supplied from Moxie Shabus's gas company in Woodridge.

Layah Ruderman always complained to Max, and this day was no exception. "Hello, Moxileh, I'm out of gas! Maybe, Moxie, you could deliver me a full tank for once, instead of the half-tanks I always get?"

And he to her, "Maybe, Mrs. Ruderman, I only send full tanks to my good customers. Why should you get a full tank? A full tank you don't deserve. A full tank is for good cooks. Do I ever get anything decent when I come over? You save the good food for your relatives. Who can eat what you put in front of me."

"Moxileh," she said in Yiddish, "I loaf you, they should only cut your head off, so you can be a half poisson, and then I wouldn't have to feed you nothing at all!"

"Mrs. Ruderman, you'd be doing me the biggest favor. You think I'd wanna die from what you'd feed me?" It was their monthly routine.

Max now owned the business of Best Natural Gas, having bought it from BuhBuhBenny in 1954. I worked for him on weekends and whenever he could after school and holidays, including Yom Kippur and Rosh Hashanah. Better than going to *shul*.

"I'll deliver to you in three weeks," he told her. "Yeh?"

"Moxieleh, for you I'll have chicken soup with mine dog's *dreck*, you should take home to your vife."

"Mrs. Ruderman, in that case, I'll have my genius nephew and Schubeck deliver to you in an hour."

"Moxie, a *bissel* more than a half tank this time. Hurry, dollinck, mine soup is getting cold."

Max turned to Schubeck, his best driver, "Take the genius with you and go deliver a tank to Mrs. Ruderman. Take whatever money she gives you and wants to pay. Doesn't matter. And don't stop for a drink, you hear me!?"

Schubeck was one of those guys who always took me with him on the road to *schlep* tanks. He forever needed a shave and always had a boozy breath from the bars and wore a dirty Best Natural Gas workshirt. He lived alone across from the gas plant and was the hardest worker Max had. But his appearance could make a customer worry.

"Let my genius nephew drive and hook up the tank himself. Noogie, don't stop at the bar for Schubeck."

"You trust that kid to drive"?

Max said, "He's fifteen. You think he doesn't know how to drive by now? Get in the truck, genius, and go deliver. Trust? Look at Shubeck, and he asks ME about trusting you?"

I said, "I never did this before."

"You heard me, Noogie. Take. The. Truck. And. Deliver. The. Gas. And. Take. Her. Money."

I was scared shitless, but off I went to Mrs. Ruderman's. I delivered the gas, hooked it up under that watchful eye of Schubeck and returned safely home. It was the first time I ever did it all by myself! I said, "Mrs. Ruderman called you a thief, a real *gonif*, and then gave me two dollars and an extra quarter for myself to go buy an ice cream, and also, a jar of her chicken soup, which she said, "Tell your uncle he should only drop dead from this delicious jar of *dreck* just for him."

"Very good, genius. Next time, you're gonna deliver bulk by yourself to one of the bungalows." That really freaked me out, thinking about it. Oh, shit, I thought. Oh, fucking shit! I did it! I'm a genius after all! There was never a thought of the local cop, "Black Dog" Ruderman, stopping and ticketing me. He was Mrs. Ruderman's son. He would simply tell us kids he knew to get their rear ends home before he locked us up.

Max called Mrs. Ruderman. "Mrs. Ruderman, you're right. What can I say about your gift of... is it chicken soup? It looks like *dreck*, it smells like *dreck* and *dreck* it has to be, and I thank you. I'm sure my wife will love it. My dog, too. I only hope it won't kill HIM! If he lives, I may try it."

Yitchy, her husband the "plum ber," pronounced in two words, the way he described himself, had just come home from a long day of threading and cutting pipes, of connecting, *schlepping*, of *schmutz* of wet shoes and excessive *schvitzy*, smelly underarms. Another day to put food on the table. He fell into his favorite velvet dark pine-green easy chair after taking off his green work shirt, exposing his stained tank top and his thick, hairy chest and simian-hairy arms, stubby and muscled, hands with short, thick, greasy fingers, permanently stained black from all the black grease and pipe sealer. He was a little *bullvan*. He could squeeze your hand and make you beg. His round, puffy face laughed through thick Russian lips and squinty eyes and rimless glasses. He had a kind face, though. He could *kibbitz* with the best of them, including Pesach Shabus, the master *kibitzer*. But he was no match for his wife Layah, whom everyone called Tanteh Layah.

He started to read his Freiheit newspaper, but she called he should come to the table for dinneh. "Come, mine guggis Yitcheleh. Come."

"What you got tonight, you should only kill me, mine Layah? Maybe save some for Moxie Shabus."

"Yeh, kill you? You should be so lucky you should die from this. I already gave Moxie some soup so he should die too." She placed a plate of steaming brisket in front of him, with roasted potatoes and string beans that looked like they had been cooking since nine AM, just the way he loved them. The aromas in their small kitchen were symphonic. Next to their plates were wedges of iceberg lettuce and tomato salad with a mixture of ketchup and mayonnaise for the dressing, and a large bowl of sweet corn that only Ray Kasofsky could grow. He grew the succulent beefsteak tomatoes as well.

"So, nu, Yitchileh, you woiked today? You look so clean," staring at his filthy work clothes. You *schmeared* a *bissel* dirt on your shirt to make me think you did something useful, like a real *mensch*, maybe?"

"Nah, I did nothing. I didn't want I should get mine nails dirty, so I set around mit the *goyim* woikers doing nothing. And you, mine *kleyn tzatzkeleh*?

"Me, mine Yitcheleh? I done nothing, too. The clothes I washed, I hung them on the line, then it started raining, you should only know from, so I hung them in the living room near the wood stove. I tooked out the meat and schmeared some seasonings on it and put it in the pot to cook mit the potatoes and onions. The string beans I started cooking later, ten o'clock, and I washed the dishes and washed the floors and made the bed and swept the porch and then cleaned the toilets and washed mine hair so I could look like a beaudelful goil just for you, and I polished mine shoes and fed the *hundt* and let him out so he could get all wet and make a new mess for me and I baked a *chollie* and I called our Doris, but the *fakakta* hoperator, she couldn't understand the way I talked, the *meshugenim*, so I had to make a transelvation for her."

"Yeh? What you tell her?"

"Well, I wanted Doris's number, so I tell her "Plummet 2- 3689 in Lost Angeles. They have big, fancy numbers in Lost Angeles, not like our 305. No Plummet. Fancy enough. And she says, " I don't have a Plummet and I keep telling her again and again the number. So I finally ask her, 'Dollinck, tell me, you got maybe a car?' and she says, 'Yes, I have a car.' "So I ask her, And what kind car you got?" and she says she has a Chevie, and I ask her, 'You don't have a Plummet?' And she says, "Ahhhhhhh, a Plymouth!' And I say, 'Yes, Dollinck, that's right, a Plummet!' And I finally got to say hello to mine Doris."

"Dat's becaussssssse, you didn't loin English good, like me. So, nu, can we eat awready?" She put the food on the yellow and pink table, covered with a flowered oilcloth.

The dishes were the everyday dishes, not the ones for the Friday Shabus. Also placed on the table was the blue seltzer bottle. They started to eat after lighting the Shabus candles and a blessing over the bread, and shared the day's stories. The dog, a black and white mutt named "Schloimie," always sat at his side, waiting for the little bite of something, anything, when Layeh wasn't looking. Yitchy had trained the dog to eat only "kosher." If Yitchy told the dog, "*treyf,*" Schloimie would know that he wasn't allowed to begin eating. It was only when Yitchy told the dog, "*kosher,*" that Schloimie knew he was allowed to begin to eat. *Treyf* wasn't *kosher.* Schloimie had a half black and half white face. He was very affectionate and eager for a rub behind the ears or on his stomach, and never left either of their sides, favoring Yitchy, though probably because of the secret feedings at and under the table and wherever else they were. Schloimie loved to drive in Yitchy's truck. His head always hung out the window, above Yitchy's sign, "Yitchy's Plumbing Co., I Make Nice to Your Pipes. Ph. 305, Woodridge, NY."

The rain was very loud and intense, machine-gunning on the roof, and the room had a chill to it, despite the clanging cast iron radiators. Layah wore a beige shawl she knitted, covering the housedress and flowered apron she never took off. When she had time, she knitted shawls, sweaters, mittens, throws. She sewed much of her own clothing and mended the many holes in Yitchy's socks, shirts and pants. The tea kettle on the old, pea green stove was whistling for their glasses of tea during and after dinner. They drank their tea through square lumps of sugar on their tongues. It was a Russian custom. Lena Shabus drank her tea the same way.

Although chilly outdoors, their kitchen felt warm and comfortable, and the table, filled with the Polish, Russian, Eastern European delicacies of dinner, was home to many guests, besides their family members, who reveled in the constant laughter of their incessant needling: sons Pittileh, Ruben, known to all as Pussy and Black Dog, the motorcycle cop, the Sheins, Katzowitzs, Kantrowitzs, Shabuses, Kaplans, Cohens, Benjamins, Goodmans, Penzirers, Alports, Kriegers and sometimes what seemed like the rest of Woodridge. Everyone contributed: Matzo ball soup, gefilte fish, latkes, kugel, chopped liver, brisket, knishes, blintzehs, pickles, rugelach. Did I forget the rye bread, bagels, lox, whitefish? There was hardly anything to eat.

And so who should bang on the door and rush in while they're eating? None other than Mrs. Schlamowitz, their tenant in the bungalow behind their house, who is screaming, "Yitchie, Yitchie!! Come! Hurry! Mine bungalow, It's drowning! It's a river! Hurry, Yitchie! Mine floor is a flood! It's ruining everything! It's pouring in. The furniture, mine shoes, a *gantseh* mess!!! Hurry, come fix!!!!"

"In the bungalow, it's raining?" Yitchie incredulously asked.

"Yeh, raining! You know what is rain? This isn't rain, this is a mess! This is a double flood, a *gantseh megillah*, you should only know! What are you sitting? Hurry before the bungalow floats away!!!"

"Oy yoy yoy, he says, I can't finish mine supper? The flood, it can't wait a few minutes? I got a boat behind mine house, Maybe I could rent it to you. Come, Mrs. Schlamovitz, sit for awhile and have a bite with us."

"Yitchie, you think this is a joke? I'll give you a joke. And you Layah, him you can live with?"

"Yeh," said Layah, "he's mine sailorman. Yitchileh, go. Put your galoshes on and your raincoat and go swimming mit Mrs. Schlamovitz to her bungalow and maybe for once in your life, you'll be able to fix something. And put a rubber tube around your waist! Bring one for Mrs. Schlamovitz too!"

"This is funny to you, Laya? A rubber tube I should wear?"

"Yeh, Yetta, it could help, you shouldn't drown in your bungalow."

So Yitchie takes another bite of brisket, sneaks a *bissel* to Schloimie, puts on his dirty raincoat and hat, grabs his toolbox and walks out with Mrs. Schlamowitz to her bungalow, followed of course by Schloimie, who stank bad enough when he was dry, but stank worse than a skunk, you should only know, when wet.

They walked through the terrible, diagonal rain, the whistling wind through the chattering twigs and soggy leaves, into her bungalow.

She said, "Oy, mine Gut, you see what I mean, Yitchie? A bigger mess you couldn't have! I should be the one to live in this bungalow? A million bungalows in the Ketskiltz and I have to live in this one! Oyyyyyyy, such a *shondah*. I'm cursed!"

"Yeh, dollinckg, a *bisseleh* rain you got, I see. So you take a mop."

"A mop?!!!!! I should take a mop to this flood??? I got the Neverstink River in mine bungalow and I should take a mop??? Fish can swim in it! I'll give you a mop, Yitchy, right on your *kup*!!! So, hurry, fix, fix awready."

"It's awright, Yetta, I'll fix. For you, I'll fix."

Yitchie had a reputation of being one of the very best plumbers in Woodridge. He looked up at the ceiling. The water was pouring in and filling the pots on the table and stove and countertop. It was dripping all over the red and white patterned linoleum floor. It was rising and almost covered their ankles. He sloshed over to the other side of the room then to see where the water was coming from. He climbed onto a chair to get a better look, while she yelled and pleaded, "So what are you waiting for? You don't see the rain? Maybe, Yitchileh, you think someone has a hose? What are you, an engineer? Hurry, awready, stop the rain! Oy, why me?????"

"Yetta, I see where the rain is coming in over there in the ceiling. Now I'll fix, dollinck. For you, I'll make a fix 'cause I love you and I want you should be heppy and you are my favorite tenant."

"Yitchie, enough awready! I'm your one and only tenant. I need your *kibitz* like I need a herring in a *tuchus*. FIX!!!!"

"Karschmer has the best herring, pickled or *schmaltz*. I'll get one just for your *tuchus* the next time I'm in his store. You like pickled or matjes? "

"Awright, no more. Just. Fix. The. Leak."

Yitchie walked slowly over to the leak with his toolbox, opened it up, pulled out the proper tool, looked up for the exact right spot, drilled a large hole in the floor below it, and exclaimed loudly, "It's fixed, Mrs. Schlamovitz!", packed his drill and other tools and walked out the door with Schloimie, followed by Mrs. Schlamowitz's haunting screams and Yiddish curses in the darkness. *"Mamzur!* This you call a fix?"

Schloimie howled too, in unison, while shaking off the rain.

# 12. Pop, Gram, Goils and That *Schmatta*

1960

It was my first summer not working in the gas plant and not having my superior intelligence reinforced day in and day out by hearing from my uncle his famous question, "Okay, genius, now what'd you do?"

Pop's face was still beautiful; thin and sculptured, white moustache (half of which, a number of years before, my grandmother Lena, tried to cut while he slept), deep-set grayish blue eyes, sensitive eyes, intelligent, probing, curious eyes, knowledgeable eyes, eyes that beckoned me over to his bed as I went to shake his hand and hug him. "What, no kiss?" he whispered from a throat that no longer had a voicebox. I kissed him. He never asked me for a kiss before. We always hugged. Kissing was embarrassing, but I did it knowing as he knew that this was the end.

We held hands, and my incredulous grandmother looked at my new goatee while I sat on the bed, a goatee I was proud of, because I was now a college student in Boston. My first time out of Woodridge, and there in Boston all us clean-cut freshmen, grew mustaches and goatees and beards and let our hair grow longer. I no longer had to go to Moe's barbershop every week. She asked me, "So Noogie, so what is that *schmatta* you got on your chin? This is what you do when you go away to college? What do you call that thing pointing out of your chin?"

"It's a goatee. You like?"

"*Oy vey. Vey iz mir.* Oy, such a fancy boy you are. Tell me, are you getting fancy grades with dat *schmatta*? The goats like it?"

"Gram, every time I feel myself falling asleep while studying, I tug on it and wake myself up to do better. How's that for 'fancy'? It's a useful thing to have in college." Besides, the 'girl goats' like it. And especially, the *shikses*, my favorites."

"*Shikses*?! You go out mit *shikses*? I''ll break your head you bring one home to me. Let the *shagutses* take the *shicksehs*. You, I want you should find a nice Jewish girl. Please, no *shicksehs*. I won't let you and her in the house. Oy, Pesach, he wants he should bring me home a *shikseh*."

"A *shikse*?" he asks. "Why not, Laya, she'll teach you how to make a nice, kosher pork brisket." Even near his death, he still *kibbitzed*.

"Okay, okay! If you feed me something I like, I won't go

out with *shikses*. But it has to be good for a change."

"What? It's not good enough mine food for you? Good I should give to a *sheygets* like you? You should starve with that *schmatta*."

"Gram, you're gonna make me starve? You want me to eat grass? I drive seven hours without stopping just to come home to see you, and you're gonna make me starve? Such a grandmother!" I go over to her and rub my goatee on her cheek while putting my arms around her so she can't squirm away.

"*Gay avek foon mir*! I'll feed you! I'll feed you! Come eat. I got some k*replach* I made for you. Your favorite you don't deserve. You take such a *shayna punim* and put a *schmatta* like that on it. Oy, look at you. A *schmutzface*. You better do good in that fancy college or I'll think you're a *schmatta* yourself. Come in the kitchen. I made some *chollah*. Do they have Jewish goils in Boston?"

"I maybe saw one or two, Gram, about three weeks ago. There just aren't any around. That's why I have to look for *shikses*. I look for the ones who look Jewish."

She raised her forearm and bent it to her as if she was going to slap me with the back of her hand. She *kibutzed*, too. But she meant it. Jewish or nothing, or else. Not to a woman from a *shteytl* near Minsk.

The *kreplach*, meat and/or blueberry, were always exquisite. If served with sour cream, they were always blueberry, never meat. After eating that *dreck* in my dorm, and forced to wear a tie with every dinner, anything would have been extraordinary, but these really were, under any circumstances. My beautiful grandmother learned how to make them from her Polish mother in Minsk. They remined me of wontons.

I never ate *chollah* so good, not before then, not since. The three-story brick house on Maple Avenue was infused with its aroma of that soft, spongy, baked bread. It embraced you. It was the perfume of a Jewish home lived in by a loving family, run by a fun-loving, smiling, laughing, humorously Yiddisheh *balabuste*, a "real balebuste" as we say, who ran the household, a grandmother who caressingly braided the bread like shoelaces, like the Helga braids I've since seen in the Andrew Wyeth paintings and drawings. Like the braids of my late Aunt Minnie from the photo I had seen, whom I had never known, my mother's sister, the one who died of scarlet fever at seventeen.

My grandmother cooked without recipes and who also made other *kreplach* and stuffed veal, *knadelach* and kasha, *latkes* and fricasse, schav, calf's liver and onions and all the other kosher meats and salami from Sam, Duddy, Moishe and Label Kessler's butcher shop, chopped chicken liver with chicken fat, which we called *schmaltz*, gefilte fish from the live carp swimming in the basement slop sink, or from the pickerel and suckers I caught in Eise's Brook, and brisket and mushroom barley soup and chicken soup with chicken feet and little undeveloped eggs, now illegal to buy, and farmer's cheese from Penchansky's and rye bread from Mortman's by Al Schwartz and lox and sable and whitefish and bagels and buttermilk from Sam Karschmer's and sour pickles and tomatoes from her own pickle recipe in five gallon crocks covered with wooden lids in the cold pantry adjoining the back of the kitchen and the door to Pop's woodworking shop from which I shoved the shavings into a hole onto the floor below of the blacksmith shop to use in lighting his forge and heating the coals to white-yellow hot.

My grandmother, who nursed Pesach Shabus, "Honest Abe Shabus," "Mr. Easter Saturday," as the "Yenkees" called him, the blacksmith with the poster of Michael J. Quill the labor leader on the door of his blacksmith shop, till his death, still cried forty years after her daughter, Minnie, died. Minnie was seventeen, innocent and beautiful in that sepia-toned three by five photo with frayed edges. I was young then and didn't yet fathom the depth of emptiness my grandmother felt over the loss of a daughter. I would sit on the couch with her and she would caressingly rub my forehead while crying and reminiscing. It soothed the eternal pain. Pop never mentioned it. Ever. He kept many secrets to himself. He was a man of his generation. He held it all in. I never knew he ran over a child many years before. She didn't die, and he hadn't driven since.

But he died the next week after I went back to school, and home from Boston I came again, for his funeral.

## 13. A Funeral Not to be Ashamed of

1960

Pop's funeral meant home again from Boston.

I made it on thirty cents a gallon gas in my green Corvair convertible stuffed with Hanna, Vivi, Oidle and Yogi, who also went to college in Boston. It cost me three dollars from Boston to Woodridge, tolls included. I got stopped going ninety-seven on the Mass Turnpike, shitting in my pants. I told the trooper I was going home for my grandfather's funeral. He was very understanding and let me go. Times have since changed. I made the five hour trip in three.

It was great to see my friends who all had stories about their first couple of months in college, stories we were to share later. We were such country people that despite living only two hours from Manhattan, I had been to the City, meaning Manhattan, only once on a school trip. Boston, my new home away from home, was initially overwhelming for a kid from a village of not quite eight hundred people at that point.

Pop had the biggest funeral I ever saw, hundreds of people, despite the cold and heavy rain. He was buried wearing shoes from Manny Perlmutter's and a suit originally bought many years before at Kulbitsky's. Our upstate family, Nainie, Florence, Barry, Susan, Jim, from Greene, NY, joined us. Hardly ever saw them, but always loved being with them. Services were conducted in the Woodridge shul, a place in which Pop refused to enter while alive because of a feud he had with a former rabbi many years before, not with Rabbi Goodman, and to which he returned only once afterward for my bar mitzvah. From there, everyone followed the hearse and drove to the cemetery. It was a hilly landscape of black umbrellas and mourners huddled in twos to stay dry, stepping all over other graves to get as close to the casket as possible.

What a miserable day for a funeral, but no Jewish

funeral can be at the mercy of the weather. The dead are supposed to be buried within twenty-four hours of death. Shoes and stockings got soaked, good dress shoes ruined, high heels stuck in the mud as people sloshed in the saturated, wet, muddy ground, but the funeral had to go on.

He was known and loved, and a shivering Chim Krieger read Longfellow's dripping wet poem, *The Village Blacksmith:* "*Under the spreading chestnut-tree/The village smithy stands;/The smith, a mighty man is he,/With large and sinewy hands;/And the muscles of his brawny arms/Are strong as iron bands. His hair is crisp, and black, and long,/His face is like the tan;/His brow is wet with honest sweat,/He earns what'er he can,/And looks the whole world in the face,/For he owes not any man. ...*" and it was very moving and very sad and we all cried. Somehow, it reminded me of the muscular marching song Max sang to me when I was a little boy, exuding power and energy. It was a perfect description of Pop. I only wish he could've heard it while he was alive. I wished also that he could've been to his own funeral to greet everyone who came. He would've enjoyed that.

From there, everyone went to the Shabus home to express their sympathy and naturally, anticipate the delicacies to come. My best childhood friends drove in from their respective colleges to pay their respects. They were the ones who practically lived in my grandmother's kitchen and fridge as we grew up together, and now went in myriad directions. We were a high school class of seventy or so kids, and I think about ninety-five percent of us went on to some college or another. It was never a question of whether we would go on to college or not; rather, which college could we get into. You graduated from high school and you're going to go to college. Period. That was the rule. First generation Jews expected that of their kids. You gotta make something of yourself. Period, again. Become a *mensch* or a "menschette," or else. Don't embarrass us. Parents and grandparents needed to brag about their brilliant kids to their friends. " Look, Sadie, I have to show you a few pictures of my daughter. She just gradulated sumana cummana something or other and she's going to Boston Univoisity," was most often heard. "Such a *punim!*" "A *punim?*" "Such a brain! Could you just *kvell!*?" "Yeh, you said it! I got one just like her, but maybe a *bissel* smarter!"

Everyone said there will never be another like Pesach Shabus and that it was the end of a dying era, you should excuse the expression, and then after his burial in the Jewish Glen Wild cemetery where all the local Jews were taken in a Garlick Funeral Home's black Cadillac hearse, we all returned to Pesach and Lena's home and ate all that good Jewish stuff that makes funerals so worth while.

You can't have a serious Jewish funeral without the food. They'd think you're nothin' but a bunch a cheap "bestids," so we excessively served, and everyone ate native gefilte fish from Eise's brook with red horseradish, pickled herring, tuna and egg salads, lox, whitefish and whitefish salad, sable, schmaltz herring, hard-boiled eggs, plain cream cheese, lox cream cheese, vegetable cream cheese, scallion cream cheese, cream cheese up the tuchus, crudités and packaged onion dip with sour cream, bagels, flagels, rye bread, cherry, blueberry and pineapple danishes, babkas, muffins, pumpernickel, strudel, ruggelehs, honey cake, marble cake, coffee, tea and hot water with lemon.

You can't cry while eating. There's no time for that. Eating at a funeral makes you feel better. It's a form of closure when you stuff your face. It's comforting. Pesach would have liked it. His funeral reception had good food. Nothing to be embarrassed about, and more than enough for seconds. His son, Sam, made sure of that with all the Jew stuff he bought in the Bronx appetizing stores. First you cry, then you eat, then you cry again. A Funeral in Three Movements in F Minor. "Yogi" Rubinowitz said the food was so good, he went back three times for seconds.

It remained a rainy, cold, November afternoon, the kind of weather that went right through you. I walked out onto the porch for a moment alone, where he once sat and smoked in the darkness of summer nights and *kibbutzed* and argued and needled and challenged and drank schnapps and got a *bissel schickered* with the nightly parade of neighbors and fellow *kibbitzers,* and where I read *Atlas Shrugged* and *The Fountainhead* while spending that summer thinking of how to change the world, caring for him with my Gram as he slowly faded and rallied a bit and then faded more quickly and then rolled in his necessary wheelchair with summer's shortening days until late November, when the leaves were no longer on the maple trees and that now looked just like the skeleton he became.

Cousins Shirley and Paul from Roslyn joined me during the reception with my grandmother's brother, Uncle Sam Fein from Brooklyn, the clothing *maven* from the Garment District and who had an office in the Empire State Building, but without a window. Shirley and I were surveying Maple Avenue from the porch and I observed that the late rain was really coming down hard. Shirley exclaimed, "Oh my Gawd, dawlinck, it's raining delusions! Do ya believe it? It's floodulating!"

"Yeah, but I think it's finally starting to let up."

Sam Siegel piped in, "No Boychick, from what I saw before, I think it's intestifying. Woise by the minute." Sam was our aformentioned official tit-and-ass-grabber uncle. No one was safe from his clutches. He walked up to my aunts and cousins from behind while they were eating and engrossed in conversation, and fingers bent, like holding softballs, he grabbed both titzkelehs at once. He did it at family reunions, anniversaries, weddings, bar mitzvahs, Rosh Hashonah, Yom Kippur, Passover, Chanukkah, and now, funerals. Why not? It's family. No one escaped. There were screams and much laughter. They knew who it was without looking up and crossed their arms over their chests. It didn't matter. He got under them anyhow. He grabbed every ass he could get his hands on too, when he couldn't get to their tits, and dropped his false teeth on purpose whenever other female relatives went to kiss him. "Feh! Samileh, you *chazeh*!" The more they called him a pig, the more he grabbed. He had very hairy fingers and a big diamond pinky ring on his cigar hand. His fat, smelly cigar never left the side of his mouth. Its tip was always an amorphous wet brown mass of slimy, raw umber tobacco. He sometimes grabbed balls, too, with a big "Helloooo!" He was an indiscriminate libertine when it came to anatomical exploration.

"What a day to bury your grandfather, heshouldrestinpeace." said Shirley. "The mud. You could get a *killa* from shoveling. I'm glad it's over, he shouldn't have to suffer any more, the poor man. Come in, dawlinck, it's cold out here. Such a nice porch. So many memories of sitting when we'd come up to the Catskills. I loved him so much. What a man! What—a—man! He was a one in a million, your grandfather. They don't make'em like that anymore." She kissed me. I kissed her. Sam pinched my cheek and grabbed my ass. I don't think he was comfortable enough to grab Shirley's anythings.

With Pop's passing, the porch lost its fighting heart and those in his age group who had visited regularly probably realized that their generation was slowly on the way out. Without Pesach Shabus, Maple Avenue became all but silent. It was all him and Lena, and without him, battles on the porch and the solving of the world's problems were now destined to become a distant verbal war elsewhere.

I was very homesick being away for my first couple of months at school and wouldn't admit it until years later. Coming home to Woodridge, my house, my old room and seeing my friends and town characters was like taking two aspirin for a headache. First you feel like shit, but you shortly begin to feel immensely better. It was two weeks before the Thanksgiving vacation, and while contemplating my drive back to Boston, I began to anticipate my return home so I could rub my facial *schmatta* on my grandmother's cheek.

## Good Bye, *Shul*

Pop died on a Thursday and was buried on Friday before *Shabus*, so, luckily (Jesus, how can I say that!), I had

Saturday and part of Sunday before my return to school. I would not go back into the *shul* the next morning. I stopped being a *shul* guy after my bar mitzvah and now, Pop's funeral. I remembered that my bar mitzvah service caused my legs to shake so badly, you'd think I was stricken with an advanced case of Parkinson's, afraid that I would screw up my *haftorah* reading with a voice paralyzed, dry and off key, and now itching from another miserably woolen suit. I was determined not to go back there unless I had another funeral or a friend's son's bar mitzvah to attend. In those days, a bar mitzvah was such a big deal, you'd think G-d would come down from somewhere and strike you dead if you messed up even as much as one word. And you'd never be able to face the rabbi again, the rabbi who spent so many months training you for the big moment, sort of like the last game of the World Series, bases loaded, two out, full count, everyone on their feet, and you're up at bat, or in this case, the dreaded bimah.

Enough was enough and since my family was religious, sort of, only during Rosh Hashonah and Yom Kippur, a little on Pesach, and some candle lighting on Chanukah if remembered, I wasn't pushed to go. But we kept a Kosher home to some extent: same set of dishes for Pesach the holiday (not Pesach my grandfather) but no bread, just matzoh.

The old, 1920s, much smaller *shul* was now used exclusively for Hebrew School and bar mitzvah lessons. Everyone went to the big *shul* for services, bar mitzvahs, wedding ceremonies, funerals, *kaddish*, the holidays. Any number of the Jews in Woodridge were "two day plus Jews": Rosh Hashonah and Yom Kippur, plus maybe another eight days for Passover, also known as Pesach. Pesach was observed by mostly everyone. In England, they had the changing of the guard. In Woodridge, it was the changing of the dishes. God forbid you eat off a non-Pesadicheh plate and all the other bullshit. You might turn into a *goy*, "and is that what you want to become?" The women sat separately, as was the orthodox custom, upstairs in the balcony. Behind them was a large window in the shape of a Jewish star. All the panes were of a different color: yellow, red, green, blue, purple, light blue, pink. Stained leaded glass artwork would've been too expensive.

There was a brown carpet between the two sides of pews, leading to the *bimah*. The railings were in need of a new paint job from all the chips in the wood. In the middle in front of the podium was a large candelabra for eight bulbs, one bulb for every day the Jews crossed the desert, maybe 25 watts to save on electric. The *torahs* were stored behind the podium. Some were elaborately decorated, others simple, all named in honor of or in memory of someone. Lots of gold thread on velvet and roaring lions. A mural of happy animals in a country landscape was painted along the walls, and above, the blue sky with wispy white clouds. It was painted by the local Woodridge artist, Robert Longo, our very own Michelangelo. He was a great talent. He was my most special high school art teacher who got me interested in becoming an artist, of sorts myself. Images of people were not permitted.

The *shul* was infused with the aroma of old prayer books of torn covers and yellowed pages that were placed behind every pew and on back benches. Others called it an odor, not an aroma, which was oppressive, especially in warmer weather. The fans were inadequate. The smell got into your clothes. It reminded me of the Bronx tenement where my other grandparents lived. You could gag your guts out when the room temperature was in the 90s in the middle of summer and you had to sit there enduring prayers and ceremonies in uncomfortable suits and ties as the sweat accumulated under your jacket. There was a rack of worn *tallises* when you walked in and a frayed, bent carton of leftover *yarmulkes* from many occasions; red velvet, royal blue, black satin and velvet, pink, yellow, white, gray, leather, large, small, gold-embossed with "The Bar Mitzvah of... The Wedding of..." names of brides and grooms "In Loving memory of; any color or style to match one's outfit if you didn't have your very own.

The large, round Jewish star above the bimah was of stained glass and welcomed the morning sun with beautiful, inviting, yellow and colored beams of light, spiritual, I guess, if you believe in all that shit. If your head is down and covered with a *tallis* and you're faking or slurring the words in a continuous moan, you're not paying attention to the light. Still, however much one might deny one's beliefs, the *shul* ultimately felt comforting and familiar and reassuring of all that we've had to endure over thousands of years. I appreciated that, but didn't believe in all that hocus pocus, even though I learned how to write letters in Yiddish to my grandparents while they were in Miami Beach for the numerous winters. And I only had to endure going to shul as long as I went to Hebrew classes and my bar mitzvah. After that, no more fucking brown, itchy suits.

I never liked striking out. Did Mantle? That's why I was such a good ball player. It wasn't the catcher I was staring at, it was my rabbi. I was driven by fear; the wrath of the rabbi, the wrath of God and the wrath of my manager-God, Frank Fairbrother, who was an inspiring little league coach. Even my itchy little league uniform was made out of wool. What a bitch it was standing in the hot sun playing ball and breaking out in temporary rashes during and after every game and scratching in front of everybody, hiding it with my glove and hoping no one would notice. But you know how it is when ballplayers have to scratch their nuts. When ya got an itch, ya gotta scratch. Baseball I loved, bar mitzvahs made me cringe. They weren't even worth a scratch on my ass, even though everyone couldn't stop congratulating me, pinching my cheeks and stuffing envelopes in my pocket for the terrific job I did in becoming, you should excuse the expression — a man. Naturally, it was a home run over the *shul* fence of "Yankileh Stadium."

Pesach's funeral was also a home run.

## 14. The King and Queen of Toilet Paper

My friends and I huddled together as intimately as possible in my grandmother's little living room, but it was no use, the room was too crowded, so we bundled up and went out onto the porch to *schmooze*. We all had college stories, new romances, tough courses to compare, wild drinking experiences, all-night-everyone-on-the-make-parties, and the different worlds into which we were now immersed and absorbed.

Donnie, who was only an hour away at SUNY New Paltz, said, "Ya know, Noogie, I didn't know your grandfather that well, but when I was a little kid, I loved to watch him bang on the anvil when we hung out. I once tried to lift his hammer and it was so fuckin' heavy, I couldn't believe it. I couldn't believe how he could lift it so easily and bang so many times and make those horseshoes and stuff."

"Yeah, he was unbelievably strong, and the only time he left the shop was to eat and take care of the chickens. My grandmother used to call, 'Pesa, come eat' and that's when he stopped. She called him Pesa. I used to bang that steel with his hammers, but I used smaller ones. I don't how the fuck he did it, but that's what he did."

Neiderschneider said, " I'd see your Pop, and I wanted to have muscles like his. Mother, I used to see him in town and his arms were so tight. I gotta write a story about this one day. Ya think anyone would give a shit about a story of a Jewish blacksmith?" He was an English major at NYU and used to be the school's newspaper editor and the best actor at FCS.

"The question is, would anyone believe there ever was a Jewish blacksmith? What Jew becomes a blacksmith? Maybe a doctor, or lawyer, or a shoestore owner, or a pickle maker, but a blacksmith? When Chim read that poem, it was sort of like Pop with the toiling and honesty and all that good shit, but I don't think Longfellow knew any Jewish blacksmiths like Pop. What an education he'd have gotten in Woodridge."

"You know," Joannie said, "when your grandfather came to my father's office years ago, my father, over dinner, told us he had throat cancer and was so upset you have no idea. He loved your grandfather and I know he didn't want to use the word 'cancer' in front of your grandmother. He didn't like to use that word to anyone, so he used 'carcinoma', figuring it gotta be something else and not so scary to people, something you could get rid of."

"Your father's a terrific doctor, but I'm glad he got Reenie Rothstein for a nurse. Those polio shots were a bitch, sorry, the most painful shots with the biggest needle I ever saw, except in a Jerry Lewis movie. And while he gave them, she would hold me next to her nice, juicy, big, round knishes, and it felt like that pain in my rear end was almost worth it just to have her grab me and squeeze me next to them. Ohhh, did-they-feel-good! Do you think she had any idea what she was doing?"

"Noogie, you're such a pig. That's all you ever think about."

"This is a funeral, you guys. Jesus Christ!" I said, laughing uncontrollably, embarrassed, unable to hold it in, and everyone started laughing non-stop and out of control and the more we looked at each other, the more we laughed and howled and screamed and pissed in our pants with tears running down our faces.

Someone saw us from the living room window and came outside to tell us it was okay to cry and that we'll all feel better later. The tears flowed that much faster, and as he walked back into the house, we were hugging each other laughing hysterically harder than ever. Thank you, Joannie.

Her father was the more popular of the two doctors in town. The other guy being Nemerson. Zimmerman used to say to me, "Come 'ere, you little sonofabitch, you little mamzur, don't you run away from me or I'll give you a whack on your goddamn ass you'll never forget," whenever I had to go in to his office and get one of his injections. My mother laughed 'cause that's the way he talked to everyone. Come to think of it, that's the way everyone talked to everyone. When I was a kid, he was scary. He had an overabundance of black hair on his arms. He always came to the house when needed.

I said, "He delivered me and Burt."

"He delivered me." Said Donnie.

"Me, too." said Arnie.

"Who didn't he deliver?" asked Mikey.

No one answered. He delivered us all, and probably most of the other kids in town. He had his hands in more Woodridge pussy than anyone I ever knew. I remember that when he delivered my brother, my mother was in the hospital for a week. It was very lonely without her and I was extremely anxious to see my new baby brother, Burt, who was named after my *zaydeh* in respect for my dad. Poor Burt. But my middle name was given after my great-grandfather on the other side, Jacob Fein. Jacob in Yiddish is Yoineh or Yacob. Can you fuckin' imagine Noogie Yoineh Ernstein? My brother didn't have it quite as bad. That's the way it was in those days.

Max told me that in his generation, all the kids were

born at home, and more often than not, he and his friends and siblings would listen to the screams of women giving birth up and down Maple Avenue, while the guys played ball outside, and thought nothing of it. We, in the next generation, were all born in the Monticello Hospital without disturbing the neighborhood. All the women were put to sleep and when they woke up, found themselves holding strange beings. It was all very quiet and discreet, the modern way of childbirth.

"Bobby, how's Brandeis? You still walking around with a roll of toilet paper on your belt?" I asked.

"Oh, fuck you, Noogie. Just because I got allergies, you gotta make fun of my toilet paper?" Bobby was a nerd, but a fun guy, and even though he was (we made him) the butt of many jokes, we all loved him 'cause he could take a joke and was smart, and unafraid, and loved baseball.

"Well, Bobby, who's makin' fun of your toilet paper now? Are there any nice Jewish girls at Brandeis with rolls of toilet paper hanging out of their purses?"

"Are you kidding? I can't even find a Jewish girl with allergies. This hayfever season is the worst. I can't stop blowin'. I tried Kleenex, but I use them up so fast, and if I didn't have toilet paper, I'd be wiping my nose on my sleeves."

"Your ass, too," wisecracked Burt, and we all cracked up. "And then you blew your nose."

"Awright, fuck you guys. I wear the fuckin' toilet paper under a jacket. I'm the only guy wearin' a jacket in eighty degree weather. What can I tell ya? I need toilet paper. No girls with toilet paper. None with allergies."

In high school, Bobby never went without a roll on his belt with a toilet paper wooden dowel attached, his invention, to facilitate the paper rolling out faster. He invented it while in the Boy Scouts camping out. He was constantly sniffling and snorting his snot in between his honking. Occasionally, we would distract him enough so that one of us could grab the roll and gently pull it while he walked down the corridor. You'd have to see that fifty foot streamer of toilet paper trailing him. No one dared step on it as it got longr and longer.

He used a plastic pocket insert in his shirt where he kept his six or eight pens and pencils. We knew he'd become a scientist some day. He wore black-framed glasses, and his pants were pulled high, which accentuated his little dick through the cordouroy, but he had a flabby belly that he tried to minimize by keeping his pants so high. From gym class, we knew he had a little one, even though he tried to hide it when he was changing in the locker room. Everyone was rated in the locker room. If you had a little dick, you'd never live it down. He was a two incher and shrinking. Butch was a four and a half and got more girls than all of us combined. I was a seventeen, of course, but didn't like to brag about it too much because I knew how jealous my friends would be. Donnie the snake was a twelve or thirteen. He used to hold it while throwing hunting knives into his bedroom door from the bed, while lying down.

"Bobby, Do you remember that time you lost control of your bike?" I asked.

"Jesus, was that fuckin' unbelievable? How could I forget it? I thought I was fuckin' dead."

"Me, too. Holy fuck, I don't know how you lived through that one. Thank God you had your toilet paper," said Shelly.

"You fuckin' guys!"

Bobby lost control of his bike coming down Hassen's Hill in the middle of town and slammed directly into the Lyceum Theatre's glass marquee and poster of a Gary Cooper war movie. His toilet paper had unraveled and was flying in the air following him as he flew down the hill inexorably into that marquee. I thought he was dead he was going so fast. His bike was bent to pieces. There was glass all over the sidewalk, and by some kind of Jewish miracle, all he got was a small gash on his forehead and knocked out briefly. When he was up and able to breathe again, he felt his head and the blood streaming out through the toilet paper we already dispensed from the unraveled roll that lay next to him, and he pulled his own piece from the small leftover toilet paper in his belt to try to stop the bleeding. We used a lot of toilet paper. He was going to need another roll for his allergies. Shelly was with us and we got him over to Dr. Zimmerman's for a few stitches and a check up. Reenie, the nurse, held him you-know-where while Zimmerman stitched, and I thought, you fuckin' lucky sonofabitch. Two miracles in one day for the toilet paper kid; his life and her juicy tits.

"My mother has to be the Queen of Toilet Paper," chimed in Janie. "You think you use toilet paper, Bobby? She has more rolls of toilet paper in her closet than most grocery stores carry, and needs every bit of it to keep her hair in place when she goes to sleep at night or when she takes her afternoon naps. She wraps her head in it by rolling it round and round and round and round and covering every hairsprayed strand and doubly protecting it with her plastic showercap. Even a roll of toilet paper could get dizzy. Her head's a mountain. Her hair is always perfect. She says it's necessary for when my father comes home from the office. "Your fawthah likes to see perfect haihr. You know, a beehive. He works so hahrd, he should see perfect haihr. When I told her that you, Bobby, use as much toilet paper as she does, ya know what she asked? She asked, 'Really? I wonder if it's two ply like mine? I wonder where he gets it? Maybe cheaper.'"

"No." I said, "He needs three for 'personal usage." My muthah dropped her panties on that one. Oh my god, did I get it for that! I hope you don't mind my assumption, Bobby," she said wickedly with a coy smile from the side of her face. We all started fake sneezing at him. Herbie sneezed while holding his crotch and moving his hand back and forth. He sneezed six times. We were gagging with laughter. Bobby, unfazed, handed us sheets of toilet paper with a flourish from the roll he had hidden under his suit jacket. This is a funeral? Janie did an incredibly wicked imitation of her mother. I'm sure she'll be on stage one day.

Mikey said, "My mother also uses toilet paper the same way. What's with these women? Maybe we should have a show, 'The Toilet Paper Follies'?" Neiderschneider, you could be the 'drector.'" We all were cracking up 'cause a couple of the other guys also had mothers with toilet paper heads. They go to the beauty parlor once a week and you never see their hair again until their next appointment and the day they return home. After that, it's toilet paper time again until the next appointment the next week.

"I don't believe how wrapped up our mothers are in toilet paper. Everything they do is toilet paper, toilet paper, toilet paper. You'd think that's all they ever think about. They're really asphyxiated on it," exclaimed the Brooklyn genius, Yogi.

"Fixated, *schmuck*. Whyncha go back to Brooklyn, moron, and learn yourself how to tawk." I said, imitating Yogi's Brooklyn accent. "How'd such an idiot like you ever get into MIT anyhow? What are you an English major or somethin'? I'm aksin' you, prickface."

I think I saw my mother's own unwrapped hair about four years ago when we went to visit my *bubbe* and *zeydeh* in the Bronx. She carried a roll of toilet paper with her in her pocketbook for the trip home and spent the entire ride wrapping her head until her turban crown transformed her into a world only imagined and dreamt about as she shortly, regally fell asleep against the car window. But I didn't want to admit to my friends that I also had a toilet paper queen for a mother.

Yogi moved from Brooklyn a few years earlier and still talked weirdly, unlike us, the proper English guys, and we kidded him mercilessly, but he was one of my super best friends and he knew how to get even. He was also an incredibly half-brilliant student. 800 in math and 410 in Brooklyn English on his SATs. His version of English came out of Ebbets field, but he was a Merlin in math.

"Fuck you, Noogie. Whyncha go fuck yourself wid that little peckah ya got in your pocket."

"Your weenie, my salami, muthah." I said, grabbing my "jewels" and going back to eating and talking to all the neighbors, relatives and friends.

It was a festive, raucous, laughter-filled funeral with so much kissing and hugging amongst us all and so many kind words about Pop and Gram and Woodridge way back when, that one would think it could have just as easily have been a bris or wedding or bar mitzvah. We remembered Pop and didn't, at this moment, wish to linger on the terrible battle he waged against the "enemy", the "Big C", whose power was stronger than his arms and hands, and his emotional grip tore out pieces of everyone's heart and left us weakened and vulnerable, mortal and worried, that his generation was forced to vacate the premises despite surviving their pilgrimages from Eastern Europe, then enduring World War I, the Depression, World War II and, to a much lesser extent, Korea. It was their time to go. My Pop was one of Woodridge's few losses that year. The Viet Nam War was was only in its infancy. Woodridge met the relatives that day and they all became part of the Woodridge extended family. My grandmother would have to wait to grieve, and we didn't want to leave her by herself, although she would soon be alone to cope with the loss of my Pop who married her when she was sixteen, and with whom the following year she had the first of their five children: Sam, Nainie, Max, Charlotte, aka "Shandie," and Minnie.

# The Expert Pickle Lover

For the moment, though, there were platters that needed filling and I shoveled it all onto my plate to ostentatious capacity. I walked over to Annie Hymowitz in the middle of the crowd, purposely crushing against her as subtly as a dog rubbing against its master and, looking at her, asked her if the pickles on the table were her father's. Annie was three inches shorter than I was and a year older. She went to Ithaca. She was also the biggest and best piece of ass in the village, eliciting furtive, leering, face forward, eyes to the side, pretending not to be looking, up and down, around front and back, with thoughts of in and out looks, by us young college guys and older lascivious admirers of juicy flesh, and blue eyes that stared you down if she caught you. She knew what she had.

I really didn't give a shit. I just needed an in to get to talk to her. Most of us were too afraid to strike up even innocuous conversations. Sid Hymowitz owned a wholesale produce business, supplying many of the hotels and bungalows in the Catskills. He always had the freshest fruits and vegetables and stored them in his warehouse/store in the middle of town.

"Your father makes the best pickles in town. Some people like Proyect's, I like your father's."

"Yeah, these are my father's. You like?"

We all liked to hang out there under the "Hymowitz's Wholesale Wholesome Produce" sign when Annie was working. Her father's slogan was, "If It's Fresh You Want, It's fresh I Got".

"Can you imagine being the daughter of a pickle maker?"

I said, "Annie, I don't know. I think your father has the best reputation around. He's a pickle expert. My father's a prescription and condom expert."

"Noogie, you have a mouth like a sewer. Do you have to talk that way? Did you learn to talk that way in Boston? So, Mr. Bigshot, what are you an expert of?"

"Actually," I said, "I'm an expert pickle lover, a pickle expert, a cuke conniosseur. It came from my grandfather when I was a kid. He used to make me breakfast every now and then on Sunday mornings, the most unique, best breakfasts I ever ate. He would make coffee first, Maxwell House, and then he would cut some of Kessler's salami in big, thick slices and stick them in the frying pan with some cut up onions and covered the salami with them to cook for a while and then he'd add a few eggs. He didn't scramble the eggs, preferring instead to let them ooze over the salami and slowly turn white in the heat of the pan he had covered. I told him his salami was as tough as and tasted like Perlmutter's English shoe leather. To him, it was a compliment. To me, I didn't care that it was sometimes tough. Salami and eggs and onions, and a pickle from Hymowitz and Mortman's rye bread and coffee from the perc at 7:30 in the morning and he would smoke a cigarette and it was the only time of day when the sun came into the kitchen. Is that a breakfast or is that a breakfast? Now I'm such a *goy*, I eat bacon or sausage and eggs. I didn't know what the hell that tasted like until I tried it in my dorm cafeteria. It was good, but if I told my mother, she'd say she'd rather starve to death and die in the desert than eat that *goyisheh* 'crep'. Now if I'm in a good luncheonette like Bushky's or Willy's or Sol's, I always ask for a pickle with it. I can tell if it's one of your father's. It's usually more rotten than Proyect's or Penchansky's."

"You are such an idiot. You think my father has rotten pickles? Really!"

"Annie, is that a way to talk to a nice Jewish boy" I asked, in my Yiddish intonation? "Such language! I'm only kibbutzing. Such woids. That's what you learned at Ithaca? I'm only kidding! Don't get so noivous. Your father's a great artist. It's a philosophy. I really think that when one loves what he is doing, when he creates the finest work of art in his profession and reaches the pinnacle of pickeldom, he is fulfilled and fulfills others in their appreciation of his creation. In your father's case, it is the ultimate pickle that satisfies man's hunger for achieving nirvana. Your father carries on the great tradition of Kosher pickle making. And being an authority of pickles, I would have to say he is the Paradigmatic Pablo Picasso of Perfectly Proportioned Pickles." I actually fuckin' came out with that one without blinking. She was laughing with her hand up to her mouth, trying to exercise discretion in a home where one could laugh only so slightly without showing disrespect.

"I know this is the wrong time to ask, but what are you doing later? Would you consider, against all odds, going out with me for a hamburger so that we may continue our philosophical discourse unfettered by my unsophisticated, unappreciative friends who would just a soon eat a Proyect's or a Penchansky's as a Hymowitz with their burgers? I gotta get out of the house and I don't want to hang out with the guys. They are ever so loutish," I remarked dramatically in an English accent. "It would be a great honor to escort the daughter of Sid Hymowitz to a location of her choice." I put my hand on her arm as I spoke. Do you believe that shit? I knew I had more balls than anyone. Any one of us would've been scared shitless to even ask her to buy a fuckin' pickle, much less ask her out to eat one. But, what the hell, I just jumped in. She hesitated at the unexpectedness of the offer, and was so very overwhelmed (oy vey) by my touch of poetry.

"C'mon Annie, you gonna waste your time with the uneducated brutes? Do they love pickles like I love pickles? No. If you love pickles like I love pickles, oh, oh, oh, what a date!" I leaned over and sang in her ear.

Annie, smiling, looked into into my killer, shiny, puppy dog, Walter Keane eyes, and said, "Okay, Mr. Philosopher singer, pick me up at eight and... oh, oh, oh, don't be late. Let's go to Dave's Diner. I love his fries and he serves 'Hymowitz's Perfectly Proportioned'." She was laughing and beautiful and amused at the guy, me, of course, who had the nerve to make the ultimate move. It was difficult to hide a pickleish protrusion when stepping away from Annie, but she caught it, duly noted without eye contact or acknowledgement as I caught her, in that minuscule fraction of a second, zeroing in on it.

The afternoon felt long, or at least it felt like it despite the quickly shortening of days in November, and twilight encroaching upon a day ready for its moment of rest, communicating its impatience to impose itself upon the gray light by turning it green, orange, purple and dark blue to bring forth the impending night. Local friends and neighbors were saying their good-byes, expressing their condolences and offering to bring food again the next day and the next. Relatives had long trips back to the Bronx, Brooklyn and Long Island, (none from Manhattan), and my grandmother's sons, my closest uncles, made plans to remain in the house for the next day or so, rearranging bedrooms with my mother to accommodate them and wives and young children. I resigned myself to a nice, comfortable, soft spot on the floor somewhere. It was much easier sleeping in the woods when I was a boy scout, though.

My favorite cuz, Jeanette, also her sister Dorothy and parents Julie and Beattie Fein, had to drive back to their home on Mace Avenue in the Bronx, and I was saddened to see them go. Jeanette and I had always been unofficial brother and sister, and she fixed me up with her Bronx girlfriends, one of whom was famous for lifting her leg when she approached fire hydrants and barked like a dog. No big deal and one date only. I didn't need to pet that barking dog. She was, anyhow. She also introduced me to White Castle hamburgers. They were little, squares of gray shit, but I liked them anyhow; ready-made and covered with little pieces of chopped, sautéed onion, slice of pickle and ketchup. One could easily eat more than a dozen at a time.

Julie Fein, my grandmother's brother, is the family's demonstrative kisser. He has a very wide mouth and two widely spaced front teeth, with an infectious smile and huge laugh and kissed every relative in monkey-lipped fashion, puckering on the lips and accompanied by a loud "mmmmmmwah!" with his big, wet affectionate kiss. It was a Jewish way of kissing; loud, boisterous and sometimes embarrassing. Did I say 'embarrassing' in relation to my family? I must have been referring to some other family. Sorry, embarrassing was not a term describing the Shabus-Fein family. None of this side-of-your-face-on-your-cheek-shit with us. It was whack, smack right on the lips. Cheek kissing and air kissing did not exist in our family. We weren't that fancy or sophisticated. Our hugs squeezed air out of lungs and caused tits to deflate. It was ass-grabbing time as well. You kissed, you grabbed, you got grabbed. "Good-bye, dawlinck, good-bye boychick, good-bye boubie, *gay gezundt a hame.* And don't come back too soon!!!" was the standard insulting *kibbutz.* Grab, kiss, hug, *potch,* pinch, fondle. Everyone got the treatment. If you didn't, you weren't part of the family.

My friends piled out together and I thanked them all and we hugged and kissed, but not before we decided to get together the next day at Bushkie's for an early breakfast when there was the most action in his luncheonette, when all the local *yenta meshugeners,* blue collar and white, arrived to talk politics and sex and business and *schmutzty* jokes, innuendoes and gossip. It was the soul of the village. I knew my family would be sleeping late, except for Sam, Max and Nainie who had their own sunrise agendas, and it was a good time to escape.

I whispered quickly, when no one noticed, to Carl that I was going to Dave's later with Annie, and he practically shit in his pants. I couldn't wait to see him tomorrow. "Fuckin' Noogie and Annie?" he said to no one in particular. "He got balls like *gefilte* fish." I didn't know *gefiltes* had balls. I wondered what kind of gefiltes he was eating. Maybe he was thinking of matzoh balls mixed with *gefilte* fish?

My mother, grandmother and the remaining relatives spent the late afternoon and early evening cleaning and straightening up the kitchen and house, trying to get it back to normal. No one wanted to move or sit in Pop's chair near the window, nor move the pillows or remove his Yiddish newspaper he always stuck into the side of the seat cushion where it met the side of the chair. His old wrought iron lamp with slightly torn shade was lit with a dull yellowish bulb, illuminating a portrait of a seated woman, a bluish, fading reproduction, on the beige wall behind. It wasn't till I studied art history and learned that that portrait residing in that one spot for all my life, was none other than Madame Augustine Roulin, "La Berceuse", the postman's wife, painted by Van Gogh.

"Van Gogh?" my grandmother asked. "He paints a nice picture, whoever he is. I always liked that painting. I don't remember where we got it, maybe in the City on the Lower East Side. I think we paid fifty cents, a lot of *gelt* in those days. It was worth it. You learned that in school, mine smart boychickel?" Maybe it reminded my grandfather of someone he knew, perhaps his mother. It had that motherly quality.

"Yeah, I also learned that he cut his ear off because he loved a girl and she didn't want him around."

"Oy, his ear he cut off?"

"Yeah, really. He made a painting of himself with a bandage wrapped around his head. It's a pretty picture. You'd like to hang it in the livingroom."

"I should hang a painting by a *meshugener* like him? Are you a *meshugener*, too, Noogileh? What kind of *meshugener* cuts his ear off for a goil? He must've been a real nut case. Better you should cut off that *schmatta* you have growing on your chin and keep your ears. You hear me?"

"He had a lot of problems, that guy, but he was a very good *schmearer*, that van Gogh."

"Pop likes the painting, too, behind his chair. It was worth the fifty cents we paid."

There was a photograph of my great-grandfather, heshouldrestinpeace, with Aunt Sadie, Uncle Hymie and my grandmother, his two daughters and son, hanging on the other side of the livingroom above my grandmother's chair. We knew from nothing about hanging art in a house. It was cozy without it, and a difference it wouldn't have made.

It was the only piece of artwork hanging in the house and it had a place of honor behind Pop's chair.

## 15. The Bronx and Greenish False Teeth

I drifted away from the funeral crowd, while standing in a quiet corner, nursing a drink, daydreaming for a few moments of when I used to visit my other grandparents, both of whom also died fairly recently.

To me, The "City" was not a place called Manhattan, but the rundown-looking stone and brick Bronx tenement where my other grandparents lived, *Bubbe* and *Zeydeh* Ernstein, whom we visited only once in a while, thank G-d. The tenement reeked of pervasive, stagnant disinfectant tenement smell, stale scent of old food and damp, soggy clothes, half-cleaned irregularly worn-down marble floors, and faded light pea green paint with beige trimmed and graying window sashes, peeling and tired and slightly ominous when looking through the sandwiched windows whose chicken wire mesh reinforced glass enhanced the effect of being either in prison or in a chicken coop, particularly that much more so when I was forced to wear my brown tweedy suit when I was a little boy, a child in a prison uniform, with shorts, instead of real pants, little bowtie and matching hat because when you went to The "City", the Bronx, you had to look like a *mensch* for Bubbe and Zaydeh. I still remember that woolen fuckin' suit itching the hell out of me and sending chills throughout my five year old body. To this day, I get the chills if tweedy wool comes within ten feet of me.

*Zaydeh's* breath fifty years later hangs over me like the dense fog of a J.M.W. Turner landscape, although I'm now a bit more nostalgic and less prone to gagging over what it once was. They were really strangers and I reluctantly pretended loving feelings in order to avoid being prodded too vociferously by my parents to hug and kiss them more than once, and hoping I could get away with only a hug and a peremptory kiss. As nice as he was, I couldn't stand kissing my *zaydeh*. His breath smelled like stale garlic vomit emerging through his greenish false teeth from a mouth that only Yiddish words came out of. *Zaydeh* wore a *yarlmulke* and he slept with it on his head. It would have been a dire sin if it ever came off.

Only my Bubbe could speak English, or her version of it. She was a very sweet lady and I never saw her with rolled down nylons. She was a city lady and perhaps wore them that way even when without company. And despite being family, we were distant enough to be considered company. They were really very sweet, but alien people living in a tiny, claustrophobic apartment with an old-fashioned half-sized fridge and stove. On the top shelf next to the glass milk bottles were blue seltzer bottles. I mixed, with parental help, some cherry syrup with the seltzer and pretended it was as good as a real cherry soda, but in reality, it was not nearly as sweet.

They also had a vertical, two-piece, long-stemmed, black telephone with a moving circular dial, and it wasn't even wall-mounted. On our phones we didn't have dials. If we wanted to make a call, we'd ask Vera Caulters, or Mavis Mednick or classmate Linda Friedberg to get us the number or name of the person we wanted to speak with. They knew most of the people's numbers by memory and all we had to do was give them the name of the person or business we were calling. Our number was 71, and later, 564. and number 9 was that of the insurance company where my mother worked by day with all her once a week Woodridge Mah Jong and Haddassah *yenta* girlfriends.

I was a country kid who threw stones to break barn

windows, shot them out as well when older, ate raw warm eggs from under the white leghorns in the chicken coops taken straight out of their straw nests to prove to my Pop that I was brave enough to swallow them. I shot a bb gun at pigeons and cleaned chickenshit out of wooden chicken crates, and I always felt so out of place standing in that odorous, dark, dingy, Jewish tchotchked, brown-furnished apartment while my father, the pharmacist, "Yussel," as he was referred to, his Jewish name  when in their presence, fawned over his parents, parents who never worked and who depended upon each son's generosity tso survive because my Zaydeh spent his days in *shul* praying to God and reading worn, Talmudic, Jewish prayer books, while slightly groaning and grunting and moaning with every move as he slowly traversed life in his smelly apartment in old, brown slippers, acting thirty years older than my Pop whom I really loved. They were about the same age, although one would never know it.

I was a kid and I couldn't wait to get out of the City and out of that fuckin' suit and back into my cowboy clothes and cap guns from Tulsa, my favorite outfit, back on the range. And the trip home was unbearable. "WHEN are we going to get there?' was my broken record question that drove my parents crazy.

"We'll get there, Noogie, when we get there." was the standard non-answer that drove me nuts. Sometimes I was lucky enough to fall asleep on the ledge above the back seat against the rear window, making the trip significantly shorter. My dog, Sporty, was always there to greet me when I got home. His breath was a lot sweeter than Zaydeh's. I liked his licks, too.

Thinking of Pop's funeral and everything that occurred early in the morning, I remembered back, of all things, to what it was like wearing a wool suit with knickers when I was a child and then, that wool suit when I became a "man," if you could call it that. Yet again, it gave me the chills.

## 16. Sour Puss Hymowitz

My mother said, "Drive carefully. Don't come home late. Oy, Noogileh, poo, poo, poo, you look like such a *mensch*." She put her hand on the side of her cheek, bending her neck to one side. I kissed my mother and father good-bye without embarrassment, since no one was around to see me kissing him.

"You hear your mother? Watch out for the deers and don't speed. You hear me?!"

"It's deer, not deers. Awright, awright, awready. I'll watch for them. See ya later. Dad, you wouldn't have an extra couple of dollars to spare?"

"Vuh den? I was waiting. Here, wise guy with the mouth, go, leave. Pew, such a stink! You think girls like to hold hands with a bottle of perfume? Take maybe a bottle of disinfectant with you just in case."

"Jesus, Dad, you never put aftershave on your face with all that stuff you sell? Believe me, it smells better than what smells like the liquid shoe polish you put on yours."

"I should tell you, boychick, that it smells a billion times better than your *Eau de Dreck* you put under your arms. That liquid shoe polish, I'll have you know, is a perfume my lady customers love, and I sell a lot if it. Say hello to the Hymowitzes. Go!" He ran down the stairs.

"Molly, open a window. It stinks worse than a skunk. What those kids do to themselves! *Vey is mir!*"

I was freshly shaved and dressed in my Boston preppy-looking button-down shirt and chinos with sewn-in eight inch belt in the rear, just under the leather belt, wearing my new dark green loafers with brass buckles on the sides just like Richard Burton wore in "Hamlet", slathered in Old Spice aftershave, stinking worse than Moe's Barbershop, stinking worse than Fox's Barbershop and Beauty Parlor combined, stinking worse than Yushka's back yard chicken pen, stinking worse than unwashed, ripe armpits, stinking worse than four gym basketball sessions wearing fermenting canvas Converse sneakers, walked up the stairs to the Hymowitz's apartment above the store and tentatively knocked on Annie's door.

The upstairs hallway smelled like my bottle of Old Spice had been emptied onto the floor, mixing with the aroma of fruits and vegetables below. It seemed like ten minutes before the door opened while I shifted my weight from one foot to the other, thinking about knocking again, fixing my jacket, rubbing the tops of my shoes on the back of my pant legs, wiping the sweat off my eyebrows, licking the salty sweat off my upper lip, rubbing my perspiring palms together, listening to my heart explode in my ears with every beat, hearing my baritone growling stomach, feeling the pulsing of my arteries on the sides of my neck, looking up at the stamped, metal ceiling, looking down at the fruit basket-patterned, worn linoleum, and questioning whether she really was at home after all, waiting to go out with me, or maybe standing me up. I was fuckin' shitting in my pants.

"Hello, Noogie. How are you? Come in. Annie will be ready in a minute," said Mrs. Hymowitz, a big smile on her face, motioning for me to come into the vestibule. Mrs. Hymowitz was a big woman, actually about my height, five foot eight, stocky, overweight, and looked to be about two hundred pounds, graying through dark blond hair, typically Eastern European-looking with blue eyes and bulbous nose, stubby-fingered with her wedding and engagement rings squeezing and inflating her fourth finger like an animal balloon finger, wearing a light blue house dress, what we call a schmatta, and a pair of black, laced, Perlmutter shoes, fitted by me, actually, when I used to work there part-time when I wasn't working for my uncle Max in the gas plant. I remembered her thick calves and slightly puffy ankles and toes and ruby-red toenails.

"Hello, Mrs. Hymowitz. Thank you. It's nice to see you. I've never been in your beautiful home before. So pretty. Oh, hello, Mr. Hymowitz. How are you?" I went over to shake Mr. Hymowitz's hand. Mr. Hymowitz gave me a crusher with a smile, which I tried in vain to return, but it was of no use and my four fingers got squeezed together. How to feel like a weakling. Made me sweat more. Luckily, Annie was still in her room.

What is it about these macho Woodridge guys with

crusher handshakes? Everyone did it. Ray Kasofsky, the farmer with the big "Hello," and even bigger smile, did it too. You just had to be prepared in advance as he lunged his arm and hand forward. I had no doubt they could all beat the shit out of me. One of our new neighbors, too, who moved in up the street, a plumber named Jerry Rudolph, loved, simply loved to shake my hand. It gave him immense pleasure. He had the biggest, warmest, wide-toothed smile and laugh. It was always great seeing him and Shirley when I came home. He and Shirley had two daughters, Melanie and Sharon, the loveleiest kids. Anyhow, I've gone off subject. Jerry had the chest of two men, and if ever there was a powerhouse, a *bulvan*, as they say, it was him. His nickname was in fact "Bull" and it was on his license plate as well. Over the years, we became good friends, and many years later, I used him as a model for a Minolta Camera ad I was shooting. It was him trying to learn yoga from a how-to learn yoga book, while his legs were up in the air in a twisted position on his livingroom floor: "Minolta Helps You To Unwind."

When I tried to withstand the slow torture of his warm handshake, squeezing my fingers while I begged for mercy, he simply looked lovingly and ever so sweetly into my eyes, blinking rapidly, smiling his mischievous smile ever more, and more, and more, and more, until the sweat poured down my face in agony. And then, when he finished paralyzing my hand, he gave me the biggest kiss and bear hug hello, forcing all air out of my lungs. That was our routine; that dirty, sadistic, fucking bastid. Of course, I loved him. Everyone did. Anyhow, just a diversion.

I said, "My father says to say 'Hello.'" Sid Hymowitz

was a big man with a protruding belly squeezed into a tight white tank top shirt that also emphasized his powerful arms. His grayish hair, combed straight back, was thin and receding. He always needed a shave and through his ample lips, one noticed that he was missing two middle bottom teeth. He sometimes hissed when he spoke. He had blue eyes and a long nose, and despite the grubby appearance, his was a sensitive, intelligent face that was capable of instantly turning from warm and sweet to loud and in-your-face dark. He had moments of anger from which you just wanted to get your fuckin' ass the hell out of the way until he calmed down or he'd chew yours up or anyone else's off until the hurricane was out of his system. His temper was legendary.

"Hello, Noogie Oinstein! How's by you, boychick. You're home for your grandfather's funeral. He was a good man, that Mr. Shabus, a good friend, one of the best, no one like him, heshouldrestinpeace. Nu? It was a beautiful funeral for a great man.

"You're here to see Annileh? And where are you going?" Questions, questions, questions.

"We're going over to Dave's Diner, Mr. Hymowitz, to get a bite. Maybe a movie. I had to get out for a few hours. It's up to Annie, but it's good to be home for a couple of days. I missed your pickles! They don't make pickles like yours in Boston, just the sweet ones from bottles. Yuck! I didn't even know they came in bottles."

"Those *goyim*, what do they know about pickles? *Gournischt*! Like shit, they know."

195

"Sid, do you have to talk that way in front of Noogie. He comes into the house and you talk about you-know-what? Vey! And his grandfather died a few days ago? You have no brains."

"Why, he doesn't know from *dreck*?"

"You're right, Mr. Hymowitz, they don't even know how to make a hot dog in Boston. They take a hot dog that tastes like *goyisheh* mush, no taste, and stick it into a funny looking roll that looks like a piece of white bread folded in half, toasted and then buttered. Would you believe they butter a hot dog roll? And they don't even serve it with sauerkraut."

"*Goyisheh dreck*. Tell me, there are no Jews in Boston who know what a hot dog and pickles is?" asked Hymowitz.

"There might be, but they're not around B.U. Maybe I should take some of your pickles back with me and show them what a real pickle is, a Catskills pickle from Mr. Hymowitz's."

"Noogileh, you got a head sticking up on those shoulders, boychick. Yeh, a *yiddisheh kup*. Annileh, Mr. Noogie is waiting for you. What's keeping you so long? Hurry up! He's oily, so you should be late? Oy, goils...."

"Coming, Papa. I'll be right there."

"I don't know what's with goils today. I never saw anyone *potshke* so much as Annie. She has to try on ten dresses and show them to my wife, and then she wears those pants like dungarees and then she needs two hours for make-up and she can't wear her hair like this and she can't wear it like that and the coil is too high and she needs a beehive and a ponytail and bangs and she has to puff it up and tease it and pump air into it until it looks like a balloon. Then she ties it with a ribbon and a barrette and she schpritzes it with Elmer's Glue and twists and toins and coils and boins it until maybe then SHE CAN COME OUT OF HER ROOM BEFORE ELEVEN O'CLOCK FOR AN EIGHT O'CLOCK DATE! Then it's the shoes. Five pairs she had to try on until they match. It's not enough to wear sneakers?"

"I'm coming!" A second later her bedroom door burst open and Annie rushed out, almost flustered. "Hi, Noogie. Sorrrrry. I got held up."

"She got held up, all right. She had to make a decision on what socks to wear!" Mr. Hymowitz yelled at her face.

" Oh, Papa, you are so incorrigible."

"I'm in Woodridge. I don't know where this corrigible place is. But if you don't leave with Noogie right now, you're gonna be *zetzed* up to the moon, I'll give you such a *potch*!"

"Okay, okay. Come Noogie, before he locks me in a pickle barrel." She gives her father and mother hugs and kisses good-bye. Her father gives her a pat on the tush. She looks beautiful in her gray sweatshirt, jeans and penny loafers, her hair in a simple ponytail.

"Don't come home late, Annie. You have to woik tomorrow. Good bye, Noogie. Drive carefully." said her mother.

"Go, awready, and watch out for deers. Not late, you hear me, Annileh, not late!" he yelled.

"Deer, not deers," corrected Mrs. Hymowitz.

"Deer, schmear, what's the difference, awready? Go! Leave! Don't hit any!"

"Good night, Mr. and Mrs. Hymowitz. It's nice to see you. I'll come visit Sunday for pickles to bring back to Boston." We quickly escaped down the stairs and into Noogie's father's 1957 Black Chevy whose rear soared like the wings of a bird. The night air felt clean except for Noogie's aftershave and Annie's Casaque. It was a combination plate of perfumes. The black bird flew to Dave's Diner in South Fallsburg.

"You smell nice, Noogie."

"You, too, Annie."

Back at the household, Mrs. Hymowitz said, "He's such a nice boy, that Noogie, don't you think, Sid?"

"Yeh, he's a nice boy, but does my Annie have to go out with a guy just a little more than her height?" She was five foot six.

What's short? He's as tall as you. And he has a kup on his shoulders. I'd like to have a taller too, but he's a smart kid and a real go-getter, a real schmoozer, but a nice one, not one of those phony baloneys."

"We'll see. In the meantime, married they're not. Maybe you should open the window. What a stink! What's that dreck he's wearing? Feh! If I let him in mine store, he'd ruin mine pickles in two seconds."

# 17. Dave's Diner

Dave's was crowded, filled mostly with Fallsburg high school kids, a few of Noogie's college friends who had been to the funeral and some of the local characters. It was loud and animated, and the aroma of French fries, pizza, grilled fatty hamburgers, bacon and cigarette smoke permeated the diner and almost drowned out their respective perfume and cologne. Mostly everyone smoked, even the kids. Dave's was the first joint to serve pizza in the area. Noogie had never tried it in high school because some of his friends said it was very spicy and he never ate spicy foods, other than Gold's Horseradish with beets on geflite fish. He finally had a slice in Boston and thought it was delicious and fun to eat, particularly when attempting to catch the hot, dripping cheese and oil and tomato sauce from the folded slice near his mouth before it reached his shirt or pants, which it inevitably did. He was the kind of guy who never wore a shirt he couldn't stain.

The diner was one of those chrome and blue jobs, the kind that is transported by tractor trailer, placed upon a slab of concrete and made ready to open in three minutes or less. The chrome was very bright and glossy. "Dave's Diner, Homemade and Good" red, white and blue neon sign hung brightly outside. Its "deLuxo Luxurio" interior had small blue plastic and fabric-covered booths trimmed with red piping and alternating red and blue counter stools that spun easily, either round and round or side to side as if on winding and unwinding watch springs. Round and round by kids who were either too young to date or older kids without dates, and side to side by kids who were on dates and engrossed in flirting, kinda like ritualized "tuggin' the putz." There were five cent miniature juke boxes in each booth and spaced evenly along the gray marbleized Formica counter. Sh-boom, Rock Around The Clock and Elvis dominated. Everyone moved to Elvis's music, mouthed his words and turned their collars up, male and female. Cool.

There were lots of greaseballs just like Elvis with goopy, slicked back hair, long hairy sideburns, and their ladies with black cavities in their hot pink lipsticked mouths, who were known as the "pickup truck scoopers." They came from a different universe, lived somewhere in trailers in the back woods, whose properties and front lawns were meticulously designed and decorated with pieces of no-longer usable burnt sienna-rusted custom-built vehicles, junk parts, weeds, truck tire painted flower beds, firewood, garbage, chickens running free, growling dogs on impossibly short leashes, greeting visitors with red, white and blue "Sta the hell out, dog bites" and "No trepsasing" warm, welcome signs.

They were twenty-four bottle week-end beer bellied, fat assed, half washed, dirty-fingered, unshaved, torn tee shirted, tank topped, tattooed, soiled dressed, five dog, six kid families. They looked at us like we were the enemy and we tried as best as we could to avoid their eyes, knowing that one wrong look could lead to the beat the fuckin' shit out of you fight. They were just hunkering for showing the smart kids, maybe the Jew smart kids, who the fuck was boss.  They  were  the  future "professionals/doctors/lawyers/scientists" of the up-raised hood and re-assembled engine. They stuck their heads and bodies under open-mouthed hoods and whose pants hung half way down, exposing the long cracks of their hairy white asses. They were the belligerent kings of the country roads, the ones who sported signs above their front bumpers, lovingly naming their trucks "Hey, Pretty Mama," "Gun Boy" and "Eat Shit and Die." They ain't nuthin' but hound dogs, and they were nuthin', except that you had to watch your ass around them, nor act like a smart ass as well.

Annie and Noogie grabbed the only unoccupied booth and slid in. The eyes were on Annie. Then they looked at me. Heads turned, whispers exchanged. Annie knew. I felt them. I acted as nonchalantly as possible, freezing my eyes on her and the cigarette butt-filled ashtray on the dirty Formica table. I knew they were sizing me up, like how the fuck did HE ever get to take HER out? And what the fuck is she doing with HIM? And, you believe that shit? But, what the fuck, I was here; they weren't. Probably they were too short and ugly for the heiress to the Sid Hymowitz pickle empire.

The waitress came over with menus and a warm hello. Her dress was slightly stained, makeup in need of freshening up and her forehead a bit sweaty, but she had a nice smile, and we were immediately made to feel diner-comfortable, now concentrating on the choices at hand, instead of the eyes of Texas upon her boobs, but not that terribly hungry after the amount of food we both had both eaten at the funeral.

The waitress looked at me and said, "Hi Hon. Take your time. Can I get youse something to drink in the meantime?" she asked.

Annie replied, "May I have a Dr. Brown's celery soda,

please?"

I asked, "May I have an egg cream, please?'

"Shoohr, no problem, hon," she said, "I'll be right back. By the way, my name is Candy." Noogie caught a glimpse of her ass as she bounced away.

"Whatta you gonna have, Noogie? I think I'd like a pastrami sandwich and fries. I haven't had pastrami since I went away to school." Annie went to Albany.

He said, "I'm stickin' to a hamburger. You know how you get a picture of what you want to eat and you just gotta have it? I missed meat at the funeral. I started picturing a hamburger as soon as I dreamed about you going to Dave's with me."

"Oh, so you look at me and you see hamburgers? Do you see fries, too?"

"How can you eat a hamburger without fries? I wasn't picturing fries, but a Sid Hymowitz pickle with my burger and you is the only way to go. It's too bad I didn't ask your father out instead."

"Do you really think my father would ever lower himself and go out with you? Are you serious? I'll have to ask him when I get home."

The waitress brought the drinks and asked, "Are ya ready to ordah, sweetie? What kin I getchas?"

Annie asked, "May I have a pastrami on rye please, with fries, and a big pickle, not just a little slice?"

"May I please have a burger, fries, fried onion rings and a Hymowitz pickle?" he asked.

"What's a Hymertz pickle?" Candy the waitress asked Annie.

"A Hymowitz pickle is like a Babe Ruth home run," I interjected. "It's number 3 (the Babe's number) hitting sixty. It's the greatest pickle ever invented. Dave buys them from Mr. Hymowitz, puts them on every plate, and you get to serve them to adoring pickle fans like us who die to get your autograph. That famous Hymowitz pickle is made by this beautiful girl's father, the pied piper of perfect pickles, Sidney H. 'Half Sour' Hymowitz. Do you not realize that you will be serving a Hymowitz pickle to the daughter of Mr. Hymowitz himself? When this lovely lady lost her first tooth, her father, the great Mr. Hymowitz, put a lucky Hymowitz pickle under her pillow and told her it was the pickle fairy who left it. It was more valuable to him than money. That's how much he loves his daughter! And you ask what a Hymowitz pickle is?"

Annie and Noogie were both laughing hysterically and loudly. Dave came out to see what was going on and the waitress called him over to the booth. "Dave, this is the daughter of Mr. Hymeretz, the pickle king."

"Oh, so you're the daughter of Sid Hymowitz? And your name, young lady? He makes a good pickle, your father. Not many people know how to make good pickles, but he makes the best, that Hymowitz. Candy, go bring them a plate of pickles. Make some extra fries too, you should bring. Maybe you know my Reenie? And who's this?" gestering toward Noogie.

"My name is Annie, Mr. Greenstein, and it's very nice meeting you." She extended her hand. "This is my friend Noogie Ernstein, from Woodridge. Reenie was in Noogie's class, a year behind me. I know who Reenie is, but just from seeing her in school and knowing she was in the A Group. Noogie was in her group, too. You make the best hamburgers and fries. I miss them in college." Annie was her charming best and Dave couldn't help but be flattered by her sweet attention.

"You're the Ernstein from the drugstore?" Noogie nodded. "You're Joe's kid? But I seen you in Perlmutter's. Look, you see what I got on? Perlmutters. You think I could stand all day on anything else? A better shoe you'll never wear, these Perlmutters. You say hello to your father and mother for me. Also, when you see Permutter, tell him his shoes are falling apart. Tell him I walk around like Charlie Chaplin with holes in my soles. Tell him I have to put corned beef inside the shoes to cover the holes. I'll come over next week for a new pair. I have a wedding. Maybe I'll bring him some mustard to glue the soles."

Annie said, "Dave, maybe you could bring him some cole slaw, too. I'll tell him hello from you and that you want more corned beef on the soles for your new wedding shoes. You want them on rye?"

"He couldn't make his shoes with the kind of fresh rye only I got. It's bad enough he uses that fashtunckineh leather. I need to buy shoes from him like I need to have my head examined."

"I'll tell Mr. Perlmutter and he'll tell me that when I come back to your place for a hamburger, I should go to the

Miss Monticello Diner instead and not eat your shoe leather sandwiches. And then what do I do?"

"Good," said Dave. "You tell him that my corned beef is softer than that English *dreck*, you should excuse my French, he makes his shoes with. Ah, here's Candy. Go eat. Enjoy. Tell Perlmutter not to step even one foot in here with his smelly shoes, and you tell YOUR father," looking at Annie, "to stop sending me his rotten pickles. Maybe a few fresh ones for a change wouldn't hoit.", he said, walking away with a warm, unshaven smile and chuckle under his white paper diner army hat with "Dave's Diner, Homemade and Good" printed on the sides.

"Bye, Dave. Thanks for the extras."

"Boy, Noogie, what a character, but he's so nice. No wonder everyone loves to come here. There's nothing like Dave's in Albany and there's no one like Dave in Albany. He's such an instigator. He's like my father." Annie's beautiful smile reflected off the chrome. The food was what diner food should be: hot, greasy, abundant, better than homemade, lots of pickles, fragrant. They were hungrier than they thought.

## Noogie Makes His Move

My plate was filled with a large handmade, irregularly shaped hamburger glistening with fat and pink and brown juices dripping into the roll and onto the plate, a mound of dark french fries, thick fried onion rings, a scoop of homemade cole slaw, iceberg lettuce topped with three slices of deep, orange-red, tomato slices, a slice of an extra large red onion and a sausage-sized Hymowitz pickle. It overwhelmed the plate.

Annie's pastrami sandwich was two inches thick on what would normally be large size pieces of rye bread, but the quantity of pastrami between those slices was like a fat woman trying to stuff herself into a girdle. The meat just spilled out over the sides unable to be contained. It wasn't lean pastrami, but had the perfect ratio of fat to meat, in that the fat was what gave the pastrami its juicy, silky, pungent, smoked, steamed taste. Alongside the sandwich was a huge mountain of fries, larger than mine, a monkey dish of cole slaw and a rotund Hymowitz sour pickle. Candy the waitress brought a ceramic jar of deli mustard from which Annie slathered the bread. "Is there enough mustard for your sandwich?" I asked, incredulous as to the amount of mustard spread upon the rye.

"I'm not sure, Noogie. I just like a little bread with my mustard," said Annie, biting into her sandwich. The excess mustard spread beyond her mouth, framing her red lipstick in yellow ochre.

I put a layer of ketchup on the hamburger, then two slices of tomato, a folded leaf of iceberg, the red onion, a big spoonful of cole slaw, two slices of fried onion rings, more ketchup and then the top of the bun. Annie said, "You gotta be kidding! Noogie, are you really going to fit your mouth into that!?"

"Yeah, I'm gonna try to break the world record for the biggest bite. Best hamburger there is." He picked up the dinosaur-sized, geological, stratified wonder, opened his mouth and jaw as wide as he could, disconnecting the muscles like a rattlesnake eating a rat, and took a huge bite, squeezing the hamburger concoction to fit into it while the rest of his sandwich juices squirted out of his hands and mouth across the table with a loud squishing sound onto Annie's plate, into her Dr. Brown's, onto her dress and face and blond hair, dripping onto the black and white checkerboard asbestos tile floor at her feet.

"Ayyyyyyyyyyyyyyyyyy!" she screamed, standing up, wiping her face, shaking her sweatshirt away from her body, grabbing napkins, squeezing the strands of her hair with a shocked look at me over the total fiasco that had her frozen. "Oh, my God, look at this! Oh, my God, I don't believe this! I don't believe what you did! Did you have to take such a big bite???? Disssssgusting!"

People came over to the table to help. Candy grabbed a towel and helped her rub the food away and helped her wipe her hair. Dave came over to wipe his floor. My friend Richie, came over to eagerly help wipe the upper portion of her sweatshirt, but we pushed him away with laughs.

Finally, she sat down and said, "Noogie, I gotta go! I gotta get home. Look at me! Take me home!"

"Would you first like a bite of pickle?"

"Oh, funny! No! Now! Home!" Good line, though, he thought.

"Annie, can ya please just wait a minute? I'd like to finish my burger first. Maybe just a minute? I'll be your best friend." Everyone was staring, but I was oblivious, wolfing down his burger and slurping his egg cream. His hands and mouth were covered with meaty grease and ketchup. She ran to the bathroom and came back as I was paying the bill with a couple of remaining bits of fries sticking between my teeth. My shirt was all stained with the stuff that came out his way. The burger was thirty cents and the pastrami sandwich, $1.25. The drinks were twenty cents each.

Into the car they went. "Did you like your pastrami sandwich, Annie?"

"You think you're so funny? Did you look at me? Did you see what you did? And I have to go home and explain this to my mother? This is a joke to you?"

"Good pickle?"

"Why I went with you, I'll never know."

"You went with me out of pity and I screwed it up, and I'm really sorry, Annie. I was showing off with that bite. Can I help wipe your dress? Can I make it up to you with another bite, I mean date, some other time?"

"Noogie, are you serious? Get your hands off me! Do you really think I'd ever go anywhere again with a pig like you? Just get me home and go 'way."

"No. I'm not doing that. You have to give me another chance. I promise I'll take smaller bites. I'll eat salami. No ketchup. A little mustard. C'mon, Annie. Just friends. I have an idea: Let's sneak into your father's store and eat a pickle."

"You have to be completely crazy! Sneak into my father's store to eat a pickle?" Never!"

"Waddaya mean 'Never?'" What's 'never?' There's no such thing as never. C'mon, let's do it. We'll go in and eat a pickle or two. No one will hear us. Real quiet. We'll be quiet pickle pickers."

A whispered, "Yes.... Yesssssssss. I wanna eat a pickle."

Annie always was brave and crazy. Noogie was a good influence. She whispered, "Okayyyyyy."

It was past her parents' bedtime and she knew they'd be asleep, and they tiptoed to the back of the Hymowitz store and went in. The door was never locked. No doors in Woodridge were ever locked. It was dark and the only light was the light of the yellow streetlights illuminating all the produce through the dirty windows, windows that had never been washed, it seemed, but good for privacy. The grimy window coating robbed the colorful vegetables of their true color.

They headed right for the pickle barrels in the middle of the store, sour, half sour and sour tomatoes. Noogie took a deep breath of the fragrant air and said, "It reminds me of Eau de Parfum Merde Alors." I was a very good French student in high school. She didn't know what he was talking about. It would smell terrific behind your ear. Try a dab," as I reached into the sour pickle barrel.

She recoiled, "Noogie! Stop!" pushing my wet hand away. "You got my sweatshirt wet with pickle juice. I am such a pathetic mess tonight." I took a big bite and crunched gently to not make too much noise.

"Here, try this one, " and extended my arm and hand to her mouth. She took a small bite and looked at me, laughter in that look, nibbling away, blue eyes on him, and I suddenly leaned into her, passionately pulling her toward me, pressing against her and planting a perfectly placed, prolonged, pickle-infused, puckered peck on her dark pink, pickle-juicy, pouty, prominent, petulant puss.

We were next to Sid's pickle barrels. I broke away for a second and reached in and grabbed a sour one in between kisses, and took a bite. In a panting whisper I offered her another bite and kissed her while she tried to chew. And she kissed me, pressing my lips against her teeth so hard that it felt like a bite. I whispered, "If only we had a pastrami sandwich to share with it, but a *shtickle* sour pickle is sweeter than I could ever wish for, Annie."

"And that's all you're ever gonna get, Noogie. I had a wonderful time tonight and I'm really sorry for your loss of Mr. Shabus. Everyone loved him."

"I have to see you again, Annie. You can't be a sour puss. Tomorrow. I need more sympathy."

"Call me when you have a free moment. My number is 842." She tiptoed upstairs.

But it only lasted for a few more hot pastrami sandwiches and more than a few sour pickle making out kisses and finally, delicious feel ups, until the barrels were emptied.

Thinking about "sour puss Annie Hymowitz," I wondered about how many sour pickles could anyone possibly eat? I had enough for one *shiva* week and couldn't wait to get back to B.U., grass, LSD, two dollar chianti, art class models and those delicious, tasteless, *goyisheh*, Boston hotdogs on buttered, folded, hot white bread. Enough with the pickles.

## 18.  Here'th Lookin' at You, Yutth

Years later, my best friend, Rick Meyerberger, was up in The Catskills visiting me in Woodridge. We continued to be roommates after B.U., but now in New York City on the Lower East Side in a loft on East Broadway, number 48, both pursuing our careers: illustration for Rick, photography for me.

"I want you to meet a good friend of mine who you haven't yet met. He owns an autobody shop in Old Falls. Don't ask me any questions." We drove over.

His glass eye really looked pretty fuckin' real. I gave him a big hello in my most affectionate manner, "How ya doin', idiot? Been a while."

"What the fuck you want, thupid thmuck moron? What are you doing here, athhole and who'th you're idiot-looking, hippie friend with the rabbi beard? Ith he a fuckin' rabbi or what? Where'th your big, black mink hat, idiot?" When he was excited, he reverted back to his lisp, but most of the time, he spoke his normal "gibberish."

We shook hands and gave each other a big hug. He

was covered in caked grease and dirt from the cars he had been working on in his auto body shop. His hands were stained black and fingernails were cracked and split. He was missing half his right index finger. His brother cut it off in a meat slicing machine when they were kids. But he still had nine and a half fingers left. He often stuck his half finger up his nose to make it look like it went all the way in. Didn't faze my friend, whose own father was missing his right pinkie.

"He's my friend, Rick Meyerberger, my old college roommate, idiot. I wanted him to meet a real, authentic *schmuckolovitch*. It goes so well with your name, Yutz Kantrowitz. What kinda name is that, Yutz? How can your wife live with such a name?"

"She loves Kantrowitz. What's wrong with Kantrowitz, putz?"

No, it's not the Kantrowitz part."

"Leave me the fuck alone, Noogie, with your sthtupid questionth, moron."

I brought Rick with me, knowing it would be an interesting experience meeting Yutz, and then we came back to Woodridge for a surprise fifty-ninth birthday party for Yutz in the Woodbourne firehouse the following evening. Woodbourne is one of the neighboring "Borscht Belt" towns.

Yutz's wife and daughters decided to throw him a surprise party for his fifty-ninth because his father died at fifty-nine and Yutz was deathly afraid, you should excuse the expression, of also dying at fifty-nine, so this was to be a most special celebration with two hundred fifty of his closest friends attending from all over the Catskills and other parts of the country.

He went to early services in the newer Woodridge *shul*, just around the corner from his home, every morning at seven before going to work in his Fallsburg body shop. He was a religious guy and going to the *shul* was a ritual and an important part of his life.

Yutz enjoyed the reputation of being the best body man around, as well as the proud possessor of a most creative, expressive, poetical mouth, from which emanated an uninhibited vocabulary of Yiddish and American off-color words and slurs that were particular to the Jewish areas of The Borscht Belt Catskills. He was a perfectionist at both his crafts. I don't think he learned his third "language" in the *shul*, though.

His property overlooked one of the most beautiful scenic spots in Sullivan County's Catskills, Old Falls on the Neversink River. It's one of the best trout and gefilte fish streams in America. Serious Jewish and non-Jewish anglers from all over the world came to Sullivan County just to fish for the elusive, wily gefilte fish, which were even tougher to catch than the native brown and rainbow trout. Across the bridge lay the detritus of injured vehicles, strewn and lined up all over Yutz's Body Shop's lot and down a hill to the stream below. It was an incongruous juxtaposition of aesthetics. The crushed metallic carcasses collided with the rough, dramatic rock formations of the falls and below, in a clanging cacophony of symphonic disharmony. It could have been John Chamberlin's sculptures set in a museum of tranquil metallic death and destruction. Who gave a shit? No one. Big fuckin' deal. Where else would ya put them?

The landscape of vehicles was what it was, and conveniently, for people wanting their vehicles to be fixed here, in this location. The tourists from the old hotels and bungalow colonies who walked along the road, paid attention to the falls as did the young idiots who jumped into the stream. Some of them were killed, injured or died by drowning. No one else paid attention to the wrecks while driving over the bridge. They were of no interest. They were just there. Perhaps of more interest were the graffiti names, dates and initials painted on the rocks by local high school students from up the Brickman hill.

"Awright, awright, so what the fuck ya want, idiot? Why'd you come here? Just to annoy me and waste my time?"

"No, prick, I invited my college roommate for the weekend and told him you would do him the biggest favor by taking your eye out for him."

"You brought that moron here for me to take my eye out? Are you a bigger *schmuck* than I thought you were, fuckin' idiot?" With that, he stuck his filthy, black, oily half-finger up his nose. It looked like his entire finger was in his nose into his eye socket.

"Jesus Christ, fuckin' *schmuck*!"

"I had to thnneeze and I didn't wanna do it all over you. So what else should I have done?"

"Disgusting, fucking pig! You embarrass me in front

of my friend, who I brought all the way from the Bronx and Boston to meet you?"

"Fuck him, fuck you, and excuse me, Rick, I didn't mean to embarrass you. Where'd ya find such a *schmuck* like this asshole Noogie? I'm embarrassed to live in the same town as your fuckin' friend."

I exclaimed, "May I have the extreme pleasure of saying fuck you both? Would you do me a favor awready and pull your fuckin' eye out so I can take my friend to lunch? You're wasting my time, fuckin' idiot. Take it out awready. It's not like I'm asking you to take anything else out. Jesus, I traveled all the way over here to introduce my friend to a genuine 'schloimeh,' you, idiot, and you can't even do a simple thing like pull your eye out? What a waste of my time! Do you think I only came to show him how you stick your half-finger up your nose and your broken cars that you didn't know how to fix?"

"Okay, thupid bathtid, here'th my eye." He put a black, greasy finger into the corner of his fake eye and extracted it, which, one could see through the grease, was exquisitely painted, and let it rest against the thick lens of his wide, black glasses. His own good eye had very poor vision. He stood in front of us, raised his four and a half fingers in the same spread-fingered victory sign Churchill made famous and asked, "Okay, you fuckin' moronth, are you thatithfied?"

"About fuckin' time you did something right, idiot," I exclaimed. "I'm really curious, though, where and what else you've done with your eye? When and how did you lose it."

"About theven years ago, I was working on an engine from a wrecked truck, started to grab a spring with my pliers and the fuckin' thing jerked loose and shot up into my eye. I knew right then I lost it. It hurt worse than a muthahfuckah and I was bleeding like a pig, screaming my ass off for a towel, anything! Hetzie, my partner, you know Hetz, heard me and ran over to see what happened, grabbed a rag and I stuck it where the eye was, I was bleeding so bad. He took one look and puked all over the fuckin' place, the pussy.

"He didn't wait for no ambulance, just threw me in the cah and we ran to that *schmuck* doctah in Fallsburg, who didn't know his ass from his elbow, much less an eye, and who passed out as soon as he took one look at my face. No shit. I'm not shitting you. Can you imagine a fucking doctor passing out like that? But he very soon came to with some smelling salt his nurse gave him and then gave me a pain shot, put a clean dressing on my wound and called an ambulance to take me to that fuckin' excuse of a hospital in Monticello, where some blind eye doctah examined me and determined, after a lengthy and thorough examination, that I lost my eye, the fuckin' genius, like I didn't know I lost my eye?

I said, "Muthahfuck!!"

"Yeah, you said it, 'muthahfuck.' So there I was with two pounds of bandages covering my eye and wondering if I'm gonna go totally blind, and scared shitless that I'd lose it all. Even with the pain shit they gave me, it still hurt like a sonofabitch, like you don't ever wanna know from it, like a white hot iron your grandfather made in his blacksmith shop sticking into your eye. I read that that's what the Nazis did to torture people or American soldiers, pull their nails out or stick their fingers into an eye and pull that out to get a confession. I'm sure it worked like a fuckin' charm, every time. Woulda got my attention."

Rick asked, "Jeeeesus, how long were you outa commission?"

"Months, moron. Hey, Noogie, what kinda idiot friend ya got?"

I asked, "I guess you adjusted to it, but what's the story of taking your eye out at odd times?"

"That's just bullshit about taking it out. Who the fuck ever told you a schmucky story like that? I gotta be careful with my eye and can't let it get dirty. I gotta keep it clean at all times. So I was at a party one night that was at Dickie Ellmont's house, and my eye got dirty from some kinda shit and Dickie was standing near me with his martini glass, talkin' to some woman and I took my dirty eye out and dropped it into his glass to clean it off. I figured alcohol would be sanitary. Did I know he was gonna take a sip before I could take it out and wipe it off? Thought I lost it, but thank God, he only took a half sip before he spit it out and his fuckin' drink went all over the cawhpit, and then I had a helluva time trying to find the fuckin' thing. I yelled out, 'Did anybody see my eye? It's on the floor somewhere and DON'T MOVE, you might step on it and then I'll really be blind!

"Dickie, who's six foot six and a real big fuckin guy, put his arm around my shoulder and said, 'Thome day, you fuckin'

Yutth, I'm gonna get even with you. You think you're tho funny thtikin' your eye in my martini? Watch out, Yutthie, your athth is grathth.' Everybody called Dickie 'Big Dick', but not to his fathe. He thounded jutht like me."

"Everyone got down on their hands and knees lookin' for it, but I had an extra eye I always carry in my pants and held it in my hand to see if I could help find the other one that fell. Dickie's wife, Eileen, came up with it in the corner of the livingroom and was afraid to touch it, so I knelt down, picked it up, rinsed it off and put it back in. I thanked her and told her, 'Ahhhh, now I can see your tits again.

"The first time I had an eye test, I had a really rough time with the fuckin' eye chart. Couldn't see it clearly. So I took my glass eye out and held it closer to the chart so I could see the letters and numbers better. Cool nurse; she told me I had perfect 10/10 vision.

"And I don't know why everyone thought it was strange that I put my eye on my grandson Austin's bar mitzvah cake just before everyone came up to light a candle. Austin was very cool. He picked it up and held it near the candles they had to light so they could see better because the room was so dark. Smart kid, that Austin."

"I told you what an idiot he is!"

Yutz, indignantly asked, "You told him I'M an IDIOT, you fuckin' thmuck moron" turning to Rick? What'th your latht name?"

"Meyerberger."

"Awright, Meyerberger, you should know I only do this

for stupid, fucking, idiot, schmuck morons like your fuckin' friend, Noogie, over here, who is the biggest putz to ever grow up in Woodridge."

Rick said, "I'm really honored, Yutzie. But Noogie told me your eye has wandered all over the fuckin' place. Is that true? Do you really take it out for everybody?"

"Only a few times here and there," laughing. "Once I was stopped by a state policeman on the Thruway for speeding, going only seventy-five in a fifty-five zone and when he pulled me over, he asked for my license and restoration, and I pulled them out and gave them to him- with my eye so he could see them better 'cause it was dark out at the time. Fucking trooper went ape shit and dropped the eye to the ground. I had to get out and find it with his flashlight. Fortunately, my record was clean and he knew who I was after I dropped the eye on him. I have a reputation, I guess."

The trooper said, "Sorry, Judge, try to slow down and keep your eye on the speedometer."

I asked, "Yutz, I hear you're going to be running for justice of the peace in the Town of Fallsburg and no more Village of Woodridge Judge."

"Yeah, *schmuck*, I am. You gonna vote for me?"

"I wouldn't waste my vote on an illiterate schloimeh like you! I'll be voting for your opponent. Who's that gonna be?"

"I think it's gonna be Ziggy Schlitzman from one of the other villages. A real schmuck, if you ask me. A dumb, fucking laundry owner whose mouth is so fuckin' dirty, you wouldn't wanna be in front of him in court. He spouts out in front of women, children, even dogs, the dick. And the fuckin' guy can't even wear a clean shirt in public, a laundry owner. Fuckin' thlob."

"Worse than you???"

"Wadda ya mean, worth than me? Do you hear me thaying the real bad shit? You think I tawk that way in front of kids. This fuckin' guy doesn't give a fuck for anyone. He thinks he's smart talkin' that way, the asshole, but he's a fat, disgusting fuck and I'm gonna beat his muthahfuckin' ass but good."

I said, "You sound pretty arrogant, Yutzie, so let's take a victory picture in advance."

"Fuck you, Noogie, okay?"

"No, not 'fuck you.' I want you to take your eye out, let it rest on your glasses and hold up your four and half fingers in a victory sign, and don't smile that stupid grin of yours. You're ugly enough as it is, moron. Just stand there and try to look like a judge."

Yutz, in his dark blue mechanic's uniform, "Dr. of Dent-istry" logo above his shirt pocket, covered in black, oily, greasy stains, stood at attention, saluted in mock-military form, and raised his four and half fingered hand in peace sign fashion with Rick, who stood at attention, puffed out his chest and saluted Yutz.

Then I took a picture of the aspiring town judge-to-be. "Don't blink, asshole, and don't smile. Be serious."

Yutzie asked, " Who was it who said that justice is blind? Not true, the *schmuck*. In my case, justice is only half-blind. Right, morons?"

"Right, your honor," exclaimed Rick.

"Noogie, your friend is an idiot. Why'd you bring him here, just to see my eye? Here *putz*, catch," and he threw his fake eye to Rick, who caught it by instinct and then yelled, 'Oh, shit, I have his eye in my hand! Oh, shit, here, take this thing! Uchhhhhh!'

"What's the mattah, *schmuck*, ya got thomething against holding my eye for me? Jesus Christ, don't drop it! I don't wanna lose it!" Rick handed Yutz his eye, frantically rubbing his hand on his pants to get the coating of eye slime off it, shaking his head in disbelief.

I asked innocently, "What the hell is the matter with you, Rick? Are you some kinda pussy you can't hold the fucking guy's eye in your hand? Yutzie, gimme the eye for a second so I can wipe it off for you." Yutz handed me the eye and I wiped it off up and down on my pants till it gleamed, and then handed it back to Yutz.

"Here's your eye, putz. I hope it saw me rubbing the shit off of it...just for you."

"You're a sick fuck, Noogie, but I've actually never seen so clearly."

"Okay, you guys, do me a favor and get the fuck outa here awready so I can get some work done. I gotta paint that fuckin' piece of shit Pontiac before I go to the dentist in Fallsburg. I'll tell you something I did to her the last time I was there: She's new and a piece of *tuchus* and I couldn't take my eyes off a huh while I was waiting for huh to come in. She finally comes in and I'm lyin' back in the chair and she introduced herself as Dr. Kaplan. And she asked me if anything was bothering me today and I told huh I thought I might have a cavity in one of my eyeteeth. She said, "Let's have a look," and I opened my mouth… with my eye on my tongue for huh to examine. She screamed so loud that everyone ran over to see what was wrong. She jumped back and I thought she was gonna have a shit fit. She was very cool and said it was okay. It was only a floating eye tooth that needed to be drilled and filled. I was pissin' in my pants. She was better than me and she was laughin' so hard, her molars were jiggling. I'm never gonna have a male dentist again!"

"Did you tell her you were a dent-ist, too," I asked?

"Actually, yeah, I did, and I told huh I'd be happy to fix huh dents, although huh dents stuck out like a thore thumb. Thome headlightth she got, too!"

"Are you saying, "She got head lice?"

" You undahsthand English, *schmuck*? Get the fuck outa here, awready, fuckin' morons."

We left, went back to Woodridge, hung around the house, had some salami and tongue "sanoviches," as my grandmother called them, with her sour pickles from the pantry, and homemade seltzer from the blue bottle with cherry syrup, took naps and got ready for Yutz's surprise fifty-ninth birthday party in the Woodbourne Firehouse. Everyone was told to get there early, which we did.

The place was jammed, including two big red fire strucks with gold lettering for the Woodbourne, NY, Fire Department and an ambulance. There were probably two hundred fifty people: relatives, friends, workers, politicians, fellow judges. Fifteen minutes after 7PM Yutz walked in with his family and the crowd erupted, in cheers and curses, "Hey, you fuckin' Yutz! Hey, thmuck! Hey, moron, idiot, utheless, putz!" Insults were and still are the way of showing affection in our Catskills. It's an expletive, followed by a hug and kiss, by both men and women. The bigger the insult, the bigger the hug. Yutz started crying in the middle of the room, tears falling from his good eye. His wife and girls were crying, we all started crying. We descended upon him in a gigantic hug. Those who were close enough grabbed his ass and crotch, pinched his cheeks the way in which bar mitzvah boys get their cheeks pinched. Between sobs, he tried to protect his privates to no avail. Everyone grabbed. One of the guys tried to pull his pants down, and almost succeeded, but his wife intervened. We saw his red boxer shorts, though, half way down his ass. She too had her ass pinched, and kept her hands on her breasts so no one could grab those. It was show time in the Catskills. No one gave a shit.

My pal, Rick, hadn't seen anything like this. But I, on the other hand, was fortunate enough to have a large number of relatives who taught at G.U., The University of Grabbit in Woodridge. Many of my fellow Borscht Belt friends and colleagues graduated from that college as well. It was a fuckin' ball.

Everyone was boozing, laughing, back slapping, handshaking, kissing, some tonguing, and eating all the homemade buffet food, a pot luck party, better than any caterer's. It was the Borscht Belt country way. Nobody scrounged on food. The pigs stuffed their faces.

## Heartfelt Tributes to Yutz, Sort of

Gloria made the first speech, welcoming everyone, theatrically asked how she did she ever end up with HIM and last as long as she did with HIM, from high school on. She didn't know what she saw in him. She told everyone that Yutz was always scared that he would never live past his fifty-ninth birthday, as his father had passed away, heshouldrestinspeace, when he was fifty-nine, and that's why we're all celebrating tonight. She told him how much she loved him and began to cry all over again, and his kids all came over into the middle of the room, hugging and kissing each other, especially Yutz. Tears flowed from his good eye again, a very weird sight, sort of like smoke coming out of one nostril when smoking.

Next to speak was New York State Supreme Court Judge Robert C. Williams, who eloquently extolled the judicial ethics and high esteem in which Judge Yutz was held throughout the County of Sullivan and Township of Fallsburg. He held up a judicial proclamation for all to see from the New York State Supreme Court, solemnly proclaiming that on Judge Yutz Kantrowitz's fifty-ninth birthday, Judge Kantrowitz finally reached an age that perfectly matched his exemplary I.Q.

The cheers reverberated throughout the firehouse as Yutz proudly walked over to accept the proclamation and whispered in Judge William's ear, "Thankth, Judge, you fuckin' moron. I love ya." With that, Judge Williams pulled Yutz's ears and kissed him on his glass eye.

Yutz wiped his tearing eye and, in front of everyone, pulled his other eye out and wiped that one, too. He held it up with two fingers to make sure it was clean enough to return to its socket. He huffed a bit of moisture on it as if one were cleaning the lenses of eyeglasses, rubbed it again, aimed it at Sylvia and then reinserted it. She mock cringed and instinctively clutched her forearms and hands close to her chest.

"Now I can thee again, you idiots!" he exclaimed. The crowd cheered. Some gagged.

There were a couple more tributes and then Big Dick Elmont, Yutz's best friend, also the same age as Yutz, walked out onto the middle of the floor, martini glass in hand, and went on to reminisce about their childhood together, growing up, going to school in Woodridge, about life in the tiny community of Woodridge. He spoke of families, wartime, politics, Yutz's high school sweetheart, Sylvia, first cars, old teachers, Yutz's father's hotel and bungalows, the Woodridge make-out movie theater, stores in town, the Kentucky Club antics, Dick's mayoralty and Yutz's position of Woodridge justice of the peace, of half-blind justice and wedding ceremonies memorized because of poor eyesight, of Yutz's judicial compassion and friendship toward all, and Yutz's extensive vocabulary in both Yiddish and Schmutzish.

At the end of his tribute, he asked us all to raise our glasses in a toast to Yutz's fifty-ninth birthday and, with Yutz at his side, said, imitating him, "Here'th lookin' at you, Yutth," and with that, with a theatrical flourish, Dickie pulled out a glass eye, or whatever it really was, from his pocket, slowly and daintily dropped it into his martini glass for all to see and… took a long swig, throwing his head back, swallowing the whole drink and eye, and yelled, "Mathel tov, you fuckin' moron!" in his best Yutz imitation.

Everyone also yelled a lisp "Mathel tov!" and cheered! Yutz and Dickie hugged each other for the longest time, this huge guy and skinny slight Yutz, who was enveloped into Dickie's crushing bear hug and lifted off the floor in awkward embrace. His black work shoes, shined for the occasion, dangled helplessly like a marionette's. "I can't breathe, you fuck!" Dickie dropped him, bent him over into a dip, and gave him a wet whopper on his lips. Yutz wiped his lips on his jacket sleeve.

"Feh, you disguthting fuckin' thhmuck." But he straightened himself and raised his hands in victory. All nine and a half fingers outstretched.

It was funny, heartfelt, loving and memorable, and everyone gave Dickie a rousing ovation as he returned to his seat, arms outstretched in victorious acknowledgement, savoring his finest hour of comedic tribute to his best friend. Yutz gave him a mock kick in the ass as he walked back to his seat, and was preparing to give a speech of his own.

Dickie sat down onto a metal folding chair near the end of one of those long folding tables, next to his wife Eileen, who was basking in Dick's ovation, gave him a big kiss, big smile, words that couldn't be made out, but were obviously incredibly complimentary, along with a hand squeeze. Everyone at the table was shouting out congratulations and reaching across the table for either handshakes or air kisses.

He smiled back that big, wide, perfect, white teeth handsome smile, and then, without warning, lurched over, his face and glasses slamming down into his plate of half-eaten food. His eyes were open, but unblinking.

Screams erupted!!!!! Cries of "Help!"

The local EMC people in the firehouse ran over to Eileen's piercing siren screams, pulling him onto the middle of the floor and attempting to frantically give him CPR on top of his chest!

She ran with them and was provided a chair almost next to him. Her head was slumped into her hands. Someone gave her a paper napkin. Women were next to her, all crying, holding her hand and shoulders.

That look on her face, that look, oh God, that look, that terrible helpless look, wide eyed, that body, the silence save but a few sobs, paper napkins to eyes, mouths open, Yutz, his family, the pounding on Dickie's chest.

The ambulance, the chair in the middle of the room.

The chair and Eileen.

Someone fuckin' idiot grabbed a cherry danish.

Dickie appeared… dead. The firehouse doors opened. An EMS crew started the ambulance, rushed Dickie into the ambulance with Eileen, grabbed the defibrillator and applied it, trying desperately to revive him, sirens wailing, onto the main drag of Woodbourne toward the Liberty hospital. It was futile.

Yutz's birthday cake was not yet cut, but the candles, all fifty-nine of them, had already been lit and were almost all melted down but still glowing.

The cake was decorated with a glass eye leaning against one lens of black-rimmed glasses next to his name in the center, a sculptured four and half finger hand stuck into the icing, and around the perimeter were colorful toy cars and trucks that had been partially dismembered, resembling those in his body shop, a three tiered cake with edible gold and silver decorations and piping on white creamy icing.

It read in dayglo blue lettering "Happy 59th Birthday, Yutth."

## 19. The Village Tavern Did Penance

I had my first drink in The Village Tavern, a dilapidated bar between Old Falls and South Fallsburg, New York, when I was sixteen. I was scared out of my mind to order one, but my pal, Joel Prattman, had done it before and told me not to worry, the guy'll serve us and he did. I didn't have a fake I.D. card.

I was shakin' like a sonofabitch and trying to act like a mature older man casually walking into a bar, something like John Wayne might do. I ordered, in as deep a voice as possible, Canadian Club, the same shit we had in the house for company, and ginger ale, and thought it was the worst tasting shit I ever drank and started coughing my fuckin' brains out after spitting it back, without anyone seeing, into my glass. And I didn't even need a fake ID. John Wayne probably would've grabbed me by the ass and tossed me out, flying through the bar door until I crash landed.

The Village Tavern was also the future site of the most educational bachelor party I've ever attended, and actually the first. Now that place is resurrected as some kind of Christian church, and encouraging all who attend to do penance for past sinful deeds within its four walls. It is now the known among us former fellow "churchgoers" as The Church of the Res-erection.

The not-so-beautiful hired female ladies of the evening were naked, and bestowed upon a number of the celebrants, in front of everyone, professional oral-erectile tactile stimulation. Among many locals in attendance was my uncle Max Shabus. Needless to say, I was surprised but happy to see him with a bunch of his older upstanding, professional friends. At one point, one of the ladies brashly walked up to him, offering her services, but like a true gentleman, he politely turned her down and repelling her advances, gently pushed her away… by placing both his hands on her breasts. I took a picture of that as proof that he was really being true to his wife, refusing her services. He asked me not to show his wife the photo, thinking she might not understand, but when I gave it to him, he ended up showing it to her himself at her weekly mah jong game, because she didn't believe him when he told her that he had truly abstained from all advances.

She got quite upset over the photo of his hands on that lovely lady's breasts, but he was able to explain that he really was trying to protect himself from her aggressiveness, and he satisfied her with his explanation. Sort of.

## 20. Kosher for Christmas

It snowed lightly on Christmas eve, coating the drab, raw umber, dead grass and petrified trees and potted plants that were left outside in the wooden and plastic planters, covered with a coating of white snowflakes, before turning brownish-gray from the sander and cars and pickups splashing the slush, disrupting the purity of the briefly pristine road, sparkling a bit from the highlight of a half moon and our outdoor yellow bug light (too fuckin' lazy to change it to white) and the few white Christmas decorative lights made to look like illuminated electric icicles our neighbors across the road hung over the entrance to their garage. Theirs was a modest display, unlike those of most of the other goyish neighbors (as my parents and grandparents would say) who seem to come out of the woodwork between Thanksgiving and a couple of weeks after New Year's, and who definitely live in a different lit up world.

But it's wonderful to share in their holiday spirit and creativity and it enlivens the short days of winter with their own country artistry better than any real artist other than Grandma Moses might dream up.

I like it best when their Christmas lights outline their homes or tractors, or barns or, in one case, a 1954 Cadillac. I like the spinning wheel lights, flashers, white, blue, red, yellow, purple, orange and green bulbs on fences, in windows, on trees and shrubs, arbors, trellises, wisteria, Santa Clauses and Nativity scenes, inflated snowmen, cartoon characters, reindeer with red noses, scrollwork on porch columns, commercial buildings, store window displays and frozen leftover sunflowers and corn stalks wrapped around porch columns. It's Las Vegas country-style, shit-kickin', fuckin' damn eccentrically good. It makes ya feel happy, and it only pisses me off that much more that we never had a Christmas tree in our house when I was a kid in Woodridge, although we've never had any as adults either because we are so "Jewish" for this holiday and found it necessary to differentiate ourselves from them and sort of worry that if you believed in God, G-d in this case, the Jewish spelling, He might get the impression you've sinned and then you're really fucked and so we've given the same excuses our parents gave all over again, and besides, having a burning bush in the living room was just too dangerous, and G-d forbid, you should only burn the house down. "Pine trees are not Jewish!" Then what? Better to stick to burning candles for Chanukkah just to play this Jewish business safe. You never know what He may think or do to you? And I really cannot figure out why Jews can't have a pine tree in their homes. Is there any logic to that whatsoever??? Maybe the kosher rabbis never thought about blessing them so that they could be Kosher for Christmas.


## Noogie Sets the Perfect Table

I set the dining room table next to all the Christmas presents, and made a big deal over my contribution and how hard I worked to make the table look perfect, impressing the women as well. My mother's best silver, a wedding present, was taken out of its 1940s box. The forks were placed on the right for righties and on the left for lefties. Spoons, too. Seemed logical to me. Knives were placed on the opposite sides of the forks. A good invention. The smaller forks and spoons for dessert and coffee were lined up in opposite directions above the plates, and a non-matching set of wine glasses, all that we had, were placed to the right of the Arabia somewhat cracked and chipped plates, but still beautiful after thirty years. The tablecloth upon which everything sat was a blue flowery April Cornell pattern. It made food and plates look like still lifes coming alive out of Matisse paintings.

Wouldn't you know that "Mme. Inspecteur Général" walked in a few seconds later. She inspected. That's what she does best. She inspects. And examines. Carefully. Excruciatingly carefully. Meticulously. Minutely. Perfection personified. She looks and searches, tight-lipped.

"What is this? Ohhh, God! How come the forks are on the right and the spoons are on the left for some people? Is this one of your little tricks to get me upset?"

"Well," I explained, "I thought it would be easier if any of the lefties didn't have to reach over anyone to get to their forks. If they were sitting in the wrong seat, they would have to reach. But this way all they would have to do is simply pick them up without any exertion or stretching. What's wrong with that, especially if they happen to sit in their undesignated seats? God forbid someone sits in the wrong seat and has to reach for a fork, then what? Would you want them to reach? Would you really want a righty reaching for a lefty fork?"

Sophie, in her incredulous mode, said, "Noogie, are you for real? Are you outa your mind? We're gonna have company tomorrow and you are putting the forks on the right, and I am going to have to explain to them that you just came out of the back woods. Really! Would you pleeease place the forks in their proper position? Girls, I want you to see what your father did this time. You're not gonna believe it. Can't we even trust you to set a table properly?"

"But I did, Sweetie. If you girls would turn to table setting chapter in that new Modern American Manners book we have, you'd see that they say it is extremely important for guests not to have to stretch for utensils, and that a proper host or hostess should discreetly inquire as to which hand a particular guest utilizes before sitting down to dinner to comfortably dine. We can make place cards so we'll know exactly where they'll be sitting and put a discreet "L" or "R" on the bottom of each place card. You could really hurt your shoulder by stretching it the wrong way, attempting to get the fork and knife and spoon. Really, I don't think you guys know anything about etiquette or table manners or about making guests feel comfortable. If all it takes is placing a fork or spoon on the proper side, it should be done."

"You are ridiculous. How can we have company with forks on the right?"

Ladies! Have pity!" Jesus Christ, they are absolutely ruthless to a poor defenseless fellow like me. Maybe I should've simply left the forks alone and just moved the spoons to the left? They went about changing everything, ruining my invention and making me feel... "defeated," and then, with hugs and kisses, we called it a night. I was feeling very guilty from causing their eyes to get stuck from rolling upward because of the way I set the table, and hoped we wouldn't have to make an emergency trip to the hospital, as a result.

We drifted off to bed, tired, expectant, after midnight, Christmas. Sophie, my beautiful artist, accomplished cook, best mother, perfect straight man to my almost funny jokes, and I snuggled under the fluffy down covers with Tarrie, the black cat, cradled in her left arm. Max, named after Uncle Max, our ninety-four pound poodle, snuggled against my bent knees, and Barnie, the twenty-six pound cat, on the other side of my legs opposite Max and Sophie's ass, pushed into the space made by my tummy and bent knees. My arm draped over Sophie's waist, although I always like to try to get a little more, like pieces of a nightly puzzle, softly stroking our twenty-five year old purring cat. It felt right and I didn't linger much, me over money anxieties and other worries, before instantly falling into a deep sleep until the siren song of Woodridge beckoned me in my fitful 4am dream.

## 21. Returning to the Ghost of Woodridge

Forty years later, the key was still there, one of those old-fashioned, long-handled, bronze skeleton keys that fit into the lockset keyhole. The once shiny brass of the lockset and glass knob was painted over with layers of paint, its raised decorative motif now obscured. I turned it and opened the hesitant, squeaking door and walked in, feeling like a criminal and hoping no one had seen me from a window across the street. I didn't want anyone alerting the police.

But nothing happened and I entered the ghost of the home that I hadn't been in since twenty lifetimes ago. The stench immediately hit me of decaying, bleeding plaster and wood. It wasn't the baked bread aroma I expected in my fantasy of home as it was. I walked to the living room and saw that the oak floor was warped as badly as a bumpy country road, and the wood floorboards were green and white with mold. The ceiling was falling down in spots, exposing wiring and supports, but the original chandelier was still hanging, slanting down on one side and held by a single wire. The decorative crown molding was cracked and broken. The walls, stained with the brown drippings of roast beef gravy-colored rainwater, filtered through old exposed rafters. Pipes were exposed and broken off from the cast iron hot water heaters that had been ripped out. Along the far wall were the remains of a left-behind bright blood red, but badly stained and ripped up couch. It was the only color in the room, the only color in the house. There was a bare mattress on the floor opposite. It too was stained.

The dining room was no different: leaks, decay, carcasses of four dead mice trapped in mousetraps, their bodies now just skeletons. The kitchen was empty: no stove, nor fridge, nor toaster, nor old sink, nor Formica table and flowered oilcloth cover and tube chairs, nor the white, painted cabinets that had been replaced by the cheap faux maple pressed board kind from a low-end box store. From the pantry, the door to the woodworking shop was open, and the metal steps my grandfather made to the woodworking shop were still there, but they ended halfway down where the landing to the shop was that no longer existed. The small table next to that door was still there, but the large crock my grandmother used for her sour pickles and tomatoes was but another memory. The odd-shaped stone that held the wooden crock top in place was surprisingly still there on the floor. I wondered how come?

I walked back into the central hallway, turned slowly in a circle to remember the space like I pictured it as it used to be, peering in the long clothes closet and in one far corner, in the semi-darkness, I noticed the framed van Gogh colored, faded lithograph leaning against the wall, glass cracked. I picked it up it, wiped it off with my sleeve, actually found the nail from which it used to hang above my grandfather's dark brown, velvet chair in the livingroom and re-hung it in the spot it once occupied and carefully eyeballed it to level.

I opened the porch door, closed it behind me, turned the old skeleton key in the keyhole, stuck it in my pants pocket and locked those memories inside forever.

I walked over to that cheap, white, outdoor plastic chair in the corner and took a seat for a few minutes, listening to those loud voices; strident, sarcastic, laughing, cursing, nighttime, mostly in that foreign language one more last time.

And with full power and authority...away I walked, down the cracked brick steps and out through the twisted, rusted, wrought iron Pesach Shabus Gate.

# Yiddish Terms And Translations In The Book

## Many thanks to Rabbi Irving Goodman and

## Leo Rosten & Lawrence Bush, authors of THE JOYS OF YIDDISH.

## I also referred to various sites on the Internet.

## A Glossary, you should only know from.

aliz gut — all is good

antisemitten — antisemites

b'rucha — a blessing

balebuste — a woman who runs the house

bar mitzvah — when a boy, at thirteen becomes a "man"

besser — better

bimah — A podium in a synagogue from where the Torah and prayers are read

bissel schickerated — a little inebriated- I made up the word

Borscht Belt — A colloguial reference of a section in Sullivan County, NY, in which many Jews lived. It was a tourist destination as well for mostly Jews from the Bronx, Brooklyn and Manhattan who visited and stayed in the many hotels and bungalow colonies in Sullivan County.

boychick or boychikel — term of endearment for a boy or man

bubbe and zeydeh — grandmother and grandfather

bubeleh — endearing word

bulvan — extremely strong man

chai — the number 18. A good luck number. Double chai is 36, and others always in denominations of 18.

chollie (challah) — braided bread

chozzer — a person who acts like a pig

davening — praying

# Raining Delusions

dreck — shit, dirt

fakakta — ridiculous, crappy

farbisseneh punim — angry face or expression

farshtunkeneh — rotten, stinky, poor quality

fartig — finished, enough

gantseh megillah — a big deal, unnecessary facts

Gay avek foon mir — Go away from me

Gay gezundt avec — Leave already! Have a good trip home!

gayn — go

gefilte fish — A wild, white Jewish fish that is rumored to be found only in The Neversink River and lakes and ponds in the "Borscht Belt" section of Sullivan County, NY. Ground up, shaped and boiled, with carrots on the side, it resembles a white log.

gelt — money

genug — enough

Gevalt! Oy, vey is mir! — Oh, no! Oh, no! Woe is me!

gluz tay — glass of tea

gonif — thief

gonseh — all, big. In this case, a heartwarming

gournischt — it's nothing

goy, goyish, goyisheh- Gentile

guttenyou — woe!

haftorah — readings from the Prophets

horah — Jewish celebratory dance

Hundt — dog

Ich gay — I'm going

Ich hub fargesn — I forgot

Kaddish — prayer for a deceased person

kazatzkehing — dancing to Klezmer music

kenen nisht — cannot, unable to

keppie — head, an endearing term

kibitz(ed) — to joke, (ed — joked)

kibitzers — people who joke with one another

killa — hernia

kinde — child and kinder- children

kleyn — little, small

klezmer — Jewish music performed at wedding and other joyful functions

klop — to strike, hit hard

knaydlekh — matzoh balls for soup

kosher — acceptable foods for religious Jews

kreplach — dumplings

kvel — to express happiness, to brag

L'chaim — a toast to life

latkes — potato or zucchini pancakes

lokshn — noodles

machetunim — in-laws. The other set of parents or grandparents

macht —make

mamzur- bastard

maven — an expert or authority in a certain endeavor

Mazel tov — Congratulations

mein gut — my god

mensch — an upstanding person

menshlichkeit —being an upstanding person

meshugenah yentas — a bunch of crazy gossipers

meshugener- crazy man or meshugene. crazy woman — meshuganim

meshuga — crazy

# Raining Delusions

minyan- A minion is a group of ten people needed to meet for prayers in synagogue.

mitzvah — a good deed. Doing something good for another.

momileh, boubileh, tzatzkeleh, tateleh — terms of endearment

nem a bissel — Take a little

noodge — an annoying person

Nu? — Well? So what's doing? What do you think? So hurry up already?

nudnick — someone who is annoying, a pain in the neck, one who acts like an idiot

Pesach — Passover. Also a Jewish name, like Pesach Shabus- Passover Sabbath

[petzeleh — little penis

pish — urinate

potch — a slap

potshka — to over-prepare, sometimes needlessly

punim — One's face

pebbe — rabbi

pugeluch — Pastry

pchav — A soup made with sorrel

pchlemiel — loser

schlep — to carry or drag

schlimazel — unlucky loser

schloimeh — idiot, useless. Also a Jewish name, but not used in this book in this manner

schluffin — Sleep — Gay schluffen — Go to sleep

schmaltz — chicken fat

schmatta — rag. Deprecating term for old, ragged house dress

schmeared — spread, wiped on.

schmeckel — penis

schmeckelpunim — dickface

schmendrick — an idiot, useless, moron

Michael Gold

schmooze — to chat

schmuckolovitch — a big idiot

schmutz — dirt. Also dirty words, pictures

schnapps — whiskey

schpritzes — sprays, schpritzing — spraying

schrei — to scream or yell loudly

Shabus — sabbath. Also the last name- Pesach Shabus

shakren — liar

shayna — beautiful. Shayna punim- beautiful face

shechit or shoychit — kosher butcher

sheygetz — non-Jewish male

shkotzim — non-Jewish males

shikkers — drunkard

shiksa — non-Jewish female

shivah — sitting shiva is mourning a dead person or persons

shlub — like a loser, lazy

shnorrer — a chiseler, a taker, a "pig", a beggar

shondah — a shame

shechit or shoychit — butcher who slaughters animals in the kosher tradition

shteytls — Jewish villages in Eastern Europe

shtick dreck — piece of shit

shtickle — a small piece

shtunks — stinkers

shtup — literally, to push, but used in the book to mean intercourse

shul — synagogue

shvesters — sisters

shvitz (ed) (ing) — sweat, etc.

242

# Raining Delusions

simcha — a happy celebration

tallis — prayer shawl

tanteh —aunt

tchotchke — knickknacks — tchotchked- filled with knickknacks

Torah — sacred Jewish scroll of Go-d's Law given to Moses

treyf — non-kosher

tsimes —to make a big deal.

tsuris — trouble

tuchus — rear end, butt

wasser — water

Vee gayst du? — Where are you going?

Vey iz mir — Oh, no! Woe is me.

Vuh den? — What do you think? Do you believe? Where else?

yarlmulke — skull cap

yenta — a person who gossips

yiddisheh kup — literally: Yiddish head. Really means a smart, Jewish person

yuntif — holiday

zayeh (good or gut) — very good

Zei gezunt — a nice goodbye

zetz zich avek — have a seat

zetz — slap

zeyde — grandfather

zin — son

# ABOUT THE AUTHOR, MICHAEL GOLD

Besides his newest book, the novel *Raining Delusions*, Michael Gold is the author of *Earn That Vote*, a grassroots political guide; *Modern American Manners: Dining Etiquette for Hosts and Guests*, co-authored with Fred Mayo, as well as contributing photographer for a children's four book series, *Where's The Science Here?*, authored by Vicki Cobb.

As a commercial photographer, he has worked on assignments for *The New York Times Magazine; Opera News; Fortune, Travel & Leisure; Esquire; National Lampoon; Reader's Digest*, and special sections for the newspapers of the *Ulster Publishing Company-Woodstock Times, New Paltz Times and Saugerties Times*. He is currently the official photographer for *The Bop Island Jazz Festival* in Woodstock, NY.

He has also produced a number of videos, including *I was Born To Fish: Lee Wulff on The Beaverkill; Grief: How To Help Children Feel, Deal and Heal; How To Tape and Interview Your relatives*; with Co-producer Dorothy Shapiro, *Team BMW*; for BMW North America, and *Taking The High Road*; a two tape biography of the late Lawrence H. Cooke, Chief Judge of the New York Court of Appeals, also co-produced with Dorothy Shapiro.

Michael was one of one hundred two writers, worldwide, invited to Yale's very first Writer's Conference in 2013.

As a photographer/artist, he has had twenty-one one-man exhibits in New York City, Philadelphia, Boulder and various locations in the Hudson Valley and The Catskills of New York State. He has also been included in group shows in The Catskills, and at MIT, in an exhibit entitled *The Metropolitan Middle Class*.

Michael's email: mgphotoman@gmail.com

Raining Delusions

# Raining Delusions

Raining Delusions

Made in the USA
Middletown, DE
06 January 2019